A Twist of the Lens
By Elizabeth S. Devecchi

Wicked House Publishing

No part of this publication may be reproduced, stored in a retrieval system, or transmitted in any way by any means, electronic, mechanical, photocopy, recording or otherwise without the prior permission of the author except as provided by USA copyright law.

This novel is a work of fiction. Names, descriptions, entities, and incidents included in the story are products of the author's imagination. Any resemblance to actual persons, events, and entities is entirely coincidental.

Cover design by Blaine Daigle
Interior Formatting by Duncan Ralston
All rights reserved. Copyright © 2025 Elizabeth S. Devecchi

A Twist of the Lens

Elizabeth S. Devecchi

To my family and the village that raised me.

"You can use a spear as a walking stick, but that will not change its nature."

— MADELINE MILLER, *THE SONG OF ACHILLES*

Chapter 1

The Village

They say it takes a village. What they don't mention is that not all villagers are created equal. I didn't have helicopter parents, or lawnmower parents, or whatever the current term is for parents who spend their lives solving problems for their kids 24/7. Mine were busy getting shit done, climbing career ladders that stretched up somewhere into the clouds. They didn't come to every soccer or softball game, but they made it to the ones that mattered. They were lovely, well-rounded, upstanding citizens. I never blamed my personal choices on them, nor faulted them for how I turned out. Besides, I'm ok with who I am. Sure, I have regrets, but don't we all? In any case, my perfectly well-adjusted, law-abiding older brother is enough—in my opinion—to get my parents off the hook.

In fact, Tom is the quintessential family man. He and his wife have the perfect little family: one girl, one boy. They live somewhere between suburbia and *out in the country* in one of those houses that looks like it should be inhabited by creepy little porcelain dolls with smooth, polished, rosy-cheeked faces, and tiny gingham clothes. A split-rail fence surrounds their entire property, which is accessible via a rickety-looking gate. A multi-colored step-stone path snakes through their xeriscaped yard, under a wooden garden arbor laced with morning glories, and up to the front door.

Not that I've ever been there. But, the pictures he sends are gorgeous.

I glance down at my phone, at his cryptic text.

Give me a call. We need to ask a favor.

We both know he's the responsible one. I can't imagine what favor he could need from me ... *they* could need from me. I examine my phone again. *We* need to ask a favor means his wife Lindsey, too. I run my free hand up the back of my neck and into my hair, letting my wavy chestnut mane slip between my fingers.

"Hey there, Sunshine. What's up? You look perplexed."

I set my phone on the kitchen counter and meet Becca's gaze. She sashays over and gives me a peck on the cheek. Then, continues on her merry way to the espresso machine.

"Still the absolute best gift you've ever given," she says, flipping a switch that illuminates an array of buttons across the middle of the coffee maker. "Should I make two?"

I muster up a smile, and nod. Sunshine is her pet name for me. Her ironic pet name. She's the one who beams. I am more of an amicable, tepid shadow.

"Tom texted. Says he needs a favor."

"Oh? Did he say what it was?"

"No. He wants me to call him."

"Aren't he and Lindsey going to Europe this summer? Maybe they need you to watch the house."

I catch my bottom lip between my teeth and nod. It's amazing how Becca can remember everything going on with everyone in both of our families.

"I forgot about that," I admit.

"Geez, Charlie. Don't you remember the pile of brochures Lindsey showed us over Christmas break?"

I shrug. I do ... vaguely.

"Maybe. But why would they want *me* to watch their house?

I've never even been there, and they know how busy I am." I take the cup of hot espresso Becca offers me.

"You have employees who are perfectly capable of holding down the fort while you are away," Becca says, rolling her eyes. "Besides, can't you oversee things remotely on your computer? I'll be away helping Mom with Dad for most of the summer, anyway. And a change of scenery would do you a world of good."

"Sure you don't want me to come help?" An impish grin spreads across my lips.

Becca shakes her head and laughs. "Right. Just what my dad needs after a heart attack."

I empty my cup, anticipating the rush of caffeine, and hand it back. Becca sets the cups in the sink and lets out a deep sigh. "You understand why I have to go, right?"

I nod. Of course I do. Even if her parents don't deserve her help, and not just because they despise me. They have been nothing but demeaning of her. But they are her parents. And she is Becca. Save-the-world-one-smile-at-a-time Becca. She's hopeful that the heart attack might have softened them, made them more reasonable. I'm not as optimistic, but have to admit that people do occasionally change. I have first-hand knowledge of that.

"Why don't you call him now?" Becca hands me my phone. "Solve the mystery."

Chapter 2

Mystery Solved

The phone barely rings once when Tom's voice sounds from two time zones away. He's waiting for my call.

"Hey, Charlie. Thanks for calling so quickly. How's Becca?"

He sounds out of breath. And is that a hint of concern in his tone?

"Good. Everything ok? Lindsey and the kids doing well?"

Becca gives me a pat on the shoulder and leaves me to my conversation.

"Everything's hunky dory."

Well, I know *that's* a lie. If everything were *hunky dory*, he wouldn't be asking me for a favor.

"Lindsey and I are prepping for that big trip we have coming up," he continues. "Everything's booked and I'm just trying to figure out the final touches. Lindsey wants everything to be just perfect."

I'm sure she does, I think, biting my tongue to ensure both the statement and my sarcastic tone remain safely confined to my head.

Not that I don't like Lindsey. She has a certain charm about her, I guess. In small doses. I'm just not mentally equipped to deal with that much pep for extended stretches of time. Her energy is what you would get if you melted together a soccer mom and a 1980s jazzercise instructor.

"I get it, Tommy. Cut to the chase. Did your house sitter fall through or something?"

He clears his throat. He hates it when I call him that, but I don't expect him to correct me. He wants—nay, needs—something from me. Why not have a little fun with it? Becca leans back into the room, knits her brows and shakes her head at me.

I wave her off and am about to needle him again, when I remember how awesome Tom was when I was going through my divorce, and all the crap that followed. How seamlessly he welcomed Becca into their lives, referring to her as Auntie Becca to the kids. Heat rushes across my face like a brush fire. I clamp my lips shut and puff my cheeks.

"Seriously though, Tom," I say, softening my tone and suppressing my impish tendencies. "I'm overdue for some vacation time, and Becca has to go help her parents for most of the summer."

"Oh, yeah. How is Becca's dad doing? That must have been quite a scare. She's going to be staying with them this summer to help? I hope they finally realize what a gem of a daughter they have. I guess sometimes it takes something like that—a health scare—to see what's important in life. It would be great if they could patch things up while she's there. I know she would be so relieved."

"He's good." I hope my voice isn't as gruff as it sounds in my head, but the fact that everyone around me seems to know everyone's business is starting to wear on me. We don't even live in the same state, for Christ's sake. "Anyhow, what I was going to say is, if you need someone to watch your house or something, I'm available. Maybe I could even scope out some opportunities to expand my business while I'm there."

I swallow hard and sigh. There. That wasn't so hard, was it? I even offered a *me* reason for the trip, so Tom won't think I've gone soft or something.

"You should absolutely consider better opportunities," he says.

Not what I said at all.

"With your expertise and experience, you could be running security for one of the big chains, some Fortune 500 company. Maybe you and Becca could move out here."

Wow. This must be some ask for him to keep changing the subject like this.

"Mom would be crushed. And besides, Tom, you know I would never stoop to working for some chain or cannibalistic corporation. I only work with family businesses and offices that actually serve the people around them. I'm hoping you have some of those out there, too."

An amused chuckle echoes in my ear. "My, my. So righteous."

Was that a note of pride in his voice? Of course, he has no clue that a significant part of my so-called *righteousness* is spurred by a perpetual need to make up for past transgressions.

"Anyhow," he says in a voice that gives me hope he is finally getting to the point. "I wanted to ask … I mean, *we* wanted to ask. Lindsey and I, that is …"

"Yes, Lindsey your wife. We've met. Is it really that hard to ask me a favor, big bro?"

"Ok." There's a pause, followed by the sound of a deep breath. "Do you think you could fly out and watch the house … and Alex, while we are away?"

My jaw skews and slowly falls open. I glance around the kitchen, hoping to reap some moral support, but Becca has wandered off. I clear my throat.

"Ummm, I thought she did those sleep away camps in the summer. Wasn't Jimmy going on and on the last time you guys called about finally being old enough to go with her? Wait … would he be home, too? Tom, you know I adore your kids, but I have zero babysitting experience."

"Jimmy is going to camp. Alex was supposed to, but she's not anymore." His voice is taking on a tenor of desperation that I don't recall ever hearing from my meticulous, organized, responsible older brother.

"Is everything ok?" I ask, a little embarrassed that I've been making it all about me.

"I don't know. She had some big falling out with her best friend and now she's refusing to go. Says if we send her anyway, she'll sneak out or get herself thrown out." He pauses and his voice dives to just above a whisper. "Charlie, I think she'd actually do it."

I believe it, but he doesn't need me to agree ... to affirm his fears and worst-case scenarios that will already be running through his mind on a loop.

"Lindsey wants to cancel, to stay home with Alex. But I really need this trip, Charlie. *We* really need this trip together."

Are Tom and Lindsey *in trouble*? Impossible. They are so perfect together. Sure, Lindsey can be annoyingly peppy and optimistic, but she balances out Tom's seriousness. And, more importantly, I know she makes him happy.

"Besides," he continues, "Alex says she doesn't want us to stay home. She was planning on staying with Mom."

This seems reasonable to me, and I'm about to say just that, when he adds, "But, obviously, I can't ask Mom. She and Aunt Cathy are going on that cruise. You know how Cathy's been struggling since Uncle Joe left."

Am I seriously the only one *not* tuned in to everyone else's drama? Ok, now that he mentioned it, Mom did say something about a cruise and Aunt Cathy. And about Uncle Joe proving to be a total asshole. But my concentration often floats off in a sanity-saving mental lifeboat when Mom starts listing off extended family dramas. And I, for one, have always known that Uncle Joe is a total asshole. He has nothing to prove to me.

"Oh yeah," I say. "I forgot about the cruise."

Tom laughs. "She's only been talking about it nonstop for

months now. Anyhow, Alex is practically a teenager. It's not like you'd really have to babysit her. When I mentioned I could ask you to come, she seemed thrilled at the possibility. Though I'm sure she'll be disappointed to hear Becca can't come."

Of course she will. The kids adore Becca. All kids adore Becca. I'm not jealous. I know they love me, too. I have a fridge covered with hand-drawn art signed with little hearts above my name to prove it. But, I tend to keep myself somewhat distant, like I do with everyone. They just seem to be more aware of it than the adults are, able to see right through the bullshit and into your core. And rarely are their questions tempered by any sort of filter. You can't satisfy them with generic answers. In short, they're terrifying.

"So, can you help us out?" he asks. "I'd owe you, big time."

"And Lindsey's on board with this?" I know I can't possibly be his wife's first choice as a sitter, even with Mom out of the running. Sure, she'd probably call me if they needed a security system installed. But she knows I am awkward with kids. "I mean, when she finds out Becca can't come, will she still be on board?"

"Absolutely," he says, after a slight but meaningful hesitation.

The line falls silent and I realize he's waiting for my answer.

"I guess I can help you out."

He releases his breath in a *whew*. "Charlie, you are a lifesaver. Of course, we'll pay for your flight. And you'll have Lindsey's Range Rover to get around in. My Beamer'll be in the shop for maintenance."

"Whoa, whoa, whoa. I'm not *flying* out, Tom. I'll drive. Actually, if you're going to leave me a car to use, maybe I'll take the bike."

"Mr. Edwards' old motorcycle? Charlie, it's a long drive. Wouldn't it be easier to just fly? Besides, we'd need you to come out a little early. You know, to get the lay of the land."

My chest tightens and my mouth feels like I've snacked down on a hill of sand. He wants me to get on one of those flying death tubes? Nope. Besides, I've spent a considerable amount of time, sweat, and money getting Bill's old bike up and running and I'm itching to take it for something longer than a running-to-grab-milk-at-the-corner-store outing.

"What is it, around twelve-hundred miles?" I ask.

"I think a little less than that. Driving with the kids, it took us a good twenty hours with all the bathroom stops. Never again. Are you sure Mr. Edward's bike would even make it? It was in pretty bad shape when we found it in his garage."

I'd forgotten Tom was with me when I found the motorcycle I now affectionately refer to as the FCC—which has nothing to do with what may have popped into your head just now, and everything to do with the fact that her color reminds me of a candy cane and she sure can fly. Yes, to me she's the Flying Candy Cane forevermore.

Honestly, I was pretty shocked when I saw her parked in the back of Bill's garage, half hidden behind boxes of old decorations and discarded items from a store he'd once owned with his late wife. I hadn't pegged him as a motorcycle guy. Of course, there was a lot I didn't know about Bill. Point in case, you could have knocked me over with one barb off a feather when his lawyer (I didn't even know he *had* a lawyer) told me he'd left everything to me.

"Yeah. It should be fine. I've put a lot of time and money into getting her running like new."

"*New* being what? Nineteen-fifty-something?"

"Nineteen-fifty-two, to be exact. I found a local shop. You probably don't remember Jay. I hung out with him sometimes. Anyway, he has a motorcycle shop. He and his crew helped get her back in shape. He wanted to buy her, but I just couldn't bring myself to sell. Besides, Becca says I look super cool on her."

"Oh, well then. Enough said. Do you think you could be out here by June first? Our flight leaves the fifteenth and we want to give you time to get used to the house and routine."

I suppress a sigh. How hard can it be to watch a house with

one almost-teenager who's on summer break? We won't even have to get up early. My hand wanders up to rake through my hair. I admit I don't know Alexandra all that well, and I have never seen her in her *natural habitat*, so to speak. But she's always struck me as an intelligent, curious kid. A good kid, with her dad's common sense and her mom's energy level, but without the cheerleady pep.

I imagine the hardest part of this job will be keeping Lindsey's plants alive. I reach back into my mind and shuffle through the Christmas pics she's sent over the years. The first thing that always caught my eye was the veritable jungle spread out behind and around each fresh-cut blue spruce. The room, which Tom told me was originally a dining room and is now affectionately called the Plant Room, contains every kind of vegetation one can imagine. Don't ask me to name any, though.

Wait. A spider plant. I do know there's at least one spider plant. Mom gave it to them when they moved into the house, making a big deal over the fact that it was grown from an offcut of a plant Tom brought home from school in second grade. I have one, too. Becca nursed it back to life when we moved in together, earning her major points with Mom.

"Will that work?" Tom's voice snaps me back into the here and now. "June first?"

"Oh, ummm ... June first?" Becca appears in the doorway, giving me a thumbs-up. "Yeah, that should work. Unless my bike breaks down somewhere in ... what states are between here and there?" Tom sighs and I laugh. "Just kidding. I will be there by June first, big bro. Don't worry, Jay and Randy say I mastered the suicide shift like a prodigy."

I'm pretty sure that was a gasp at the other end of the line, followed by a sigh. "I don't even want to know what that means," says Tom.

"And, man, I hope Alex has her mom's green thumb, for the sake of that jungle in your dining room."

"Lindsey is in the process of writing out directions for all of her babies," he says, his voice relaxing into the light back and forth I love. "Prepare for some heavy reading and training that'll make whatever a *suicide shift* is seem like a walk in the park. Gotta go. Someone's knocking on the door. Oh, Charlie?"

"Yeah?"

"Thanks. This really means a lot to me. To Lindsey and me. To both of us."

"No worries. I've got your back." I hang up and stare at the floor for a moment or two. The question of whether Tom and Lindsey are having trouble has edged its way back to the top of my mind.

Chapter 3

The FCC and Becca

"What's this I hear about you going out there on the FCC?" Becca's brows are practically smothering her eyes, and the color is being pursed from her lips.

"Oh, that. Yeah. You know how I feel about planes. So, I figured I'd take the FCC. Give the old girl a spin for real." I flash one of my widest grins, hoping to enchant her away from the lecture I feel coming on. There's no way she'll drop it as quickly as Tom did.

"Emphasis on *old*," she says. "You've never ridden that thing for more than a few miles at a time, and now you want to go halfway across the country on it? And what the hell is a *suicide* shift?"

"It's nothing," I say, laughing, hoping to lighten the mood. "It's just a silly name for the shift mechanism on my bike. You know, like with cars? A stick shift as opposed to an automatic? Some people are scared of them, I guess. Anyway, Randy says she's ready for the open road."

"Did you mention to Randy how long that open road will be?" Becca gives me a knowing look before heading over to the coffee machine for a second round.

"Well, no. Not yet. Though, to be fair, *I* didn't even know how long the road would be until just a few minutes ago." My million-dollar grin morphs to a more comfortable, impish smile. It doesn't have the disarming effect I was going for.

"Ok. Point taken. I'll go down to the shop tomorrow and tell Randy what I'm thinking. If I get a thumbs down, I'll take the Jeep. I promise." I cross my index finger across my chest and soften my eyes. I know she's just worried about me. "Oh, and Tom wants me out there by June first. So, it looks like we'll be leaving around the same time."

"Why so early? I thought they were leaving on the fifteenth."

A quick burst of tension rides up my spine before I can shake the feeling of standing alone outside of some giant family loop. I take a deep breath in, resigned.

You can't complain. There are plenty of things they don't know about you. I push the voice from my head. It's one I haven't heard in a while, and don't care to hear from again.

"Well, they want me to get the lay of the land and master the study of the sacred plant manual before they leave." Becca giggles at this, as expected. She always gets a kick out of my Jungle Book comments or faux-horrified *wait, is that the plant from Little Shop of Horrors? Run kids, run!* exclamations when the annual Christmas card arrives. "Oh, and Alex will be there, too."

"Alex? Isn't she going to camp?"

I shake my head. Ha! This is a loop I'm actually in on, mainly because I wanted to go away to a summer camp as a kid. My parents had even suggested one, but circumstances never allowed for it to happen. I always grin when I get Alex's postcards from camp. You know, kind of a living-vicariously-through-my-niece thing. I love reading about campfires and canoeing, and even admit to having been a little jealous when she wrote about learning archery. Hopefully, Jimmy will send some this summer.

"She's refusing to go this year. Something about a falling out with friends. She wanted to hang out with Mom, but ..."

"The cruise," says Becca, nodding. "Yeah, that wouldn't work. And Lindsey's ok with this? I mean, obviously you'll be an excellent babysitter. Not even that, really, since Alex is practically a teenager. You'll be a wonderful house sitter and it'll be a great chance to bond with your niece, since we only see them around holidays ..."

I hold up a hand and laugh. "I know what you meant. I'm sure Lindsay will be a little nervous when she finds out you can't come with me, but Tom says it'll be fine. Besides, like you said, the kid's practically ready to move out on her own, start a career. She'll probably be more the babysitter than I am, especially when it comes to those precious green babies in the dining room. She might even end up saving my life if I get lost in that jungle."

Becca sets the cups under the spouts, flips a switch and the java begins to flow. She takes my hand, draws me close, leans her forehead against mine, then kisses me.

"That's one of my favorite things about you," she says, giving my hand a squeeze. "You always find the positive and you can always make me laugh."

"I love you, too," I say. If she only knew the paths of negativity and doubt my thoughts almost always trudged through before I can filter the darkness out, quash my cynicism and speak. I pull her into an embrace as she picks up her cup.

"Careful," she says, finishing her coffee before it spills.

I take her cup and place it next to mine. Now free, her hands rest between my shoulder blades, her arms tight against my sides. She nestles closer and runs a hand up the back of my neck into my hair. I take a deep breath, intoxicated by the mix of her perfume— a light and enticing scent—and the lingering smell of fresh coffee.

Chapter 4

The FCC and Me (Randy's Blessing)

A few days later, I'm cruising along on the FCC, almost home from trying to lengthen my ride-time endurance, when I notice a package on the front stoop of our little ranch. I don't recall having ordered anything, but the packaging will be useful. Becca had the wonderful idea of shipping my things out ahead of me, so I won't have to worry about overloading the motorcycle—something I'll need to do soon if I want my stuff to arrive on time without paying those ridiculous express or overnight fees.

That's right! I will be riding the FCC all the way to Colorado. At this thought, my cheeks pinch, forced up by a wide, toothy grin. Randy gave her a once over yesterday, took a ride alongside us to see how my skills have progressed, then gave her opinion over a hot cup of coffee and pancakes. My treat, of course. I insisted after she gave the ok.

"Yeah, you can totally do this. And I know your bike can after being restored and maintained by such a talented mechanic," Randy had said while drowning her pancakes in syrup.

I laughed and reached over to give her a pat on the back. "Here, let me take over so your arm doesn't get tired," I said. "Oh, and breakfast is on me. Wait, you didn't just say I could do the trip to get a free breakfast, did you?"

"Are you kidding me? And risk getting murdered by that hot lady of yours?" said Randy. "Not worth it. Seriously, though, you have some time before you need to get going. Do some longer rides, maybe test your mileage with some highway riding. You should get maybe thirty to forty-five mpg. Oh, and Becca said I should remind you to map out your stops. I'd say you can maybe get a little north of two hundred miles on a full tank. What is it, eleven or twelve hundred miles to your destination? Maybe five or six gas stops?"

I nodded. I had done the math.

"And I won't mention security, cause I *know* you've got that covered. What'd you call that crazy science fiction tracker you put on her?"

A smirk creeps up the left side of my face. "Shadow. Impossible to find, and always finds its way home. Like the dog in that movie, Homeward Bound. Also," I tapped my watch, "if you even look at the FCC wrong, I get a rumble on my smart watch. All that and I've been thinking of getting a set of disc locks …"

"Newsflash. Disc locks got no place to go on your old bike. But you can pull the spark plugs, maybe get a chain lock for an extra layer of protection. Oh, and you still haven't told me what FCC stands for," she said, chuckling. "I asked Becca, but she said it's your bike and you named it. So, it's not her place to tell."

"And that is why I love that woman," I said, raising my brows and nodding.

"Fine. Knowing you, you probably can't say it out in public anyway. There might be little kids listening." Randy had turned her focus back to her breakfast, and I laughed to myself thinking about how silly *the Flying Candy Cane* sounded and imagining her reaction if I told her.

THE BOX HAS Becca's name on it, but no return address. I take it inside after parking my bike in the garage and set it on the floor next to the kitchen island. My bet is that it's equipment for her job. She's a physical therapist. A damned good one, too. So good that she quit her job at the clinic a few years back and became an independent contractor. Patients seek her out and can only hope they are lucky enough to fit into her schedule.

That's actually how we met, having sought her out following my dad's first stroke. It's also one of the many reasons my mom loves her so much. Her patience with Dad was nothing short of angelic. Not that he was a horrible patient. He wasn't. But when something like that takes an active person like Dad completely out of the game, there's going to be a fair amount of frustration. Frustration that tends to rear its head and gnash its teeth at the people who are the closest.

Becca and I didn't start dating until about a year after his sessions finished. She wanted to make sure my feelings weren't due to transference, or hers to the Florence Nightingale effect. She was there for my dad, but essentially helping the whole family deal with our new situation.

When we did make it official, my parents welcomed her with open arms because it already felt like she was a part of the family.

"I never did like that last one you chose," Dad said when I finally worked up the courage to tell him that we were an item. Mom stood beside him, nodding in agreement.

A smile had melted the nervous strain tensing my face, and my jaw slacked. Of course, my parents had been there for me during the divorce. They were my support system, always there to listen to my rants, but I had never heard either of them express such a stark opinion of my past choice.

And, Tom ... well, Tom later told me he could see how happy I was around Becca from day one, despite my sadness for Dad.

Dad's second, and final, stroke came a few months later, and Becca was there with us through his last days on earth.

I reach up, catching a tear that's gathering mass before it can escape and slide down my cheek. This happens whenever I think of Dad and the way he was taken from us. I shake my head and walk to the fridge to find myself a snack.

"Whoa there, sweetie," says Becca, walking into the kitchen and putting a hand on the fridge door. "Aren't we going to meet Randy and Jay for dinner pretty soon?"

"Yes," I say, scooping her into a hug. "But," I spin her around and turn back to the fridge, "I'm hungry *now*."

Becca's brows climb in a faux-shocked expression. "Well, I never. I suppose one little piece of the peach pie I made this afternoon won't completely spoil your appetite."

"Pie? You made *pie*? Cancel the dinner. I'm set for tonight!"

"Very funny. Seriously though, we have about twenty minutes before we need to leave. If you're going to savage my pie, you'd better be quick about it. I'll be upstairs getting ready."

I turn from the fridge, pie in hand, brows furrowed. "This isn't a fancy dinner, right? I mean, I don't think I've ever seen Randy or Jay in anything other than jeans."

"No, nothing fancy. I just need to change. I had kind of a rough session with Mrs. Kline. You know how she can get."

I nod and offer a sympathetic smile. Mrs. Kline is a seventy-five-year-old ex-marine. She recently suffered a fractured hip and makes no qualms about showing her frustration at the speed at which her rehabilitation is proceeding. This includes not only hurling insults, but the occasional plate of food as well. The insults are never personally aimed at Becca, and she always apologizes and pays for dry-cleaning if necessary, which isn't often because Becca knows not to wear anything that can't be quickly thrown into the washing machine ... or the trash ... without any fuss.

"Guess what, though? We actually made a lot of progress today, and when I left, she was smiling."

My mouth forms a gawping hole and I bring a hand to my heart while the other balances the pie. "Smiling?"

"And, I only counted ten F-bombs, total" she says, laughing when my eyes pop open.

"No. It can't be true. Are you sure she's ok? Ten has to be an all-time low. Just that one time I accidentally trampled her flowers when I was a kid brought on a string of at least fifteen! And that was all in a matter of seconds. There may have been more, but I was too busy running to hear them."

"Ok, goofball. We can talk about your childhood transgressions later on at dinner. I know for a fact that Jay has some stories. Now, I'm going to get ready and I suggest you do the same. There's something I need to show you before we leave." She throws a mysterious wink my way and saunters down the hall to the bedroom.

I look over at the pie. It's still calling to me, but intrigue takes the upper hand. I put it back in the fridge and head after her.

"Something you need to show me?" I call, curiosity raising the pitch of my voice.

WHEN WE RETURN to the kitchen after getting ready, the pie calls to me again. I gaze at the fridge, and my stomach gurgles its opinion.

"You can wait until after dinner," says Becca, poking my ribs. "I promise, if you're still hungry when we get home, we'll have ice cream and pie with a big ole heaping of whipped cream on top."

"We have ice cream, too?"

"Focus," she says, lifting the package I brought in earlier onto the table. "Open this."

I slide over next to her and lift the box, giving it a little shake next to my ear, as if willing it to reveal its contents.

"Open it." Becca is having trouble containing her excitement now. It is contagious.

I fetch a pair of scissors from our everything drawer and spread the blades.

"Careful," she says, when I rest a blade on the edge of the tape.

I nod and slide the scissors the length of the box, freeing the cardboard flaps from the strip of brown packing tape. Then I glance over at Becca before parting them for a look inside. The sides of her eyes are crinkled and a grin is pushing her rosy cheeks into plump little cushions. The right side of her lower lip is tucked between her teeth. She is radiant.

When I look inside, my breath fails me for a few beats. My eyes feel like they must be glistening like the sea on a sunny summer day. I reach inside and pull out a striking navy-blue jacket with red shoulders and silver reflective stripes, followed by some kind of vest, and a pair of protective pants. I lay everything out on the table and go back in for a pair of riding boots that look like they were flown in from the future. They are surprisingly light. One more trip into the box lands me a curious-looking light gadget and a set of reflective helmet strips that match my new ensemble. I am speechless.

"Do you like them?" Becca's staring at me, trying to gauge my reaction. Her smile is infectious and she's rising and falling on the balls of her feet, waiting for me to speak.

I clear my throat and run a hand under each eye.

"Becca, this is too much. It's awesome, but it's too much." I hold the jacket up in front of me, admiring its sleek design. She rushes to take it so I can slip it on. It is, of course, exactly the right size and feels airier than I expect.

"Reach into the left pocket on the inside. Your left," she says.

I do and pull out a little packet of gummies. I love gummies and Becca knows it. "Hors d'oeuvres?" I ask, my brows arched. I lick my lips.

Becca bats my hand. "That's for the trip, Sunshine. Not for now. They are energy gummies with electrolytes."

"But I love gummies, babe! Just one?"

"You know you won't just eat one, Charlie. And, those aren't candy! Put them away for when you actually need them. Like, on your way or if you guys go hiking."

I shrug, slide them back into the pocket, and zip it closed. Then run my hands down the front of the jacket, doing a little spin like a model on a catwalk.

"It has a waterproof membrane you can put on if it rains and air mesh fabric inserts so it won't get too hot while you ride. There are aluminum plates in there somewhere and shoulder, elbow, back, and chest protectors. The pants are made of mesh fabric, too, and have all sorts of protective inserts. They actually zip together, the jacket and the pants. The vest ..." She holds it up, "is like an airbag. Randy says it's state-of-the-art." Of course, Randy was in on this. Becca and I know very little about the motorcycling world. She sets it back down and picks up the gadget with the lights. "This is a brake light that attaches to the back of your helmet. Cool, right?"

"Very," I say, trying to figure out how to wire it to the bike.

"No connecting wires," she states, anticipating the question. "Randy says it has something called *smart brake detection.*"

"Cool. Babe, how much did all this cost?" I pick up one of the boots and turn it over.

"That's for me to know and you to never find out. That's how presents work." She laughs, obviously happy with my expression of awe. "Don't worry. Randy knows people and got me a phenomenal deal. She knows this trip has had me a little on edge. With all this safety gear, I feel much better about you taking the FCC all the way to Colorado. Besides, you look really hot in that." She slides her hands inside the jacket and around my waist. "You should wear it to dinner tonight."

"Well, I will now," I say, pulling her closer and kissing her.

"Look at the time," she says, pointing to the digital display on the microwave behind me. "We'd better get moving. We don't want to keep them waiting." She trots over to the hallway and stops at the foyer closet to pull out a matching jacket. She grins up at me. "Got a jacket for myself, too, to complete the look when we're riding together."

My brows shoot up. Becca has never shown any interest in boarding the FCC, with or without me. My heart flip flops, forcing a gasp through my teeth. I'm certain this day cannot get any better.

"Let's get moving," she says before I can respond. "I got myself a helmet, too. It's in the garage. We can ride over to The Hilltop on your bike. Just go slow. Remember, I'm a newbie."

From the very first—somewhat awkward—ride, cruising around on the FCC has always felt liberating. Not that I otherwise feel trapped. It's hard to explain. The closest thing I can compare it to is when I was ten and got my first real bicycle, a ten-speed Schwinn. I went everywhere on that thing. It felt like flying. I even named it. Red Lightning. Yeah, I've never been great at naming things. Another good reason not to have kids. Anyhow, the bicycle opened up a whole new world for me, expanded my horizons. The FCC has done the same. Riding her just makes me feel lighter—carefree. Riding with Becca cuddled up behind me, her arms wrapped around my waist, is perfection.

Cruising down Main Street, my mind drifts to when I was sixteen and mentioned to Bill that I might ask my parents for a scooter for Christmas.

"That's really all I want from *Santa* this year," I'd said.

He had turned and looked at me with disdain. It was a look that cuts my breath off to this day when conjured from my memories.

"Kids who ride scooters and motorbikes look like punks." The words had fallen on me like a sandbag, a punch to the gut. "I can't have you looking like a punk now, can I? The image you project is essential. You are an excellent and obedient student, and that is what people should think when they see you." A solemn nod and I never spoke of wanting a scooter again. Which is why I couldn't believe it when I saw the motorcycle in his garage.

"Let the past live in the past," Becca always says. Of course, she's generally referring to my divorce when she says it. She knows next to nothing about my childhood.

Chapter 5

Old Friends, New Lives

Randy and Jay are already seated when we arrive at the restaurant. I get a text teasing us for being late and letting us know where to find them. We ended up leaving the house in plenty of time, but I took the back roads.

"Why'd you go the long way?" asks Becca. She pulls off her helmet and leans down to use one of the side mirrors to adjust her hair.

I grin. I was going to take the direct route, but it felt so good cruising along with her tucked up against my body, her arms cinched around me. A little too tightly at first, then relaxing into the rumble of the 1300cc motor. I didn't want it to end.

"I wanted you to get the full experience," I say. "Didn't you see all those people admiring us in our matching outfits, floating along on this stylish beast of a vehicle?"

"Anyone ever tell you you should be a writer, what with your flare for poetic descriptions?" She hands me her helmet and I cable them both to the FCC. Then she takes my hand and we make our entrance into The Hilltop Tavern to find Randy and Jay.

We get to the table just as a waitress arrives with a tray full of beers and a huge plate of fries.

"We went ahead and ordered some refreshments," says Jay. "You guys can get the next round." He stands and extends a hand, pulling us in for a quick squeeze.

"Nice digs," Randy says, winking at Becca. "You have great taste for someone who doesn't truly appreciate the beauty of a great bike."

Becca laughs and loops her hands around my arm. "That might be changing. Guess how we came here tonight?"

"Hear that, sweetie?" Jay says, tapping his wife's arm. "She may be coming around, yet. How'd she do, Charlie?"

I gesture an unsure motion with my hand. Becca lets go of my arm and gives me a playful push.

"Fine. She did just fine," I say.

We have been out with Randy and Jay a few times now. It's always pleasant. The conversation flows easily like a rain-swollen creek, filled with wisecracks and belly laughter. I'm glad I ran into Jay at the end of my divorce. After being suffocated socially by someone who used my insecurities as a bludgeon against me, it felt good to reconnect with someone from my pre-marriage past.

I hadn't seen him in years, about ten if I remember correctly. He wasn't exactly an angel when he was a teenager, when my group of friends scattered. It was good to see that he'd turned his life around, met Randy, and opened a shop with her.

"You guys sell motorcycles?" I could totally see it. He went for the punk image while I was the Goody Two-shoes.

"Sell, restore, repair. We do it all. My wife's a killer mechanic. I prefer to work the floors, seal the deals. We've built up quite a loyal following. You should check out our website," he'd said, his voice and posture reflecting a pride I'd never seen when he was a teenager.

"What a coincidence. Did you know Bill had a motorcycle? I found it in his garage. I don't think it runs, though. I have it in storage with a bunch of his stuff I still have to go through."

Jay's eyes widened. He shook his head and laughed. "Didn't he always say ..."

I nodded, a burst of laughter rushing out through my nose.

"Bill, the punk. Who knew?"

We both laughed until tears shimmered in our eyes and any apprehension about our shared past had melted away. The air was clear and a new friendship was born.

"What is it? Want me to come take a look at it? I can bring my wife, Randy, give you an estimate."

"I think it's called an Indian, or something like that. It looks pretty old. I'd love to get your opinion."

"You have an old Indian motorcycle stashed away in storage?" Jay gave me a pat on the shoulder. "Do you believe in destiny, Charlie? Because I'm pretty sure fate brought us back together. Think you'd want to sell her?"

My brows furrowed and I gnawed at the inside of my cheek. I'd never thought of selling anything of Bill's. It kind of felt like a betrayal, though I knew that was totally irrational. If anyone was the betrayer in our situation ...

"Nah. If you think you can get it running, I'd like to learn to ride it." I'd hunched my shoulders and watched his expression, worried he might be disappointed.

An easy, sincere smile lit his face, crinkling the corners of his eyes. He reached out and gave my shoulder another pat. "Yeah. Even better. Man, I think I just heard someone rolling over in his grave."

"Charlie? What do you think?" The sound of Becca's voice yanks me back to the present. She reaches over and nudges the bottom of my chin with her index finger—her solution for when I slip into daydreams and let my jaw slack open. It's a habit I've had since I was little, despite my dad's warning about flying insects swooping in if I wasn't careful.

I refocus my eyes and scratch the back of my head, as if considering the question. The one I didn't really hear because I was daydreaming. What is it we were talking about? The last thing that pops into mind is the discussion about the different ways to get from here to Tom's place. I wonder if the question has anything to do with that. I decide to throw out an answer.

"I was thinking on the way out, it might be nice to swing south and stop in St. Louis to take a look around."

"Right, but do you think you're going to break the trip up or try to make it there in one day?" Becca knows I was in a completely different world and I appreciate her efforts to bring me up to speed.

I shrug and take a quick sip of beer. "I'll probably decide on the way. I'm giving myself a few days to get out there, just in case. I might even want to take a peek at some sights, maybe check out the St. Louis Arch and stuff."

"Seems like a good idea," says Jay, nodding. He reaches into his pocket, pulls out a folded paper, and hands it to me.

I open it and look over the list of names and numbers organized by state.

"What's this?" I ask.

"That, my friend, is a list compiled by my much-more-worldly-than-I-am wife." He puts an arm around Randy and kisses her on the cheek. "She knows mechanics in bike shops all around the US of A."

Randy grins and shakes her head. "Maybe not *all* around the US of A. I don't know any in Alaska, for example." She pauses and scrunches up her face. "Wait, I take that back. I think Pete Greene moved there when he left Wisconsin. Anyway, the numbers there should cover most of the road you'll travel if you head south and through St. Louis." She hands me another piece of paper, and a twenty-dollar bill to her husband. "This one has numbers for the route that would take you through Chicago and across Iowa, which is, by the way, the fastest way to get there." She shoots a knowing look at Jay, who flashes a toothy smile.

"She thought you'd wanna get there as soon as possible. I told her there was no way you were gonna waste your very first road trip on a highway through corn fields. And so a bet was born." He makes a production of carefully folding the bill and sliding it into his shirt pocket, then gives the pocket a couple taps.

"I guessed that if you were one for meandering, you would have got the heck outta here years ago. Didn't you inherit an entire house or something when you were a kid?"

I shrug off the question, but Jay nods an affirmation.

"Man, I would've sold that thing, jumped on a bike, and hit the road until the money ran out. Of course, then I might have missed out on meeting the love of my life here," says Randy, leaning her head on Jay's shoulder. "But I would be twenty bucks richer." She reaches over to his shirt pocket like she is going to lift the bill, and Jay's hand flies up in defense.

I attempt to swallow a sudden lump in my throat, feeling my pulse quicken—my body's usual response when my mind wanders to my unexpected inheritance. The rest of the table does not seem to notice my discomfort. I'm glad. I don't want to taint an otherwise pleasant evening.

The ride home is just as magical as the previous journey, and helps to bring my mind to a better place. As we cruise along, I find myself wishing that Becca could come to Colorado with me and that *my* first road trip on the FCC could be *our* first road trip. But I know that isn't going to happen. So instead, I start thinking of places we can go when we are back together again.

Maybe a trip to the East Coast? I've always wanted to see New England. We could go in the fall, when the leaves are those unbelievable colors I've seen in calendars at my mom's house. We supposedly have a great-aunt there somewhere. I don't remember meeting her, but she sends a new New England fall calendar every Christmas like clockwork.

That night in my dreams, I ride serpentine backroads flanked by vibrant splashes of scarlet, orange, and gold foliage, Becca snuggled up behind me.

Chapter 6

Ready to Roll

It's three days before my departure and I'm ready to roll. Becca and I have decided to leave for our separate destinations on the same day. That way, nobody has to spend any time in the empty house, pining for the other. She took a few days off to pack and get her car ready, and to spend some more time with me before saying goodbye.

I've been taking longer and longer rides on the FCC, mostly with Becca. I told her about my idea for a trip to New England in the fall. We are going to make it happen. First, though, I'll have to get through the summer ... and house-sitting ... and babysitting ... and plant sitting.

My phone buzzes in my pocket. It's Tom.

"Hey Tom, what's up?" Maybe Alex decided to go to camp and they only need a house-sitter. Or maybe they won't need me to come at all, which would honestly be a little awkward since I already shipped my stuff. Oh well, he can ship it back just as easily. Then I could hop on my bike and follow Becca to her parents' place. Of course, I would book an Airbnb so they wouldn't even know I was there. We could—

"Charlie. Can you hear me? Are you there?"

"Yeah. Sorry, I got distracted. Everything ok? Are we still on?" I try to keep any traces of concern out of my voice.

"Of course we are. I wanted to let you know that your stuff got here. That's an awfully small box. You sure that's all you'll need?"

"I like to travel light."

"I wasn't aware that you liked to travel at all." He laughs and I hear a rimshot in my head.

"I'm warming up to it. Though my mechanic warned me that I'm going to be a little sore for a few days after the ride out. Ask me how keen I am on travel then."

"Are you all ready? Sure you don't want to take the plane? I can still get you a ticket."

"No planes. Geez, Tom. I'm finally going more than a few miles out of this town. One step at a time," I say in a playful tone.

"Sorry. I just worry about you. Pretty sure that's my job as an older brother. Anyway, I'm glad you're finally coming to see where we live. You will love it out here. And, next time you come ... because there *will* be a next time ... you have to bring Becca."

"Definitely. She's sad she can't come this time." I pause, allowing the image of the two of us riding across the country to form. "And, so am I."

"Well, when you do bring her, I know she'll love it, too. Hell, maybe I can convince you guys to move out here. Mom has actually been considering it."

This is news to me, though I'm not completely surprised. I know she'd love to be closer to her grandkids. I haven't given her any and there is no way in hell Tom will move back. Not only is Lindsey's whole family in Colorado, but I know Tom loves it out there.

"I don't know, Tom. It sounds beautiful and all, but I have the business."

"Becca says you've set it up so that you can run it remotely. She says you have a great crew there. You could open an office here and head back occasionally to make sure everything is running smoothly."

I pinch my lips and shake my head.

"So, you two have been conspiring?" I say in an exaggerated *a-ha* voice. I am a little hurt that Becca never mentioned even considering a move to me, but I know why.

"Nah," he says. "Just making small talk. But I know you guys would love it here."

"Ok ok. I get it. Let's just get through this summer before you guys completely plan out my life." There's a slight edge to my voice this time, as I contemplate yet another loop of which I am not a part.

"Agreed. But don't be surprised if you fall in love with life out here." He lowers his voice. "Charlie, I know that Mr. Edwards was like a grandfather to you, but when he died, it kind of felt like you gave up on a lot of your dreams. You never even came out for family weekend at CU like we planned."

What would he think of our loop? I ignore the voice, jaw clenched.

"You're not still mad at me about that, are you?" This conversation is beginning to wear on me.

"I never was," he says. "Just disappointed. I was secretly hoping you would decide to go to school here, I guess. I missed you." He successfully disarms my rising ire with this last statement. I am silent. When did my big brother become so dang sentimental?

"Anyway, I'm glad you agreed to come and hang out with Alex. She kind of reminds me of you when you were a kid, you know. She has your snarky humor, which is not something her mom appreciates."

"I think that's just called *adolescence*," I say, laughing. Though I am genuinely flattered. "PS, Becca doesn't always appreciate *my* snarky humor, either."

"Great. You two can commiserate."

"Hey. Did you ever find out why she doesn't want to go to camp? Anything I can help with while I'm there?"

"All I know is that a few weeks ago, she and her best friend, Chloe, were looking forward to it. Those two have been inseparable since kindergarten. Then, suddenly, they aren't speaking to each other. Chloe is going to camp and Alex is refusing. She won't tell us what happened. Chloe's mom is just as confused as we are." He takes a deep, calming breath. "Alex is happy that you're coming, though. The other day, I caught her writing some kind of list of things for you guys to do."

"Well, maybe she'll end up telling me what happened. Sometimes it's hard to tell your parents things." *Even really important things you should tell them. Life or death things*, I add in my head.

"I'm kind of hoping she will. She and Chloe were so close. Kind of like you and Sarah were." Now there's a name I haven't heard in a long time, though I'm not totally shocked to hear him say it. "Man, did I have a crush on her when I was in high school."

"I was well aware of that," I say. "And, so was she."

"Was I that obvious?" He adds an embarrassed chuckle.

"Was our blacktop driveway a million degrees in the summer?" This brings up some belly laughs on both sides of the line.

"Whatever happened to Sarah?" he asks.

"Not sure. She took off after some guy when I was all tangled up with Bill's estate. Not an easy maze for a teenager to navigate." A sigh slips out before my throat tightens.

"I'm guessing he thought you'd be a little older when you'd have to deal with that. Too bad you didn't have your kickass lawyer brother to help you. I wasn't even in law school yet, when all that went down."

"Nope. But you did help Mom when Dad passed away. And you and that friend of yours were lifesavers during my divorce. So don't be too hard on yourself. You haven't been completely useless."

"Tom, is that Charlie you're talking to? If so, say 'hi' from me!" Lindsey's peppy, cheerleader voice sounds from somewhere on Tom's end.

I roll my eyes and laugh. "Tell Lindsey I can't wait to see her, too. Sounds like you've gotta go, big bro. I will see all of you soon."

"Can't wait," he says, genuine excitement in his voice. "Remember. You don't have to do it all in one day. And maybe call from time to time to let me know you're ok."

"Will do, Tom. Bye." I hang up the phone and find Becca standing in the doorway holding our spider plant.

"I think I should take the baby with me," she says. "That is, unless you want to take him out to visit his cousins in Colorado."

Man, am I going to miss her.

Chapter 7

The Adventure Begins

We wake up at 4 am on the big day, so we can have a relaxed breakfast together before heading out. I go extra heavy on the coffee. I didn't get much sleep. My mind kept tossing up worst-case scenarios and how to overcome them, running through lists of things I didn't want to forget, and trying to recall everything Randy and Jay had taught me: from tips on how to avoid cramping up, to a variety of hand signals useful for communicating with other bikers on the road. I caught a few hours of sleep somewhere in between, but not nearly as many as I wanted.

"Whoa. Slow down there, champ," says Becca. "You're going to need to hit the restrooms before you get to the end of our street if you keep downing coffee like that. Remember, what goes in eventually needs to come out."

"I know. I'm just a little nervous." I set my mug on the table.

"Oh, well, then you should definitely load up on caffeine to calm those nerves." She rolls her eyes, then gets up to clear the table, starting with my not-quite-empty coffee mug.

"No. Not my fuel. Don't take my fuel," I whine, pretending to reach for it with a weak, floppy arm. I get up to help, heaving a fake sob when she empties the remaining coffee into the sink.

"There are snacks in the saddle bags. I put in some of those energy gummies Randy suggested. They'll give you a boost without filling up your bladder."

"You and Randy have really hit it off," I say. "I like hanging out with her and Jay. They're fun. Wouldn't it be cool if we did a couple's road trip sometime? Even just down to Indy or something for a night on the town?"

Becca nods, smiling as she wipes down our breakfast plates. Then the corners of her lips turn down, gravity stepping in to pull us back to reality. It's time to go and we both know it.

We head outside and I do a double take. Something furry is stretched out against the front tire of the FCC.

"Hey! FFFFTTTTT! Beat it!" I yell, running and clapping. A large, brown tabby cat pauses from sharpening its claws on my bike, and turns its head to look. It's glaring at me like *I* am the one out of place. The one disturbing the peace. It wanders a few steps away, then sits and regards me with what I can only describe as an expression of complete boredom and a hint of contempt. Then it sees Becca. The change in its demeanor is immediate. The beast hops to its feet and trots over to her, head and tail held high.

"Hey there, handsome," Becca croons, leaning over to receive the affection this now bouncing, purring ball of fur is exuding. "Is this scary human bothering you?"

She smirks at me, then crouches to shower the feline interloper with attention. The cat looks at me. I swear to God the SOB is smiling. And is that a wink?

"I see you two are acquainted," I say, throwing a dash of contempt into my voice. "Maybe tell your *friend* it's not cool to touch other people's motorcycles. I believe that's part of Motorcycle Etiquette 101. And I'm guessing that sharpening one's claws on someone else's bike is an even more serious offense."

Becca laughs and scoops up the cat. She walks towards me, despite my obvious body language against said approach. "Oh, come on, Charlie," she says, the cat rubbing against her cheek, "it's just a cat. He's really sweet. Some of the neighbors and I have been feeding him. We think he's a stray." Great. A conspiracy. "I call him Kitty."

"Very original," I say, putting up a hand and shaking my head when she leans the cat toward me. "No thanks. I'm not a huge fan of cats."

I'm more of a dog person, and even more of a no-pet-at-all person. Dogs don't ask questions. They seem to love you no matter what. Cats? Cats are like kids ... like teenagers. Becca puts the beast down. It snakes around my legs, purring and looking up at Becca, like it's trying to show her that *it's* not the problem. Like I'm the one being unfair and unreasonable. *It* wants to be best friends.

"See? He likes you," says Becca, reaching down to give *Kitty* a pat on the head.

You lose, the cat says with its eyes. It's on.

"I have actually been thinking that maybe we should get a puppy when we are both settled back into our routines," I say, taking Becca's hands into mine. "Didn't you say your grandparents had a German shepherd? 'Best dog in the world,' were your exact words, if I remember correctly?"

"Really?" Her eyes widen and go dreamy. I bet she's thinking of a name right now. She throws her arms around me and squeezes. I smirk at Mr. Kitty over her shoulder. "I'll bet Pluto and Kitty will be best friends," she adds.

Time to move on from this conversation.

"I guess we'd better get going," I say, releasing her and looking at my watch.

"You good riding all the way to Indy, then filling up and going our separate ways?"

I nod. "I did the ride down there and back last weekend, no problem. Though I'd rather keep on going together."

"The next time you go to Colorado, I'm coming with. I promise. Let's go ahead and say goodbye here, so we're not doing it at the gas station."

She hugs me and plants a kiss on my lips. In that moment, I don't even mind the fact that Kitty is giving my leg one last rub and leaving a patch of brown fur behind which static has now made an integral part of my new pants.

The ride to the gas station in Indy is uneventful. I'm glad because I don't want Becca worrying about me the rest of the way. I'm sure she's already worried enough about how her parents are going to act while she is there. She calls to chat as we make our way south. My helmet Bluetooth attachment makes it seem like she's on the bike with me, whispering into my ear. We top off our gas tanks, lean in for a quick hug, and head off toward our destinations.

About ten minutes into my solo ride, my phone rings. It's Becca.

"Hey. Long time no see," I answer.

"Hey, Sunshine. I just wanted to let you know that I put together a playlist called Road Trip for you. Just promise you won't let the music distract you while you ride."

"Cross my heart. Thanks. Love you, babe!"

"Love you, too! Call me every now and then, and definitely let me know when you get there. Gotta go. Mom's calling. She probably wants my ETA." The line goes dead.

I instruct my phone to pull up the playlist "Road Trip." The first song that plays is "Fast Car," by Tracy Chapman. Well, that's a bit depressing. Wait, is she trying to send me a message? When David Bowie's "Rebel Rebel" comes on next, I decide I was just being paranoid. When my head starts bobbing to "I Ain't Worried," I relax into my ride and my mind wanders, even as I focus on the road ahead.

I slow down when I see a biker riding in the opposite direction tap his helmet to give me a heads up on a speed trap. My left hand comes off the bar and I drop my arm to 45 degrees, two fingers extended down. The other rider reciprocates. The biker wave. I've been practicing. It feels good, like I am part of a tribe. But not one that keeps me tethered through emotional blackmail.

Ungrateful, the both of you. After all I did for you. I practically raised you. I shake my head.

I am almost to St. Louis when I stop for gas. I could probably make it into the city, but prefer to do that on a full tank. Besides, I have been on my bike for around six hours now and am definitely starting to feel it. I pull up past a colorful metal rooster set on the side of the road to welcome incoming travelers and am elated to see that the gas station is also a diner. I close my eyes and breathe in the heavenly perfume of burgers on a grill. And are those onion rings? A look at my watch tells me what my stomach already knows. It's lunchtime.

I ride to the front of the diner so I can park the FCC where I can see her. I'll fill her up after I fill my stomach. Then I pull the spark plugs and set the motion detector/tracker. I'm nervous about leaving her there all by her lonesome.

"Sweet ride."

The voice comes from the direction of the pumps. I turn to see an elderly gentleman walking toward me. He's wearing dust-stained blue jeans that rest atop a pair of brown leather work boots. Dried mud crumbles off the bottom of his boots with each cloud-stirring step. The collar of what was most likely a white t-shirt in its younger days, but has since taken on the yellow crusty tone of years of hard work and sweat, peeks out over the highest button fastened on his long-sleeved, burgundy shirt. A straw Stetson with a thin black band sits atop his head. He removes it to run his hand through his salt and pepper hair, before setting it back on its perch. Then he turns his gaze from the FCC to me, giving my outfit a once over with eyes so dark I can't tell where his irises end and pupils begin.

"Someone sure wants to keep you safe," he says, his voice like gravel on a back road. I'm guessing he is or was a smoker. Probably was. I would expect to smell it on him with a voice that coarse.

"*I* want to keep me safe," I say, donning a cautious but friendly smile.

"Let me guess. With a bike like that, you're either a collector, or you inherited ... maybe from your grandad or even great-granddad. I'm guessing it's a fifty to fifty-three? The last years of the original Indians. That getup you're wearing looks pretty fresh from the box, so my guess is that you inherited that beautiful machine. And good for you, learning to ride her. I'm sure you got more than one generous offer to take her off your hands."

"Those are pretty close guesses," I say, even more nervous about leaving her parked outside now.

"Worried about someone taking her?"

I hunch my shoulders and raise my brows. My stomach growls loudly enough that I shift my gaze to the window of the diner, half expecting the people inside to be craning their necks, wondering if there's a storm on the way. A waitress is setting down a plate of what looks like steak and onion rings in front of a young couple seated next to the window. Once again, my stomach tugs and gurgles. Thankfully, much quieter this time.

"Food's real good in there," he says. "I should know. My wife's back there cooking it." His mouth curls up into a slow, easy smile. The kind you generally save for family or close friends. He holds out a hand. "James," he says, and somehow the fact that he leaves out his last name makes me feel more comfortable. Besides, he shares a name with my dad, another plus in my book.

I shake his hand. "Charlie."

"Good strong handshake says a lot about a person." I nod, trying to figure out what exactly my handshake is saying about me. I guess it's something good; he's still smiling.

He points up at the corner of the roof, just next to where I parked the FCC.

"Put in new cameras just last month. Not that we've ever had any real problems other than the occasional youngster trying to figure out right from wrong. It was my granddaughter's idea."

I nod. I can appreciate good security, obviously.

"Tell you what," he continues, "Let's head inside. I'll let Chris know to keep an extra eye on this fine machine of yours, so you can have a seat and enjoy a nice hot plate of home-cooked food. It's hard to appreciate a good meal if your head's all tangled in worry."

"Thank you. That sounds wonderful," I say, reassured.

The moment the door opens, and I'm engulfed by a wave of sweet and savory aromas, I know I have made the right decision. The only trick will be not eating myself into a food coma down the road. I think of the gummies Becca packed for me, but decide I won't deny myself a cup of coffee.

We walk through a small convenience store to a sign indicating the waiting area for the restaurant. James waves to a young lady standing by a refrigerated bakery case loaded with goodies and points to me. She nods and rushes over.

"Booth over by the window," he says. She nods again, walks to the booth, pulls a white cloth from her apron and gives the table a quick wipe down. Then she smiles and waves me over. "Jen will take care of you," James says, giving me a fatherly pat on the shoulder. "I'll go back to make sure there's an extra set of eyes on your bike. It was nice meeting you, Charlie."

"It was nice to meet you, too, sir. And, thank you."

"Folks gotta keep an eye out for each other," he says with a wink, before walking away.

He's right. I enjoy my meal even more knowing that the FCC is safe. Sure, she's parked practically on the other side of the window flanking my booth, and she's fitted with the latest in security tech that works with a bike her age, but knowing there's an extra set of eyes on her allows me to relax, fill my stomach, and prepare for the next leg of my journey. I'm tempted to hang out a bit longer, maybe stay overnight in St. Louis. But, I still feel pretty fresh and my preference would be getting to Colorado sooner rather than later. Besides, if I'm nervous about leaving her parked outside a diner for a meal, how am I going to feel about leaving the FCC overnight?

It's about four hours to Kansas City, allowing for a stop to stretch and get gas along the way. That'll be the perfect time to get dinner, though I doubt I'll find anything as good as the food I just ate. Randy gave me the name and number of a garage there where I can park the FCC overnight, and there's a Holiday Inn practically next door. Also, I don't want to make Tom and Lindsey wait up for me. If I try to make it tonight, it will end up being really early tomorrow morning at this rate.

I call Tom and leave a voicemail when he doesn't answer. Then I text Becca to let her know. Becca and I agreed we would text before any calls so that her parents wouldn't know it was me and start in on how much they disapprove.

I pay the check and include a large, well-deserved tip and a "thank you!" penned at the bottom. Then I make my way to the convenience store, hoping to find one of those cold coffee drinks and a few bags of chips to add to the stash of healthy snacks Becca prepared. I am waiting in line to pay when I see a little boy with a dark blue coat in the candy aisle. He's probably around six or seven years old. His coat looks like it's at least two sizes too big, his dark brown peach fuzz hair barely poking over the top of the hood folded down against his back.

I scan the area around him, but don't see any signs of a parent. The few people in line in front of me don't seem to notice the boy. He stares longingly at the rows of sweets, then reaches for a bag of Twizzlers, turns it over a few times in his hands and slides it into his sleeve.

My jaw slacks and my throat muscles tense in an effort to keep my heart from climbing right out of my mouth. My eyes flit back and forth, but the rest of me is frozen, my mind floating somewhere between the past and the present.

Not much skill and absolutely no technique, but he's got the balls. The voice is getting clearer, crisper somehow. I push it away.

The boy turns his head and catches me watching. He stands, pie-eyed, his mouth set in a determined pout. I'm about to look away, to inch my way up in the line as if nothing happened, when a movement behind the boy catches my eye. My new friend, James, walks up to him and taps him on the shoulder. His little body jolts at the touch, as if it holds the voltage of a lightning bolt. James lowers himself to the boy's level and puts a firm hand on each shoulder. He tips his head down and raises his brows. His lips are moving, forming words with soft precision. Deep creases line his forehead, but his eyes are kind.

The boy nods to whatever is being said. He slides the Twizzlers out of his sleeve and points to the woman in front of me in the line. She's holding a plastic basket filled with grocery items in one hand. The other is wrapped around the handlebar of a pram. She is moving it in short bursts, forward and backward, I assume to appease the happy-looking baby lying inside.

No doubt this is the boy's mother. He looks like a small version of her, and the baby looks like an even smaller version of him. The baby sees me looking and smiles with a gurgle, forming a tiny bubble at the corner of its mouth, which makes its way down a rivulet of drool. The woman turns to see what is so amusing. My cheeks flush, a voyeur caught in action.

"Cute kid," I say, my comment feeling somewhat obligatory given the circumstances. Besides, the kid is actually kind of cute, as babies go.

She smiles, then her expression shifts when she spots James approaching with her son by his side. The boy trudges along, his eyes studying every inch of the floor.

The bag of Twizzlers is dangling from his right hand.

"Hello there, young lady," says James, after giving me a quick nod. "What a beautiful little sweetheart." He wiggles his fingers at the baby, who answers with an infectious, gurgly belly laugh. "This delightful young man tells me you are his mother." He looks down at the little boy, who has lost all color in his face.

The woman regards her son with a certain intensity flashing in her eyes. It sends an inexplicable tingle up my spine.

"Yes, sir. This is my son, Danny. Everything ok?" Her lips slide up into a smile that doesn't quite make it over her cheekbones to her eyes.

"Right as rain now. I was just explaining to young Danny that this is a store, a local store that serves this community. And, that in a store," he is speaking to the woman, but it's obvious from his tone that the words are meant more for young Danny, who is absorbing each and every one, "we need to pay for the things that we want. There is no hide-and-seek with the merchandise."

The woman's smile fades and her brows pinch. She releases the pram and grabs hold of the boy's arm, spinning him to her side. His lips part and he sucks in a startled gasp, dropping the Twizzlers.

"Did you try to steal those, Danny?" Her words are a sharp hiss. Danny's gaze bounces between his mother and James, catching mine on the way by. He has the appearance of a small animal trapped in a cage.

"No need to get overly upset," says James, his voice slow and smooth. "Danny and I had ourselves a little talk, and he has apologized."

Danny nods. He slides from his mother's grip, picks up the Twizzlers and hands them to James. Then he steps beside his mother, a hopeful gaze fixed on the elderly man.

"I am so sorry about this," his mother says, setting down her basket. "I am so embarrassed. I'll come back for this stuff later, if that's ok. I need to get him home." She turns to her son. "Danny, we're going right home and you are gonna stay in your room at least until supper. Say sorry to the nice man, again."

"I'm sorry, sir," he says, his voice a squeaky whisper.

"Apology accepted, Danny." James holds out a hand. The boy

looks at his mom, who jerks her head toward the extended hand. He reaches out and they shake on it. Then his mother marches him and the pram out of the store, giving a tug every few feet to supplement the boy's short steps.

When they are outside, James turns to me. "I sure hope poor Danny doesn't get it too bad at home. I think he may have learned his lesson."

"He looked pretty sorry to me," I say. He did, though something in the back of my mind wonders if he was sorry he did it or sorry he got caught. Or maybe I was wondering that more about his mother.

"Got any kids?" asks James.

"No, sir."

"Suzy and I have seven," he says, running a hand around the back of his neck, then laughing at my shocked expression. "Sounds like a lot, I know. Every one of 'em is different from the others. One thing I learned, Charlie. Parents are only a part of what shapes 'em. It really does take a village."

After I pay for my items and thank James for his kindness, I walk out to the FCC, still parked safe and sound where I left her. Once I stash my purchases in the tail box and slip my helmet back on, I move to the pumps so I can fill up and get going.

To my surprise, Danny and his family are still in the parking lot. They are behind a large blue minivan on the other side of the pumps near the main road. The slider-door is open and the baby is fastened into a safety seat which is belted in close to the opening. The boy, Danny, is on the floor of the van, seated just inside, feet dangling over the edge. He pulls a big red sucker from his mouth and licks at it happily while his mother pulls items from deep inside the pram and loads them into the back.

I freeze, pump in hand, when I remember she didn't buy the things in her basket.

The magic of misdirection. Now there's a proper pro. Perhaps little Danny isn't quite as inept as we thought. A shiver runs through me. "Shut up," I hiss in a whisper, thinking of the kind old man, James, and his optimism.

Danny's mom catches me staring and gives a whistle, prompting Danny to pull in his feet and slide the door closed. She tosses the pram into the back of the minivan and rushes to the driver's door. She gives me a wink as she drives off.

Danny's gonna need one helluva village, I think to myself.

Chapter 8

Road Trip Reverie

I get on the road again and head toward Kansas City. I already called the garage to let them know the FCC will be spending the night. The moment I dropped Randy's name, I went from total stranger to trusted friend. The guy on the phone, Carl, gave me a guest code to punch into the keypad at the entrance, in case nobody's in the office when I arrive, and told me to park in any open space on the second level. I will sleep well tonight.

Since I already know I'm not driving the whole thing today, and Kansas City is only about four hours away, I decide to swing south and jump off Interstate 70, once over the mighty Mississippi River. I cruise down 44 into the heart of St. Louis so I can get a look at the Gateway Arch. After riding along miles of highway flanked by nothing but open landscapes of mostly browns and shades of beige, peppered by the occasional farm, it's nice to be back riding on roads lined with leafy green trees. It's a lot cooler, too, thanks to the proximity of the river and I am awed every time a bald eagle soars over on its way to snag a meal from the flowing waters.

The arch is as impressive as I expected it to be. I pull to the side of a lush green park and snap some pictures with my phone. I'll send them, along with the others I've taken along the way, to Becca when I'm in my hotel room for the night. I turn off my bike and sit staring at the enormous strip of steel and concrete, bowing up toward the sky. It stirs memories of a road trip I had planned to take when I was younger, with a friend. The arch was going to be one of our stops. She'd shown me a postcard of it. It was a road trip that never happened.

A young boy runs across the grass chasing a soccer ball. He catches my gaze and waves. I wave back, thinking of the boy at the diner, Danny.

It takes a village.

Perhaps it does take a village, but I would add a caveat or two. If you catch the eye of the village thief, your life is going to turn out differently than if you caught the eye of, say, the village minister or a dedicated village teacher … depending on the type of eye-catching we're talking about. I think about Bill.

Chapter 9

Bill

I was only five when I first met Bill. That meeting took place at the pharmacy downtown. It was supposed to be a quick trip, in and out. My mom needed to pick up some meds. She was going to leave me in the car while she ran in, like she usually did, until she was challenged by some lady parked next to us.

"It's dangerous to leave a child unattended in the car," she said, raising a brow.

My mom bit her bottom lip, no doubt deeply perturbed at the notion of being seen as an unfit mother, even though it wasn't that hot out, and I had long since proven that I could hang out in the car until she got back without incident.

"It will only take me a minute, and it's cool enough for long-sleeves. The doors will be locked."

The woman in the car glared. "Well, I'm pretty sure it's against the law. I could find a police officer to ask, if you prefer."

My mom took a deep breath, walked over, and opened my door. When I climbed out of the car and took her hand, Mom gave a quick, tight smile and a nod to the intrusive woman. Later in life, I would learn that this particular tight smile was my mom's civil, ladylike way of flipping someone the bird. Whenever I hear someone say "you have your mother's smile," this is what comes to mind.

Once we were inside the pharmacy, she released her grip on my hand and motioned for me to keep up. She made a beeline to the pharmacist's window at the back of the store. Mine was less of a beeline and more the path of a meandering fruit fly, but I was keeping up. My mom had begun her conversation with the pharmacist when a glint caught my eye. Beside the counter's reading glasses, a teardrop magnifying glass dangled from a silver chain. It turned slightly, catching the lights from the ceiling and casting a bright, magical beam onto the back of the display. To my five-year-old eyes, it held the radiance of the crown jewels of England.

I didn't know exactly what it was, but I wanted it. I looked up at my mom, who was digging through her purse for money to pay the pharmacist. I knew there was no way she would buy it for me. My mom was not the type to buy things on a whim, and my brother and I knew not to ask for candy or toys when we were in the store with her. Sometimes we could guilt things out of our dad, since he worked longer hours, but he wasn't there.

My mom placed a few more coins on the counter and zipped up her change purse. She was reaching for the small paper bag that contained her prescription, when I felt some kind of primal instinct take over. I picked up a pair of glasses from the display, the pair that sat just above the necklace. When I reached out, I maneuvered my arm so that the glass tear slid smoothly into my sleeve. The chain lifted from the peg and followed the cool glass down against my arm. I quickly switched the reading glasses to the other hand and tucked my arm in at an angle against my stomach.

"Mom! You should get these glasses," I said, tapping them on her arm. "You would look really good in these."

She looked down at me, seeming a little startled, and took the glasses from my hand.

"Do you think so, sweetie?" She laughed and opened them, taking a better look, then put them on, tilting her head down to peek at the little mirror on the display. She looked back at me. "Well, what do you think?"

They actually looked quite good on her. I nodded, enthusiastic.

"I don't need reading glasses yet, sweetie, but I will be sure to bring you along when I do, so you can help me pick out a pair. You have good taste." She removed the glasses, touched them to the end of my nose, and put them back on the display.

We turned and headed toward the front of the store. My heart quickened with each step, and by the time we were almost to the door, its spastic pounding covered all other sounds around me.

"Oh shoot." My mom came to a sudden halt. Did she know?

"I forgot to ask if I need to take these with food. Sweetie, can you stay right here next to the door while I run back? It'll just take a sec."

I nodded. Did she notice the sheen of sweat on my forehead? Apparently not. She strode toward the back of the store.

A large hand clamped down on my shoulder. "Hand it over, kid."

I tilted my head up to see an old man. I remember thinking that he had to be at least a hundred years old. But dang, he had a strong grip. His expression told me that denial would be useless. I let the necklace slide out of my sleeve and passed it to him, ensuring my mom's attention was fully on the pharmacist who was pointing to something on a medicine bottle.

"Please, don't tell my mom." My voice was only a decibel louder than a field mouse, but he heard me all the same.

"Don't worry about it, kid. I just wanted to confirm what I saw. You've got skills. How old are you?"

I held up my right hand and wiggled all five fingers. My mom turned and walked in our direction. When she reached me, the man gave me a pat on the head.

"Is this your young'un, ma'am?"

"Yessir." Apprehension rippled from the bridge of her nose up to her forehead. No doubt the recent accusation of bad parenting was still weighing on her conscience.

"You are raising a polite child, ma'am. I don't see many polite children nowadays. It is downright refreshing. My compliments."

The words put a huge smile on my mom's face, and I could tell she was mentally sending a *bad mother, my ass,* to the woman from the parking lot. The old man shook her hand.

"William Edwards," he said. "My friends call me Bill."

"Linda Blake. Nice to meet you. And," she looked down at me, "this is Charlie. Close your mouth, Charlie."

I hadn't realized my mouth was hanging wide open, but quickly closed it. Bill reached down and shook my hand.

"You need to work on that handshake," he said with a chuckle. "It's important to have a good, firm grip. Your mom here has a respectable handshake."

My mom smiled even wider and blushed. I had never seen her blush before. Bill opened the door for us and we all walked out to the parking lot.

"It was nice to meet you, Bill. Right, Charlie?"

I nodded, still confused as to what was happening.

"It was nice to meet both of you, too." Bill looked down at me and winked. "Oh, and before I forget, I like to reward polite behavior." He reached into his pocket and pulled out the teardrop-shaped magnifying glass, its shiny silver chain trailing behind. He held it out to me. The price tag had been removed.

I looked up at my mom, not sure what I should do. She seemed a little unsure herself.

"Think of it as an acknowledgement of excellent parenting."

Damn, he was smooth.

"My late wife used to make these magnifying glass necklaces and we sold them in the little shop we owned. Children love playing detective with them." He sighed, as if remembering better times.

My mom directed an empathetic smile at Bill, then looked

back at me. "It's ok, sweetie. You can take it. And, don't forget to say thank you. Otherwise you would prove yourself—and me—unworthy." She laughed at her little joke.

Bill set the necklace into my palm, chain and all, and I folded my fingers over it.

"Don't go burning too many ant hills with that," he said. And, when my mom stepped over to unlock the car, he whispered, "Here's a tip, kid. Don't give up so easily. They aren't allowed to strip search a minor. See you around."

"What a sweet old man," said my mom on the drive home. "I sure hope we run into him again. Columbia City isn't that big, so we just might. He kind of looked familiar. I wonder if I ever shopped in his store."

On the ride home, I sat in silence, my mind spinning like a hamster wheel, powered by a rodent on speed. How did Bill see me take the necklace? Why didn't he tell on me? Did he pay for it? Why did he give it to me? Wait, was it still stolen? Did I steal it, or did he? Would God still be angry if I wasn't actually the one who stole it?

This last question lingered for a moment. We rarely went to church, but I knew "thou shalt not steal" was a Big Deal from the Sunday school classes I had attended. For some reason, though, I didn't feel the least bit guilty. Maybe it was because, in the end, *I* had not stolen the necklace.

Chapter 10

Checking In

I slowly drift through the hustle and bustle of St. Louis, with the occasional stop alongside the groomed, green grass of the city parks to stretch and grab a snack from my packs. I go light on the fluids in favor of the caffeine gummies, as once I'm out of the city and past the little towns on the outskirts, there'll be a stretch with no rest areas.

Before I leave the city, a text from Becca is read out through my helmet. I wish it was her speaking to me instead of the tinny, distant AI voice. A shiver runs down my spine when it tells me how much it loves me. But she tells me I can call when I stop for the night, as her parents should be in bed by then. So, I have something to look forward to.

When I roll into Kansas City, the first thing I do is locate the garage. It's just after 7 and I don't see anyone in the office, so I enter the code and ride in to find a spot. Once the FCC is parked, I retrieve a small travel bag from the trunk box, add some of the snacks from the saddle bags to it, and swing it onto my shoulder.

"Hey there," calls a deep, rich voice from behind me. I spin on one heel. There's a figure walking toward me. "You must be Randy's friend. Man, she wasn't kidding. That's one sweet ride."

The garage is lit well enough, but numerous overhead fixtures cross-light the space, striping shadows across the approaching man. The rim of a baseball cap further darkens his face.

"Didn't mean to startle you," he says, extending a hand. He tips his head up, revealing a set of piercing blue eyes—they remind me of the glacial waters in the environmental documentaries Becca loves to watch. I suppress a grin at the thought of seeing a baby harp seal reflected if I lean in close enough.

"You must be Carl," I say, shaking his hand. "Charlie. Thanks for the parking spot. How much for the night?" The truth is he already told me over the phone there'll be no charge, but I still feel awkward about the arrangement.

"That ground's been covered. Any friend of Randy's is a friend of mine. And Randy and I have a rule about math between friends. There'll be none of that shit going on. As is, she dragged my ass through math classes K through 12. I can never repay that debt."

I beam, making a mental note to send a thank you text to Randy. Maybe I can bring her something back from Colorado? I've always been more of a tallying kind of person. I suppose that has something to do with the way I grew up. Bill was big on keeping track of debts and favors.

Good people settle their scores.

"Can I at least offer you a drink?" I ask.

"Well now, you've got me there." A wide, roguish grin flashes across his face and sets his cerulean eyes twinkling. "I will never say no to a drink with a friend."

"I just have to check into my room next door and change out of these clothes. I'll defer to you to pick a place, being a local and all."

"Not quite a local, by locals' standards, but I've definitely lived here long enough to know where to wet my whistle." He gives me a pat on the back. "Tell you what, I have to tend to a few things before I can lock up and get out of here. Why don't you head over and do what you gotta do. I'll be in the lobby when you come down and we can head out for a bite and something to drink. I'd love to hear what you think of that suicide shift. Never tried one, myself."

I nod and he heads back toward the office, a hand extended in a wave. I'm not sure what I'm going to say about the suicide shift, seeing as how I have nothing to compare it to. Randy and Jay have asked me many a time if I wanted to try one of the bikes at the shop. Something more modern with more bells and whistles. But, I've been happy limiting my motorcycle adventures to the FCC. The thought of riding anything else somehow feels like cheating, as silly as it may sound.

When I'm checked into my room, I set my things down and pop in an earbud so I can call Becca while I'm getting changed. As comfortable as my new motorcycle gear is, peeling it off feels heavenly.

"Charlie?" Becca answers the phone just as my pants are sliding to the floor. I kick them off, making more of a racket than I intended. "What's that noise?"

"Sorry, babe. That was my armor ... I mean my pants ... sliding across the hotel carpet. I feel about ten pounds lighter now. How is everything? I was going to change and *then* call you, but I couldn't wait."

"I'm glad you didn't," she says, giggling. "Now I get to talk to you while picturing you with no pants on."

"Sadly, I'm about to slide on another pair. I'm going to take Randy's friend out for a drink to thank him for letting me park the FCC in his garage. He won't let me pay for the spot, and you know me."

"Ah yes. Heaven forbid we let someone do us a favor and just say 'thank you'."

"Rebecca! Rebecca, where are you? Are you in your room?" Her mother's shrill voice assaults my ears. I roll my eyes.

"Sorry, Sunshine," Becca sighs. "It's been a rough night so far.

Dad wasn't quite as far down the road to recovery as I was led to believe."

"Rebecca? Are you on the phone?" The voice sounds much closer now. "Are you talking to that *Charlie* person?" Her disdain tells me everything I need to know about how Becca's visit is going thus far.

"I'm sorry, hun," she says, her voice dropping to a whisper. "I thought they would be in bed by now."

"Rebecca!" A door opens on Becca's end of the line. "Dr. Charles wants to talk to you. He needs to talk to you."

"Mom, I'll be right there. Tell him I will be right there." I hear the sharp clap of the door against the frame. "I'm sorry, Charlie. My dad's doctor stopped by to check on him. Actually, I'm pretty sure my mom called him over to meet me in the hopes that I'll fall head-over-heels for him. They just don't get it. I'm starting to think it was a mistake coming here."

"Don't worry about it." I'm starting to think the same about her going there, but I know she's strong and needs to set some things straight with her folks. Besides, she would have felt guilty not checking up on her dad after his heart attack. "Go ahead and take care of things there. We can talk tomorrow when I'm on the road. Call me when you can sneak away."

"Love you. And thanks for understanding. I guess I'm off to talk to Dr. Charles. Goodnight and have a drink for me. Make that a few!"

A juicy kiss sounds through my earbuds, followed by dead air. I imagine Becca heading out of her room to meet Dr. Charles. I wonder if Charles is the doctor's last or first name. Maybe he's a Charlie, too. The right kind of Charlie. The kind of Charlie Becca's parents were hoping their daughter would end up with.

I shower, throw on some jeans and a t-shirt, and run a comb through my freshly washed hair. After a quick glance at the hotel hairdryer nested in a pile of cord, I decide my hair will dry fast enough on its own. Besides, I've toweled most of it, and the cool air feels even more refreshing against my clean, damp head. I vacate the room, grabbing my wallet and phone on the way. In the elevator on the way down, I write a quick 'goodnight, see you tomorrow' text and send it to Tom.

Carl is standing by the front desk chatting with the receptionist on duty, a young woman with long dark hair. He waves at me as I approach.

"Mary, make sure you take good care of my friend here," he says. The young woman smiles before reaching for the phone, which has come alive in a sudden burst of rings.

"That's Mary. Sweet kid. Her dad's a good friend of mine. She'll be at the desk or back in the office if you need anything tonight."

"Thank you."

"I'll bet it feels nice to get out of your travel gear."

"Yes, it does," I say with exaggerated relief. I run a hand through my hair, happy to be helmet-free.

"How do you feel about walking a couple blocks for the absolute best barbecue around? There's a couple closer places, too, if you're tired. They're not too bad, either."

My stomach gurgles and crescendos into a strangled howl. I laugh and clutch my gut.

"I think that means we'll go the distance for the absolute best."

"I was thinking maybe it did," he says, gesturing for us to walk on.

I'm not sure how the food at the closer places would have compared, but he is correct about one thing; the barbecue at the joint we end up in is the absolute best I have ever tasted. It's a pleasant evening of good food and conversation. I do most of the listening. After a brief discussion about my trip and what to expect for the remaining miles, I sit back, drink in hand, to enjoy tales of Randy's younger days. Sipping my beer and mentally taking notes on all of the embarrassing stories I can use to tease her when we next meet.

I look at my watch. It's almost 9:30. Early for a night out, stretching toward late given the miles I will need to cover tomorrow.

"Well, Carl," I say, setting my empty bottle next to a plate piled with the remnants of the most divine ribs, "I'm gonna call it a night. I think you've given me enough embarrassing historical ammunition to hold Randy hostage for at least the next ten years. And, for that, I can never repay you."

Carl breaks into a bout of gut shaking laughter, which proves to be more contagious than the common cold. So much so that when the waitress comes over to hand us the check—which I promptly snatch—she can't help but giggle.

"You don't need to pick up the whole tab," Carl says, reaching out a hand.

"Nope. I don't. But I'm gonna ... and still owe you after."

"Can I at least pick up the tip?"

"I'm putting in a tip, but I can't stop you adding a little something for our wonderful waitress." I tip my head and throw her a wink.

Carl takes out his wallet and hands me some bills to add to mine. I'm not a fan of credit cards.

Just another way to end up owing someone something.

The clarity of the voice surprises me and I give my head a little shake. I guess I thought that distance would weaken it, thin it like pulling a thread of taffy across a room. I wonder if talking about Randy and Carl's younger days has pulled me back into my own. My mind turns back to the store where I first met Bill. When my mom wondered if we would run into him again.

Chapter 11

Aspirations

As it turned out, we ran into Bill quite frequently after that first encounter. One of his favorite things to do, it seemed, was sit on a park bench feeding the pigeons. Since the park was central to the downtown area and parking, we often passed him while running errands. He always waved and said something like "how are my favorite people?" or "there's that sweet family." Usually, we were in a hurry and would holler a quick "hello" and wave. But, on those rare occasions when my parents had some time to kill, we stopped to chat.

"Always so busy," said Bill, maybe a year after our initial encounter. I was in town with my mom and brother, who needed new shoes. I was being dragged along because our dad was away on business, and I was still too young to stay at home alone. "What are we up to on this fine day?"

"Tommy needs some new shoes," Mom said. "He's poked his big toe right out of these." She pointed to his left foot, where a socked toe could be seen wiggling through a small tear in the top of the shoe.

Bill laughed. "They grow so quickly." He looked over at me. "I'm planning on sitting here for some time. I've got a bag full of seed I still need to spread among my friends here." He swept out his hand toward the pigeons that had gathered, tossing some seed and sending them into a frenzy. "If you'd like, Charlie could sit here and feed them with me, so you have one less on your hands."

I could see by her signature lip bite that my mom was conflicted. She looked toward the shoe store across the street, then at me, and finally at Bill. "I wouldn't want to inconvenience you."

"Absolutely no inconvenience. Charlie, I am sure your mother has taught you not to go anywhere with strangers or people you don't know well, right?"

I nodded.

"I knew it. She has you two dressed *and* educated to the nines." He tossed another handful of seed toward the birds. "Well, you all have a lovely day, and you stop growing so quickly," he said to Tommy, flashing a grin. "You are going to wear your poor mother out trying to keep up with you."

My mom looked down at me. "Do you want to wait here and feed the birds while I get Tommy his shoes? I'll be right across the street if you need me."

I nodded without hesitation. I wasn't looking forward to pacing the store while my mom had Tommy try on a million different pairs of shoes.

"Thank you, Bill," Mom said. "Remember, I'll be right over there. If you need to go, just bring Charlie over."

"I have absolutely nowhere to go. That is one of the perks of being old."

My mom thanked him again and grabbed Tommy's hand. They rushed across the park and crossed the road before disappearing into the shoe store.

"How's your life of crime going?" asked Bill. He reached into the seed bag and handed me some to throw to the birds.

"What do you mean?" I had shoplifted some candy a few times since the pharmacy, but it hardly seemed like it could be defined as a *life of crime*. I tossed the seeds and watched the pigeons scramble, trying to beat each other to the jackpot.

"Have you been working on your skills?" He pointed to the chain that was visible just above my shirt collar. I pulled out the magnifying glass and inspected it.

"I guess. Maybe. A little."

A small group of teenagers strolled into the park and sat on the bench next to ours. They were talking, laughing, and sharing fries from a fast-food bag. Bill gave a quick wave and a lanky brown-haired girl in jeans and a Disney princess t-shirt stood up and walked over with the bag. She set it on the bench next to Bill.

"Sarah, this is Charlie. Charlie, Sarah."

"This the kid you told me about? Cute." Sarah studied me for a moment, then held out her hand for some seed.

I watched Bill reach into the bag. He dug a little deeper this time, and along with the seed, he pulled out a small wad of cash. He placed it all in her hand. Sarah shifted the pile of seed to her other hand while palming the cash. The movement of her hands was smooth, almost artistic, and in a second, the money had disappeared, leaving only the seed, which she tossed to the pigeons.

Bill laughed. "Close your mouth, Charlie. One of the pigeons might fly in."

Warmth rushed to my cheeks. I shut my mouth, staring at Sarah in awe. I wanted to compliment her for her magician-like hand movements, but I couldn't think of any way to say it that didn't sound, in my head, like it was coming from a stupid little kid. Sarah smirked and gave me a pat on the head.

"Cool necklace, kid." She walked back to the other teens and they walked across the street.

"Who was that?"

"That was Sarah."

"You know what I mean," I said, growing impatient. I knew my mom would be back shortly. "Who *was* that?" I motioned toward the fast-food bag Sarah had left on the bench.

"Now there's the kid I've been waiting for. The one from the pharmacy. Sarah and her friends do some work for me from time to time."

"What kind of work? Can I do some work?"

"Don't get ahead of yourself, Charlie." He held his hand out with a huge amount of seed in it, enough that I had to take it with both hands cupped together, and still spilled some on the ground. "Start small and build. That is how any successful business works. Start small and build. Otherwise, you may find yourself overwhelmed." I nodded and tossed the seed. "Earn your keep and it's best not to owe anyone anything, if you can help it."

I saw my mom and Tommy coming back in our direction. Tommy had a brand new pair of sneakers on and was carrying a box that I assumed contained the old shoes destined to be labeled "play shoes only."

"Listen, kid," Bill said. "When you are a little more independent, we can talk about some training. In the meantime, don't get caught. I have no use for a kid with a record."

Before I could consider his words, he rose to meet my mom and Tommy.

"There they are," he said in an exaggerated voice of relief. "This one was such a handful!" He laughed. "Of course, I'm joking. Angels raised by angels. That is what we have here. And I have to add that my day has been brightened by the mere presence of your fine family. Thank you."

I thought he was laying it on a bit thick, but my mom was lapping it up. I decided that maybe she wasn't that great at reading people. She thanked Bill, and we went on our way. I spent the way home trying to calculate how long it would take me to become more independent.

Chapter 12

Twelve

As soon as I'm back in my hotel room, I slip into some boxers and a t-shirt. Then, I gather my discarded travel clothes from the floor and lay my riding armor on the little desk in the corner next to one of those pod coffee machines you find at every hotel now. I take a picture of the machine and send it to Becca with a crying face emoji, then reach over and pick up one of the packaged pods set in a little basket to the side, wondering if anyone actually uses the decaf. I laugh and toss it on top of my pack. Maybe Alex will want it. I'm guessing her mom doesn't let her drink the caffeinated kind.

After balling up my dirty clothes and shoving them into the side pocket of my overnight bag, I pull out one of the two changes I brought along for the trip. Everything else was shipped ahead. I want my things to be laid out before I go to bed so that I can get an early start tomorrow morning. I have between eight and nine hours left, depending on stops. So, calculating the time difference between Kansas City and Tom's place, I should be there in plenty of time for dinner.

The moment my head hits the pillow, my phone rumbles. I reach over and pick it up, the charging cord pulling taut like a leash, hoping maybe it's Becca wanting to chat a little before going to sleep. She's bound to have some funny stories about her encounter with Dr. Charles. I hope. Ok, I'm a little jealous ... not because I think they're going to go riding off into the sunset together, but because he got to hang out with her tonight and I didn't. Not only that, but her parents obviously like him ... and they definitely DO NOT like me.

Sure enough, there's a message on my phone. But it's from Tom, not Becca.

Still up? If not, just give me a call tomorrow before you leave.

By the way it's worded, it's surely not an emergency, but I decide to give him a call. It's getting late, so he must have something on his mind. I sit up, pile the numerous pillows against the backboard, and sink into them before dialing his number.

"Hey, Charlie." His voice is quiet, barely above a whisper. "Hang on a sec. I'm gonna go downstairs so I don't wake anyone up. I was pretty sure you were already sleeping."

"No problem," I say, then clear my throat. My voice tends to get a little crackly when I'm about to go to sleep. Becca calls it my sleepy frog voice.

The sound of a door latch followed by footsteps distracts me while I wait. Then the creaking of hinges and I can make out the gentle closing of another door.

"Ok," he says, his voice louder and clearer, though still not at full volume. "Sorry if you were already in bed."

"No worries. I was just getting set for tomorrow, so I can leave right after I drag myself out of bed. That is, if I can still move." I laugh, hoping that my little white lie and levity will help him to relax. He sounds pretty tense even at low volume. Tom has always been easy to read.

"A little sore?" he asks. "Wishing you took me up on that plane ticket?"

His voice smooths into the easy familiar tone I prefer from my big brother.

"Sore, but definitely not *that* sore," I say. "Remember the summer I wanted to try horseback riding? Mom and Dad got me some lessons and I ended up volunteering to help with the girl scout trail rides one weekend for extra riding time and community service hours? I think I was in the saddle for something like sixteen hours and could barely move on Monday."

"God, I remember that. You and your whole room smelled like a barn. We were supposed to go to the pool that Monday morning and you flaked out. Wait, if memory serves, I believe you threw something at me when I tried to convince you to get up. Or, at least you tried to."

"I don't remember that part," I say, laughing. "Anyway, I'm thinking this is going to be a close second in body aches after another full day tomorrow. That said, I'll take walking funny for a couple days over one of those gravity-defying metal tubes any day of the week. I am glad I'll have a little time to stretch and wander at your place before I'll have to jump back on the bike and head home."

A smile spreads across my tired face. I haven't thought of the horseback riding thing in a long time. A silent chuckle pushes a puff of air from my nose at the memory of young me sliding out of the saddle at the end of the second day and trying to walk, mini-wannabe-girl-scout Daisies and Brownies running circles around me. I did end up with a ton of volunteer hours for school, though, and added to my Goody Two-shoes reputation. I remember Bill being a little too entertained by my attempts to walk at the park later the next day, but also happy to hear that I had volunteered.

It's important to give back to our community, Charlie. There are so many forces that come in and try to take over, push good people away. In the end, it's the local folk who are the lifeblood of any town.

"Charlie?"

I snap back to the phone call. "Sorry, Tom. I drifted for a minute. What's on your mind? I'm sure you didn't just call to wave that plane ticket in my face again. Everything ok?"

Silence hangs in the air for a moment, but this time he is the one prolonging it. I wait patiently.

"I'm glad you're coming," he says.

"I'm glad I'm coming too and glad you're glad I'm coming." I'm trying to lighten up the sudden shift in mood. Swing it back to where it just was. But I don't hear laughter from his end.

"I mean it, Charlie. I'm hoping that maybe Alex will open up to you about what's going on. She's not acting like herself. And, as much as I adore Mom, I really don't think she's that good at reading people or situations."

No kidding, I think.

"Alex looks up to you. She thinks you're cool ... or whatever the word is nowadays."

"Don't ask me," I say, laughing. "I'm only a few years younger than you are and totally isolated from teenage banter. She's probably just doing what teens have done since the beginning of time, rebelling against her parents. I remember you sneaking out a couple times to hang out with friends. You're welcome for not telling, by the way. Anyway, I'm sure she's not up to anything nefarious, Tom. She's a good kid. Relax. It's probably just a phase. You and Lindsey worry about having a good time on your trip. I'll hold down the fort while you're gone."

A yawn, a deep breath and a sigh meet my ear.

"Yeah," he says. "You're probably right. I mean, she's twelve. What kind of trouble could a twelve-year-old really get into in our small town?"

"Right," I say, wishing he hadn't said those words. "I'll see you tomorrow, Tom. Goodnight."

"Night, Charlie. Can't wait."

What kind of trouble could a twelve-year-old really get into?

My mind wanders back. I was twelve when I started my training. That thought hits me like a wet sandbag. Not that I think Alex is getting into the same kind of trouble that I was at her age. Twelve seems so much younger on my niece than it did on me. I mean, wasn't she just toddling around in diapers, like yesterday? Reaching her little arms in the air for me to scoop her up and plop her onto my shoulders, so we could run around my parents' backyard like a jockey and her racehorse ... her Charlie Horse, Tom would say, laughing.

I push all but two of the pillows to the side and snuggle under the crisp hotel sheets, tugging at the comforter to get it up under my chin. I think about my early teenage years in Columbia City. About Mom and Dad and Tommy. About the fact that none of them really knew me.

Chapter 13

Independence

At the age of fifteen, I'd been allowed to take the bus to the square downtown by myself for almost three years. Well, not exactly by myself. Tommy, now seventeen and officially only 'Tom', had to ride with me, but once we were downtown, we went our separate ways.

"Just be back at the stop in time to catch the bus home for dinner or we're both screwed," he told me every time we went. Then he would hurry off to meet his friends.

I always went straight to the park to feed the pigeons with Bill.

"Want me to go to Fuller's Jewelry store today?" I asked quietly. "That would totally be worth the trip."

Bill tossed some seed. "Fuller's? Seriously? You know how much security they have in jewelry stores, Charlie?"

"Sarah and the others can keep the clerks' eyes on them and I wouldn't go for anything too big, nothing the cameras would catch."

I looked over to the other side of the park where Sarah, now in her early twenties, was hanging out with a small group of teenagers, and pretending not to notice us. Over the years, some of the faces had changed. Some moved on. Others were caught and cut out of the group. Bill didn't want anyone with a record hanging around. He would give them what he called "severance pay" and wish them luck. Most of the older kids ended up striking out on their own eventually, which was fine with him as long as they asked permission and left town. Sarah stayed. She still looked around fifteen and was as good at playing the innocent kid and lifting merch as she was at punking out her look and drawing attention to herself to keep it off of me, or us. She had mentioned a few times that she wanted to leave, but Bill wasn't ready to let her go.

"Charlie." Bill sounded a little frustrated. "What did I tell you about the local stores? Fuller's is a family business. Fuller's is good people, like Esther and I were. We only hit chains. Chains don't care about our community. Chains don't care who they run out of business."

"Sorry. I didn't know they were local."

"Well, you still have a lot to learn. How are your grades, kid? Still my Goody Two-shoes straight-A scholar? Reputation is everything."

"Yessir. How about the Wally's down on the end of Main?" I was getting restless. My palms tingled.

"Always in such a hurry. Fine. Go down and head for school supplies, notebooks and such. I'll have Sarah and her crew head over about five minutes behind. Stay small and stay away from electronics. I heard they have new security and the guy's a little jumpy."

I reached into the paper bag and tossed more seed. Then I turned to leave.

"Hey hey," said Bill. "You forgot something."

I turned back, gave him a peck on the cheek, and skipped away. I saw him flash Sarah a W and a five with his fingers. She nodded slightly, all the while chatting loudly about boys and homework with her cohorts.

About an hour later, I came skipping back to the park toting a

Wally's bag and sat down with Bill. I pulled out a bag of licorice and handed it to him.

"I got this for you with my allowance. It's the old-fashioned kind you love."

He raised an eyebrow. "Well, that was thoughtful of you."

He set the bag on his lap and looked inside.

"Charlie. I told you not to go into electronics. You could have been caught."

I grinned. "But I wasn't and that'll get you more than school supplies would."

"You are a magician, a master of illusion," he said. "That is why I will never let you leave. But, you are going to give me a heart attack. I will process this and get you your part next week. Now, go get yourself an ice cream, and bring me back a coffee, black." He handed me a twenty.

On the way to the creamery, I ran into Sarah. She was by herself. Her eye make-up was smeared, like she had been crying. I walked up and tapped her arm, startling her.

"What's wrong?"

She wiped her eyes with her sleeve. "Nothing. It's just allergies."

I put my hands on my hips and tilted my head so it was obvious I was not buying it.

"Ok, fine." She wove her hand through my arm and started walking, bringing me along. "There's this guy."

"Do I know him? Is it one of our guys? Is it Peter?"

"Whoa, whoa. Peter? No way. Why? Do you think Peter likes me?"

"I don't know. Maybe. So, if it isn't Peter, who is it?"

"You don't know him," she said. "He isn't one of us. His name is Lucas, and he goes to a law school in Colorado. He was here visiting family a couple months ago. I met him at a bar and we've kind of kept in touch. I really like him, Charlie."

"That doesn't sound like a reason to cry." I reached over and wiped a small clump of smeared mascara from the corner of her eye.

"The other day, he asked if I would think about moving to Colorado, if I ever thought about taking classes. He thinks I'm super smart."

"You are super smart. And pretty badass, too. I mean, I would miss you and be completely crushed and all, but maybe you should go."

"I can't," she whispered. A fresh tear shimmered in the corner of her eye, threatening to drop. "Bill won't let me."

"What do you mean, Bill won't let you? Why not? Other people leave. People leave all the time."

"Only if they get caught or they have permission. He said he needs me. He said he would release my file if I try to go. If Lucas finds out who I really am ..." The tear escaped and slid down her cheek.

"What file?" I was confused. This wasn't the Bill I knew. He cared about us.

"Never mind," she said. "I'm just being silly. Lucas is coming to visit next week, so I'll get to see him. Please promise you won't say anything to Bill. I don't want him to get upset with either of us."

"I promise," I said, and I meant it. "I'm getting a coffee for him. Want to grab an ice cream cone?"

She nodded, and we waltzed into Madigan's Creamery, separately, of course.

Chapter 14

The Last Leg

A blaring, squawking tone jars me awake. At some point, while reminiscing about my youth, I apparently fell asleep. Despite it feeling like I settled into bed mere minutes ago, an entire night has passed. I reach a hand out and fumble for the hotel alarm clock. My phone alarm will be ringing in about five minutes, as a back-up. So, once I am able to silence the obnoxious sounds blasting from the clock, I shut off the alarm on my phone. No danger of falling back asleep, thanks to that rude awakening.

Thin threads of last night's dreams wisp through my mind like spiderwebs cut loose from their anchors. I rub my eyes and clear the images of my childhood friend Sarah that appear behind my lids. Sarah staying over at my house to watch movies. Sarah as I remember her ... before she disappeared.

The faint smell of smoke tickles the back of my nose. My eyes fly open. I sniff at the air around me, then relax. It was my imagination, a remnant of a bad dream my mind has already forgotten. My phone rumbles. It's Becca.

"Hey babe," I say, yawning audibly.

"Hey there, sleepy frog. Did I wake you up?" Her voice is low, but I can tell she's been up for a while. She is wide awake. "Want to make yourself some of that delicious hotel coffee and call me back? Dad's asleep and Mom's at the market."

I swing my feet over the side of the bed and stretch out the arm not attached to my phone.

"Nah. I can chat and make coffee at the same time. All I have to do is fill the water thingy and throw a pod in."

I do just that, while we talk about the pictures I sent her and about her parents. When my coffee is ready, I dump both sugar packets and the little thing of creamer powder into it and sip between stories.

"Man do I miss our espresso machine," I say after a few gulps of the tepid brown water. I pour the rest down the sink and toss the cup.

Becca laughs. "You'd better get going if you want to get there before dinner. Maybe have some afternoon tea in the plant room, or a real cup of coffee," she says, her voice painting a smile in my mind. "Keep sending those pictures. It kind of makes me feel like I'm there traveling with you. Love you and miss you!"

"Will do. Love you, too." I keep the phone to my ear even after the line goes dead.

I wonder why I've never told Becca anything about Sarah. There was never anything more than friendship between us. She was first a mentor, then an accomplice, then a dear friend. It's been years since I last saw her. I take a deep breath in through my nose and slowly release it through pursed lips. When I get back from this trip, I'm going to tell Becca a lot more about my past. Not everything, mind you, but a lot more. It's only fair. I want this to work. I want someone to know me.

Are you sure about that? Are you sure she would be ok with the things in your file? Are you sure you want her to know who you are?

My breath catches, forming a tight ball in my throat. I squeeze my eyes shut and will the voice away. Then a thought occurs to me: maybe telling her would silence the voice. Maybe he doesn't want me to tell her—or anyone—because it would finally silence him for good.

There are plenty of people in the world who believe in ghosts. I never thought I would be one of them. I don't believe in the pale, floaty spirits you see in movies and shows. My ghost isn't like that. If he's even a ghost at all. He's more of a stoic presence. His voice is an inconvenience ... a growing inconvenience in my head. Maybe the way to banish him for good is to bring him out into the light. Maybe he suspects what I'm planning and wants to scare me off. A survival tactic of sorts.

I look down at my phone, which has fallen onto my lap. It's 7:30 am, which means it's 6:30 at Tom's place. I have time for a nice cool wake-up shower and some coffee from the shop I noticed across the street when I was checking in. Last night, I told Carl I'd probably be taking off at seven. He told me he'd be in the office and to make sure I say "hey" on my way out.

The coffee shop latte hits the spot, removing the stale acidic taste of the hotel coffee, despite a round of heavy tooth-brushing and rinsing. I pitch the empty cup into the recycling bin before heading to reclaim the FCC.

Today's ride is different. Yesterday, I was leaving the familiar and venturing into the unfamiliar. This morning, my voyage begins from deep within the unfamiliar, and as I ride through sleepy towns, past silos and factories, the land transforms from familiar greens to tones of beige and brown. Before lunch, I make two stops: one for gas, and another to take some photos of the endless, peaceful farmland—pump jacks dotting the landscape, and hundreds of feet of raised water pipes on wheels looking like the skeletons of gigantic alien creatures.

My stomach starts growling sometime after noon. And though I cannot hear it over the steady rumble of the FCC, I feel it churn and twist, telling me it's time to stop. Thanks to Becca, I still have some snacks left in my saddle bags, but decide I want to find a place to sit and eat, maybe people-watch for a bit, before finishing my trip and landing back in the world of family drama. I pull off the road when I see a sign for gas and eats in a quaint town called Colby. After filling up at the gas station, I cruise past a motel and park in front of the restaurant attached to it, the City Limits Grill.

This is only my second day traveling, but after hundreds of miles of exchanging friendly greetings with other bikers, and even being enveloped into a group of fifteen to twenty bikes for a stint as they cruised along, heading off to who knows where, I'm feeling like an old pro. The thought of parking the FCC (after I lock her and remove her spark plugs) so I can grab a bite to eat no longer concerns me.

I saunter in and a young man in a white t-shirt and jeans greets me. He's wearing a name tag, but the way he's standing wrinkles a fold of his shirt over his name. He cranes his neck, looking over my shoulder. Then straightens, revealing his name to be Christopher.

"Sweet ride," says Christopher, sizing me up. I'm guessing he's probably in his late teens.

"Thanks. Table for one." Becca always uses a server's name as soon as she reads it on a tag. She waitressed when she was in high school and says that it made things feel more personal and friendly when people did that with her. I have never been able to do that even after they introduce themselves as my waiter or waitress. To me, it feels invasive. I guess it's good that I never waited tables.

"Right this way," says Christopher, leading me to a table by a window where I can see the FCC. The boy has read my mind.

Nicely done, Christopher.

"My uncle has an old Indian, but his has a sidecar," he says handing me a menu. "They're pretty cool. I've got my eye on a Ducati Scrambler. I'm about halfway to earning the money for it."

"Cool," I say. I have no idea what a Ducati Scrambler looks like, but it sounds cool and the fact that the kid is working to save up for one impresses me. I make a mental note to leave a big tip.

After asking for some advice, I order a Jack Daniel's burger and an iced tea. The Chicken fried steak sounds delicious, but I don't want to doze off into a food coma in my last few hours on the road. The food comes out quickly. There's only one other table occupied in the restaurant and that's by an older couple.

Their familiarity with each other sparks a warm feeling that starts in my chest and washes through me like hot chocolate on a cold winter's day. When the waiter brings them coffee and a slice of cake, the woman reaches over and adds sugar and cream to both, while her companion cuts the cake into two pieces and passes her a fork. The way they look at each other, as if engaged in a deep, secret, wordless conversation, stirs something in my mind.

That's what I had with my Esther, says the voice. This time tied to a memory, a conversation I recall from long ago.

A bell rings to announce the arrival of more customers, its peppy chime pulling me back to the here and now. I close my mouth when I realize my jaw has slacked in my reverie and watch a young family enter the restaurant. The parents look exhausted, but content. A little boy skips around them, making faces and eliciting giggles from a toddler secure above him in their father's arms. I smile to myself when the elderly couple engage the young boy in conversation as they pass by. His parents are visibly happy for the distraction of their little ball of energy.

My check arrives and I'm ready to strike out on the last leg of my trip. I hand the cash, including a generous tip, to Christopher and wish him luck on purchasing his Ducati Scrambler. Then I make a quick stop in the restroom and head out to the open road once more.

I make one more stop to top off my gas in the town of Limon, Colorado. The FCC is starting to feel a little sluggish, and I want to make sure I can make it to Tom's place. I fill up and take some quick pics for Becca, checking the internet for some factoids about the town to include in my text.

My heart sinks when I read the information on-screen. It's a quaint town with an indelible stain woven into its fabric in the year 1900. A chill winds its way down my spine as I read about the young black boy, Preston "John" Porter Jr., sacrificing himself so his father and brother could go free, and how a bloodthirsty crowd intercepted him and burned him alive. What does redemption look like after such a horrible act? I shake my head and slide my phone back onto its holder.

Just outside of the town, the Rocky Mountains suddenly appear before me, lifting my spirits. I have never seen mountains up close before. I pull to the side of the road and take some pictures for Becca, opting to send those instead. As I attempt to pop my phone back into the grips of the holder, a movement to my right catches my eye. My jaw slacks and my pulse quickens at the sight of a herd of pronghorn deer, the American antelope. They race away at incredible speeds, their fuzzy white hind quarters blurred by the dust they stir.

I'm a little disappointed that I didn't have the presence of mind to grab my phone to get a video for Becca. She would've loved it. Instead, I write a descriptive text about my encounter and send it off to her. Then I head toward the mountains, my brother, and his family.

Chapter 15

Into the Drama

It's early evening when I finally find Tom's house and pull onto his long, winding driveway. The pictures I've seen don't do the place justice. And that view of the mountains ... damn! I toot the new and improved horn that Randy installed on the FCC, then turn her off and dismount. I'm almost at the front steps when Tom appears in the doorway.

"Hey, big bro. Long time no see," I blurt out.

"A whole five months since the last family shindig, if I'm not mistaken," says Tom, pulling me into a bear hug, complete with sturdy back thump.

"Charlie, you made it!" Lindsey rushes over to convert our greeting into a group hug.

"How was your trip?" they say in unison from either side of me, treating me to the full stereo experience.

A movement at the top of the stairs pulls my gaze upward. It's Alex. Despite the passage of less than half a year since I last saw her, she looks different. The easy smile I'm used to seeing when she bursts through my parents'—now my mom's—door, always the first in when they visit, has somehow soured. She's smiling at me, but it's a jaded smile, one I did not expect to see on the face of my preteen niece. I guess preteen is the new teen.

"Hello Tom, Lindsey. Nice to see you again, Charlie," she says mid-stairway.

My brother and his wife flinch. Though Alex has never called me just by my first name, and it takes me by surprise, she does pronounce it with a modicum of grace and warmth, as if to indicate that I am in a separate category to her parents. Maybe she is still deciding whether I am to be friend or foe.

Tom pulls in a deep breath, I imagine to steady his emotions, and Lindsey tries to mask the pout that flashes across her usually cheery face.

"Alexandra Parker," says Tom. "Really? This is how we address family now?"

Alex glides down the last few steps as smooth as a phantom.

"Hey, Alex!" I've decided to try breaking the tension with axe-like delicacy. "You can absolutely call me Charlie. Look at you. You're what? Twenty, twenty-five now? Seriously though, you've matured so much since Christmas. I feel like I stepped through a time warp."

Alex grins and I catch a glimpse of the sweet, clever kid I know.

"Charlie it is, then," says Tom.

Just then, Jimmy bursts into the foyer from a side room and throws himself full speed at me.

"Do I look bigger and more *mature*, too? I'm going to camp this year, you know! Can I call you Charlie, too?"

Now this kid is 100% Lindsey's offspring. Obviously her genes felt slightly under-represented the first time around, so they made up for it tenfold with the second born.

"Of course you can, Jimmy. Or should I call you Jim?"

His brows shoot upward and his eyes illuminate as if I have lit a fuse.

"Don't encourage him," says Lindsey, ruffling his wild, dirty-blond hair.

She is visibly happy to move the conversion ball from the court of the sullen child to that of her more agreeable one. She must know that the teenage years creep closer for both her progeny and that her days of motherly bliss—or at least the illusion of control—are numbered. May as well enjoy the relative glee remaining with the second born.

I actually don't mind them calling me Charlie. In my mind, it moves them a little farther from the child category toward one I'm more prepared to handle.

"Can we call Auntie Becca, Becca, too?" Jimmy asks, now fully invested in this turn of events.

I laugh when I imagine Becca's reaction. She adores the kids. She also adores being called Auntie Becca. Her estranged sister has three kids, but she's never met them. On the rare occasions that she mentions them, the pain in her voice is palpable.

"Hmm," I say, scrunching up my brows and crinkling my nose. "Maybe we should leave that up to her."

"One partner should never presume to speak for the other, Jimmy," says Alex, side-eyeing her parents.

Damn, that's something I never expected to hear from the mouth of a twelve-year-old. Though, maybe I should have, her dad being an attorney and all. I look at Tom, who seems to be developing a sudden sunburn on his cheeks. Lindsey puts a hand on his shoulder and gives it a quick squeeze. Her tight smile acts as a huge red banner, letting me know that I do *not* want to know what that was all about.

Her shoulder squeeze works to disarm Tom, his color normalizing. Once again, I observe how perfectly they complement each other. And, once again, I hope their trip is more of a couple's respite and less of a couple's re-connection.

"Hey, Mom." Jimmy seems oblivious to the undertones circling him like ravenous sharks. "I want to send postcards from camp like Alex always does."

"Did," Alex reminds him. Jimmy doesn't flinch, which makes

me think maybe his is more a strategy of avoidance than a state of oblivion.

"Where do I send the ones for Auntie Becca and ... Charlie?" He exaggerates the pronunciation of my name after his slight hesitation, obviously enjoying this new development.

"Easy," I say. "Just send them to our house. That way, when I get back, Auntie Becca and I can enjoy them together."

"Hear that, Mom? Remember to write their address in my camp notebook next to Grandma's."

"Will do, sweetie. Now, why don't we let ... Charlie ... go upstairs to change and freshen up?"

"You look pretty cool in that jacket, Charlie," says Alex, ignoring her mom and also emphasizing my name.

"Thank you, Alex. Auntie Becca got it for me. It has all the bells and whistles for a safe motorcycle experience."

"Oooh. Can we see your motorcycle?" asks Jimmy, his eyes widen at the reminder of how I got here.

"Tell you what. If you let me run up and change out of my travel clothes, I'll show her to you *and* let you sit on her."

A squeal slips through Jimmy's toothy smile. Lindsey's face is strained. Her eyes are fixed on me and I meet her gaze with an apologetic nod. I've overstepped and I want her to know that I'm aware.

"I won't turn it on, though," I say. "She needs a rest after all those miles. This is her first big trip in a long time."

"Will you give us a ride later?" asks Alex, raising a brow. She looks from me to her dad.

"We don't have any helmets," says Lindsey. "And I *know* Charlie would never take a passenger for a ride without a helmet."

"Absolutely," I say, edging toward the first step up to sanctuary. "Totally up to your parents, kid."

I give Jimmy another quick squeeze and look at Alex, unsure of what kind of greeting to offer. I don't want to start our time together by overstepping boundaries with her, too. She puts out a fist and I give it a bump.

"It is great to see you guys again, and to finally get to see where you live. Sorry it took me so long," I say, walking up the stairs. "Hey Alex, will you show me where my room is?"

She nods and walks ahead of me.

"We are really glad that you were able to come, too," says Tom.

"Can I show Charlie my room?" asks Jimmy, starting toward the stairs.

Tom slides an arm out and redirects him to the hallway.

"You, sir, are going to set the table. I'm sure Charlie's hungry after that long trip. Right after you guys take a look at the motorcycle, we're going to sit down together for a meal. You can give a tour of your room after dinner. Hopefully, it looks better than it did this morning."

A rosy blush tints Jimmy's cheeks and his eyes dart to the side. I stifle a laugh at the top of the steps.

"Let me know if you need anything," Lindsey calls up as I head along the hallway. "I put some towels on your bed, but there are more in the little closet inside your bathroom."

Inside *my* bathroom? Alex opens the door to what she refers to as the "guest suite." My jaw slacks, and a breath remains suspended in my throat. The wall on the far side is entirely made up of windows—almost floor to ceiling—and the view leaves me without words.

"That's Pike's Peak," says Alex, when she sees me marveling at the mountain centered like a painting in the window frame. "There's a cool train you can take up to the top. I heard Mom and Dad talking about going up this weekend. There's a road, too, but Jimmy's a wimp and cried most of the way up the last time we went. There are practically no rails. Anyway, they want to make it a fun family thing, so we'll probably take the train."

I raise my brows and nod. I think I might be with Jimmy on this one; I've never been a fan of heights. We took a trip to Chicago when I was younger and there was this building, Sears Tower or Willis Tower or something, where you could step out onto a glass panel over the city. I put one foot on there and backed out. It was like someone had flipped a switch in my brain, shutting down any forward motion motor skills. Reverse was the only option, no matter how much Tommy had teased. And that was a strong, completely encased structure. The words "no rails" were all I needed to hear to know that I wouldn't be driving up that road.

"Alex, come help, please," Lindsey's voice called upstairs, mixed with the sounds of plates and utensils clanging.

"I'd better get down there before Mom, I mean *Lindsey*, bursts a vein," Alex says, and takes a step toward the door.

A short sputter of laughter escapes before I can close off its exit. I'm no expert on kids, but it probably isn't a good idea to encourage her.

"I'll be down in a minute," I say. "I just want to wash the miles off me and get changed for dinner so you don't all pass out when I sit at the table."

Alex grins and exits the room, then turns and aims her dark eyes at mine. And there it is, that drill-like intensity kids muster without even a hint of disconcertment. I smile, squirming inside.

"Is it *really* ok for me to call you Charlie? Cause I won't if you don't want me to," she says.

The tension building in my shoulders melts away. This is a question I can handle.

"I really, *really* don't mind, Alex. To be honest, I actually prefer it. Not sure your parents are too keen on you using their first names, though."

She shoots me a sly grin. "Oh, I *know* they aren't," she says and heads back down the hallway.

Note to self, this kid is starting to sound like a younger me, which is flattering and concerning all at once. Perhaps I am the best one to try to figure out what's going on with her.

You were a cheeky little kid and an even cheekier teen. I tried to mold you, to prepare you for life, but you were reckless. Look where that got us.

I take a deep breath and hold it with my eyes closed. Then I let it slide between my gently pursed lips while I observe the mountains outside my room ... the *guest suite*.

"I don't know, Bill. Things are looking ok from where *I'm* standing.

Chapter 16

Settling In

The atmosphere at the dinner table is much lighter than when I first arrived. It appears that while I was upstairs showering and unboxing the things I shipped to the house, the air was clearing downstairs. Even Alex is smiling. She's still calling her parents by their first names, but she's dropped the snide tone, and Lindsey and Tom are letting it slide completely. I'm guessing they're using the age-old parental tactic of picking their battles.

"We were thinking you might want to go to the top of Pike's Peak," says Tom, between forkfuls of Lindsey's tasty lasagna. "There's a train that goes all the way up."

"Sounds good," I say, nodding.

"We'll also introduce you to some of the neighbors, the ones that aren't away on vacation, and show you where things like the grocery store are before we take Jimmy to camp," Lindsey says, and I can see a hint of anxiety on her face.

"When does Jimmy head to camp?"

"In ten days, Charlie! We're going to be in these really cool cabins. Scott and Jay are going to be in mine and we're going to be The Bears." Jimmy grins, then opens his mouth to keep talking, but Alex interrupts.

"Only if the other campers in your cabin agree," she says, rolling her eyes. "There are six kids to a cabin and they vote on the name."

"Well, we are going to convince them," says Jimmy. "We're going to be The Bears."

"Anyway," says Tom, placing a hand on Jimmy's shoulder and looking at me, "that's why we wanted you here early. The plan is to drop Jimmy off at camp, then head to the city for the rest of the day until we need to go to the airport. First stop, Paris!"

"And, if you need anything, we got the international plan for our phones so you can call at any time," says Lindsey.

"Alex and I will be just fine," I say. I can see Alex nodding out of the corner of my eye.

I spend the next nine days touring the area with my brother's family. He joins us for a trip up to Pike's Peak and a hike around the Garden of the Gods on Saturday and a walk around Estes Park with a tour at The Stanley Hotel on Sunday, but is at work the rest of the time. The day before they leave, he comes up to my room and apologizes for his absence.

"You have nothing to apologize for, big bro. I get it. You need to tie-up the loose ends at work so you can enjoy your vacation." I give him a light punch to the shoulder. "This is a work trip for me, too. Remember?"

"Speaking of work, how's the wifi treating you?" He waves a hand at the laptops I have set up on the desk in the sitting area of my suite.

"Well, now that I amplified the signal, it's perfect."

"Quite the command center you have here. Is that your place?"

I point to one of the screens. "That's my place. The one over here is Mom's, and the one down there is the shop. That's Rick in the shop." I click on a little microphone and lean toward the laptop. "All good, Rick?"

Rick turns around and looks up at the shop camera, flashing his pearly whites. He gives one thumbs-up, then another.

"That's two thumbs-up. Rick must be having a particularly good day. I wonder if he finally asked the chick at the coffee shop out."

Tom laughs from over my shoulder.

I click the mic again. "Hey, Rick? You asked her out, didn't you. You devil."

The thumbs go up even higher, now, as do his brows. "Yessir, boss. We're going out when we both get off work tonight. Everything ok out there in the mountains?"

"Yup," I say. "Just showing my big brother the set-up."

Rick waves at the camera. "Hey there, Charlie's big brother. Got any embarrassing stories for me about the boss?"

"Not today, buddy," I say. "Keep at it and remember to give Mrs. Wilson a call. She said she's having trouble logging into her account again."

"Sure thing, boss. I'll have to get those stories next time. Oh, and how much do you want to bet Mrs. Wilson accidentally changed her password again?"

"I don't make losing bets, Rick. What's the crew up to?"

Fact is, I know what the crew is supposed to be up to, but I want to hear it from him. It's not that I don't trust them. I'm just feeling a little anxious about being disconnected.

"Kim's got an installation—the Jones' are finally upgrading, keeping up with themselves, I suppose." He laughs. "Mickey and Teens got a call to check out a faulty camera. We got this, boss. Take some real time off and enjoy your family."

"Will do," I say. Rick rolls his eyes, a knowing smile spread across his lips. I turn and see that same smile on my brother's face. "What?" I say, clicking off the screens.

"Nothing. He just seems like a nice, responsible guy," says Tom. "Someone you can trust to run things once you set up your Denver office?"

I laugh. "A little premature there, aren't we?"

"You like it here, right? And we like having you here. Think you can hang around a little when Lindsey and I get back? I know Jimmy wants to spend some more time with you. He's jealous that Alex will see you more than he will."

"Well, that depends on Becca, and when she plans on heading home."

Tom nods and rests his hands on my shoulders, something he used to do when he helped me with homework.

"I really like Becca," he says with a sappy smile. "We all like her. You guys need to come visit together next time. She's the reasonable one. Bet we can convince her to move here." He winks and rustles my hair, making me feel like a kid again.

Lindsey calls up, announcing it's time for dinner—our last one together before Alex and I are left to fend for ourselves. On the way out the door, Tom taps the enormous binder that's sitting on the dresser, the words *Plant Instructions* written on its cover in large, loopy black sharpie letters.

"I hope you've been studying," he says, his voice overly serious. "Lindsey will personally check each leaf on every plant when we return."

"Well then," I say, slipping past him and heading toward the stairs, "I hope Alex is really good at taking care of plants."

I'm not about to tell him that although I found the plant room in their Christmas pictures amusing, in person, it's freakishly intimidating. When I told Becca on the phone, she was laughing so hard, I could hear the tears forming in her eyes. For some reason, that room really gives me the heebie jeebies. It's filled with a million different kinds of plants, some hanging, some on shelves. Some are in vases set on the floor and stretch up to practically touch the ceiling. Hell, some have leaves bigger than my head! I, of course, toured the room with Lindsey, nodding and forcing a smile while she showed off her *babies* and told me what they were and the care they needed. But, other than that, I have tried to steer clear of the room altogether. To me, it looks like a jungle ... and the jungles in the books I read always come with danger hidden in the shadows.

Dinner is once again delicious and I can't help but think that poor Alex is going to get a rude awakening when I try to put together a meal. From the looks of the camp brochures that Jimmy showed me about a million times, even the camp food these two are used to is better than anything I can whip up. Becca does most of the cooking for us. I like to joke that my cooking was one of the things that ended my first marriage, but sadly wasn't bad enough to work as a poison.

"Are you all ready for camp, Jimmy?" I ask, reaching for a plate stacked high with homemade rosemary focaccia.

"Yeah," he says, "but I kind of wish I could stay with you guys." One side of his mouth pinches and the other sags into a pout. He shoots a jealous glance at his sister.

"I'm sure you will have an awesome time with your friends and I'll be here when you get back, so you can tell me all about it."

"I'll have a lot of stories. So, that means you'll have to stay for a while."

I nod. "I'll stay as long as I can, buddy. But I'm pretty sure Auntie Becca's gonna want me back before too long."

Lindsey sweeps the table with a gaze, assessing the situation. Then announces, "Who wants some dessert? Alex and I made pies from the berries you guys got at the market Saturday morning."

"Wow, when did you do that?" I ask, eyes wide and stomach recharged at the suggestion of pie.

"While you were upstairs working," says Alex, grinning. "We wanted to surprise you."

"Consider me surprised." I stand up and gather some dirty plates from the table.

"Sit, Charlie," says Tom. "You're a guest."

I gather a few more and head toward the kitchen. "Nope. Lindsey and Alex made pie. I am forever in their service."

"Sure wish that worked with the kids," says Lindsey, laughing.

"Maybe you just need to make more pies," Alex says, an impish grin on her lips.

The family atmosphere remains light and cheery for the rest of the evening. After dessert, we all lend a hand cleaning and play a few rounds of cards once the task is complete. We decide on the game Bullshit, though Lindsey and Tom are calling it "No Way" for the kids' sake. I have to bite my tongue a few times not to slip up. There are a few close calls when I end up calling "buuu—no way", to everyone's delight. I win almost every round; I guess I'm a good bullshitter. That and it's easy to read everyone else. I individuated all their tells the very first time we broke out a deck of cards. Well, all except for Alex's. She's good, and manages to pick up a few games.

It's around 9:00 when Tom finally gives a lengthy look at his watch and declares it a night.

"We have to get up super early tomorrow morning and it's a long drive to camp. So, off to bed!"

"I'll see you all in the morning," I say, pushing my remaining card to the center of the table.

"If you want, we can say goodbye tonight, so you don't have to get up so early," says Lindsey.

Jimmy gets up and launches himself at me. I put out my hands to save myself from being knocked over, then redirect him to the chair in front of me and turn so that he can jump up for a piggyback ride.

"Want a ride up to your room?" He nods and hops onto my back. "I already set my alarm," I say, shifting my weight back and forth, and brushing the ground with my feet mimicking a horse raring to break through the starting gate. "I will be there front and center in the morning to send you off on your adventures."

I bow and head toward the stairs, my jockey giggling as I bounce him about.

Chapter 17

The Send Off

The next morning, my alarm's screech shatters a pleasant dream involving Becca and a cool mountain lake. A deep breath and a thorough eye-rubbing bring me further into the real world, though my mind fights to return to the lake. It's still dark outside.

My complete return to reality takes some time. But, when the aroma of coffee sneaks under the door, I'm finally able to hoist my eyelids from half-mast and to roll out of bed.

I slip on some sweats and wander down the stairs, drawn by the promise of one of Lindsey's signature cappuccinos. I am the last one to the kitchen, which is already bustling with those members of the family preparing to leave. Alex is seated at the table in stark contrast, watching the frantic back and forth of the rest of her family as they simultaneously eat breakfast and go over lists of things they don't want to forget. I catch a subtle look of longing before she notices me and smiles.

"Passports?" Tom looks up from a paper he is holding.

"Yup." Lindsey pats a small pouch attached to a strap she has draped from one shoulder to the opposite hip.

I sigh. I should probably get a passport. Tom and Lindsey's impending trip to Europe has me thinking of places I would like to visit. Becca and I have been dreaming up plans during our nightly calls. I'm a little jealous, to be honest.

"Jimmy? Did you toss your sleeping bag into the back of the van, like I asked?" Tom peeks over the top of his list, pen in hand. "Jimmy?"

Jimmy is in the process of devouring a plate of scrambled eggs. He pauses, holding up a finger while attempting to swallow the heaping forkful he just shoveled into his mouth.

"Yes," he says before his mouth is completely empty, making his answer sound more like "efth," He reinforces it with a head nod for those who might need a translation. Then swallows again and adds, "I put my backpack in, too, and my duffle bag."

"Good man," says Tom, sweeping the pen over the paper in what I imagine must be a large checkmark.

Lindsey hands me a cappuccino, then heads over to the sink and starts to clean up the plates they used for breakfast.

"Leave them," I say. "Alex and I will tidy up."

Lindsey looks genuinely relieved. And who knows, maybe I've slightly boosted her confidence in my housesitting abilities. That bar was at sea-level when I got here. In fact, there have been several times since my arrival when her doubts were almost palpable. Tom says it's just my imagination. I don't think so. I've always been good at reading people. Anyway, maybe it's just the rush to get on the road or the excitement of the upcoming trip overseas setting in, but Lindsey looks like she's no longer worried about leaving her firstborn, her house, and her jungle in my care.

"Thank you, Charlie," she says, giving me a tight squeeze and a kiss on the cheek. "I trust your judgment, and I know that Alex will be just fine with you."

Part of me thinks that maybe she's saying it as a sort of self-assuring affirmation. The other part appreciates her effort, even if she's maybe not 100% certain.

"Really," says Tom. This time, he's the one to piggyback onto Lindsey's hug, once again making me the center of a sandwich. "You're a lifesaver."

Lindsey walks over to Alex, who stands up from her place at the table and allows herself to be pulled into a mamma-bear hug.

Tom leans in to talk to me. "I left the keys to the Range Rover on the key-holder in the foyer closet."

That is a bad security decision. It's one of the first places thieves look when they break-in. I decide not to say anything. Talking about break-ins as they head out the door for a vacation would definitely be bad form. I'll do some rearranging and tightening up once they are gone. It's the least I can do for my big brother and his sweet little family.

"Oh, and the keys to the cabin are also in there."

Strike two, I think.

"You are welcome to take Alex there while we're gone. It should be ready. The cleaning company was scheduled to stop by, and I asked them to make up the beds. I was hoping we could all spend the night there after the Ghost Tour at The Stanley, but I had to take care of something at work. Maybe we can all go when we get home ... you know, before you head back."

I nod and make a mental note to ensure the keys don't have one of those little labels with the address attached to the ring, like I suspect they might. Another suboptimal security decision.

"That would be fun," I say, then whisper, "if the plants let me leave."

A snort of laughter escapes before he can cover his mouth.

"What?" asks Lindsey.

"Nothing, dear. I was telling Charlie about the cabin."

"It's almost like being here, but higher up and with larger animals," Lindsey says, laughing. "So many of the neighbors have bought houses up there, too." She looks at her watch. "Ok! Everyone leaving needs to head to the van so we can get on the road."

Jimmy nearly tackles me. By some miracle, I manage to stay on my feet.

"I'll miss you, too, buddy," I sputter. "You are going to have so much fun at that camp. I'm kind of jealous, to tell the truth."

"Maybe you can come, too. You could be a camp counselor!"

"Well, then. Who would babysit your sister?" I ask, winking at Alex who is giving her father a goodbye hug.

"Right," she says. "Besides, I'm sure Charlie would rather be relaxing here than stuck in a cabin with a bunch of stinky middle schoolers."

"The Bears," says Jimmy.

I give him a thumbs up. "The Bears, right."

Alex and I stand in the driveway, waving as the van pulls away.

"Ok, kiddo," I say when it's out of view. "I don't know about you, but I'm heading back to bed. I need more sleep before beginning the day."

She nods and we walk back into the house, lock the door, and head upstairs.

"Wait here," she says when we reach the top. "I'll be right back."

She takes off down the hall to her room and emerges a few seconds later holding something. The hallway is dark and shadows mask the object until she is right in front of me. I stare at it for a moment, then look at her.

"So you can take me for rides," she says, holding up the powder blue motorcycle helmet.

My jaw hangs open and my brows waffle. I try to find a response, but my brain comes up empty, as if all vocabulary has suddenly been flushed from my consciousness. I'm at a loss and she takes advantage.

"My mom said you couldn't bring anyone for a ride without an extra helmet. So, I borrowed one. Problem solved."

I'm fairly certain, given the smug grin pasted below two wide, faux-innocent eyes, that she knows this wasn't her mother's only concern. I'm also suddenly aware that this housesitting gig is going to be more challenging than I imagined.

Chapter 18

Day One

My original plan was to go back to sleep after seeing off Tom, Lindsey, and Jimmy. But I find myself wide awake. I grab my phone off the nightstand to see if there are any messages. Nothing. I know Becca is having a rough time with her parents. On our last call, she told me it might be hard to keep in touch for the next few days. I tap at the letters with clumsy fingers.

Hope all is well. Miss you tons! Give my deepest love to your folks.

I backspace until I've removed that last sentence. She may not be in the mood for jokes right now. I hit send, roll off the cloud-like memory foam mattress, and trudge to the bathroom to take a shower. I can always take a nap later, and it's not like there's anything planned for the rest of the day. With all the wandering about doing touristy things since I arrived, I haven't had much time to explore the immediate area ... aside from shaking hands with the neighbors on either side. I wouldn't mind taking a nice walk later to familiarize myself with my new surroundings. Lindsey mentioned a trail that leads to the little downtown area. Maybe Alex and I can go for an ice cream or something.

After showering, I throw on some sweats and sit at the window to gaze at the world awakening before me. The mountains bask in the rising sun that paints them with hues of pinks, reds and oranges, making them look like something from a dream. Purple mountain majesties, indeed. Hints of snow grace the highest peaks to my right, and I wonder if there are people skiing upon them at this very moment, microscopic disturbances from my current vantage point. Is it possible to ski there year-round? I've never even put on a pair of skis, though I came close once.

There was a winter when my parents had decided we should give skiing a shot, but I broke my arm two weeks before we were supposed to leave. My parents took it as a sign, and we did a *staycation* instead. Which was just as well. Bill wasn't too happy at the prospect of me heading off to try a "rich man's sport." Besides, my cast and sling turned out to be a bit of a windfall. Though I did have to explain how a pack of licorice ended up trapped in there when the pediatrician finally cut it off. Thankfully, none of the jewelry that sojourned in there got stuck, or I would have had to cut the damn thing off myself.

I'm about to check the camera activity on the laptops and run through customer emails, when I see something move in the backyard. A small fluffy fox bounces across the spikey tan grasses of the xeriscaped yard, sending an explosion of grasshoppers into the air. It turns and crouches, its over-sized ears poking up through the plants, as three more fox kits dart out from a nearby shrub. They tackle the first, a festive free-for-all of jumping, running, and pouncing about the yard. I slowly rise and walk closer to the window until the glass fogs with each breath.

One of the kits notices me and freezes, holding my gaze. It yips and nips at a littermate which has chosen this moment to pounce. Then they all direct their attention to me, their ears aimed like radar dishes. It looks like they are lined up to watch a show on the screen of a drive-in. I wave, giving them a start, but they don't run. The one that saw me first takes a cautious step toward the house, tilting its head with obvious curiosity. I wiggle the tips of my fingers at it. It sits and wraps its gorgeous, full tail around the tops of its front paws. The others creep closer, but are not quite as brave.

Time smudges and I lose myself to the moment. The courageous kit and I stare at each other, shifting our heads ever so slightly, each taking in the other's presence. Its mouth is open, set in a panting smile of sorts, and there's something slightly elfish about the way its eyes twinkle. They are mischievous and merry.

I hear a light knock at my door, but cannot pull myself away from the small furry admirer below.

Another knock, a little less gentle.

"Come on in," I say, just above a whisper, my gaze still fixed.

The door creaks and footsteps approach.

"Slowly," I say.

Alex steps up behind me, and the eyes of my new wild friend shift back and forth between us. The new presence is too much for the rest of the litter, and they scramble away under a nearby bush.

"I see you've met our fox family," says Alex in a scratchy morning voice that gives sleepy frog a run for its money. "They're early risers."

"That one's a bit cocky," I say, giving an almost imperceptible nod toward the last remaining kit in the open. A close look at the bush reveals a group of little, black, shiny noses at its base.

"Dad ... I mean *Tom*." She clears her throat. "Tom calls that one Charlie."

I turn my gaze to her and raise my brows. My head is tilted down so that I can look at her with eyes near the tops of their orbits, as if glancing over the rims of invisible spectacles.

"We both know the person that's meant to annoy isn't present at the moment," I say, then glance back at our little furry friend outside, who is obsessing over a brazen grasshopper clinging to its fluffy tail for dear life. "It's fine if you call him *Dad*. I won't tell."

Alex cinches the corners of her mouth and shrugs.

"Charlie, huh? Your dad is much more adventurous than I am.

He's the one that was brave enough to wander out into the world. Maybe we should call our little friend out there Tommy."

"He says when you were kids, you were the brave one, curious and sly like a fox. Then, when your friend Mr. Edwards died, you changed." Alex bites the inside of her cheek and stares outside, grinning at the small fox who has managed to shake the giant insect off its tail and is now hopping along trying to snap it up.

Silence falls over the room while I take in what she has just said. I'm surprised Tom mentioned Bill to his daughter. I always felt he wasn't all that fond of Bill, or Mr. Edwards, as he insisted on calling him even after Bill gave him permission to use his first name. When I was a kid, I discounted it as jealousy over the attention the elderly man showered on me, like a grandfather playing favorites. But now I'm wondering if it wasn't something else. Maybe Tom could sense something about Bill that I just couldn't see through the filter of awe he inspired.

"I suppose he's right about that. He was kind of like a grandfather to me ... Mr. Edwards. A complicated grandfather." My tone is soft and distant. I half expect the voice in my head to interject, and am happy when it doesn't.

"Dad says you felt responsible or something."

I stiffen. Laughter reverberates through my skull. Deep, dark, spiteful laughter. Bile burns my throat. Once again, I have to contend with the people around me sharing my business amongst themselves, passing it around like a bowl of candy. My features harden, but I take a deep breath, steady myself.

If those words had come from Tom, I would have snapped, maybe even stormed off. But they didn't, at least not directly. They came from the mouth of my niece ... the niece I'm here to watch and protect. The niece who's obviously struggling with some issues of her own. Tom entrusted me to watch her and to see if I can help her. If I'm to take this responsibility seriously—and I intend to—I'll need to set my defensiveness aside. After all, I want to be a positive member of *the village* that's raising Alex. And I need to prove to myself that I am capable of being a good influence.

"Well," I say, "sometimes things happen that we can't undo ... we feel responsible. They weigh on us."

She doesn't need to hear the rest of the conversation spurring in my head. How easy guilt and self-loathing can consume you once you let someone take control of who you are. How easy it is to simply fall under someone else's control once that first person is gone. She doesn't need to hear that. And hopefully she never will.

Alex chews her lip for a moment, her brows furrowed. I brace myself for a barrage of youthful, unfiltered questions, and focus on keeping my cool. Despite the many years gone by, this subject is a raw, open wound. I suppose it always will be.

"I get it," she says, surprising me. "I kind of messed up things with my friend Chloe. I didn't want that to happen either. But I don't really want to talk about it, if that's ok."

I jump at the offramp. "Why don't we go downstairs? We can get some coffee and figure out what we want to do on our first day together. I just need to take a quick look at my emails and make sure everything's ok with the security cameras. It won't take long." I walk around to the desk. Alex follows and lingers behind me when I sit.

"Can I see?" she asks. "Dad says you are a *security guru*, whatever that means. Mom likes the system you gave us for Christmas, but she's pretty sure Dad set it up wrong. We don't really use it all that much. This is a quiet neighborhood."

I laugh. "Well, I can certainly make sure it's installed right while I'm here. Don't tell your dad, though. I wouldn't want to hurt his pride."

My fingers race over one of the keyboards. I log into work and small video boxes jump onto both screens.

"How are you making both laptops work with just one keyboard?" Alex asks, leaning her chin on my shoulder.

These are the kinds of questions I don't mind at all. They have nothing to do with emotions or personal information. I reach over and flick a cord between the two computers.

"They're connected. They think they are only one computer, a two-headed beast. At home I have multiple monitors, but it's much easier to travel with laptops than with my monitors. So, I rigged these two together for better visuals of multiple cameras at a time."

"Hmm-mmm," she says, the sound vibrating into my clavicle. "What's that one?"

"That's my little office downtown. It opens in about an hour. And the one over here—"

"That's your house," Alex says. "I've been there lots of times, silly." She lifts her chin and knocks a fist into my shoulder. "And that's Grandma's place. Look, those are last year's school pictures. Ugh, mine came out gross. Charlie, can you hide that one when you get home?"

"You want me to mess around with Grandma's stuff ... in Grandma's home? You must think I'm crazy," I say, dodging another punch to the shoulder.

I'm enjoying this *bonding* thing much more than the usual interactions I have with Alex when they come visit ... the *how's school going* line of questioning gets old quick and I never know what to ask after.

"What's the little one on the bottom?" she asks, stepping closer to the screen and leaning in. "That looks like my bicycle."

"Is your bicycle in your garage?"

"Well, yeah. You have a camera in our garage? Where is it?"

"Would you believe me if I said I have little camera drones everywhere? Maybe I'm actually a spy?" I lift one brow, trying to keep my face serious and mysterious.

Alex squints, scrutinizing my expression. One corner of her mouth is turned slightly in a grin, but her eyes say she's not completely sure I'm joking. After all, there is currently a small image of her bicycle on my computer screen.

"That's my FCC camera," I say, smirking.

"What's an FCC?" Her head is tilted and her hands are on her hips. She's staring like she's trying to figure out the joke, or if there even is a joke.

"What, indeed." I click on the image to enlarge it. "It's a little hidden camera I put on my motorcycle. It points toward the person riding it. There's a motion detector on the bike and when it's disturbed, it activates the camera and a GPS. See the time signature on the video? It must have been bumped when your mom went in this morning."

"But what's an FCC?"

"That, dear Alex, is the name I gave that glorious machine I rode out here."

"What does it stand for?"

"Becca and I are the only ones that know."

"Can you tell me?" She's giving me the infamous puppy-dog eyes that children have used for generations. Hell, I used them more than once back in the day. They always worked best on my dad, though, not so much on Mom.

"Hmmm," I say, scratching my chin. "I'll have to think about that. It's a pretty big secret. Many have tried to pry it from me with no success."

I fold down the laptops. I'll look through emails later. A preliminary scan didn't reveal anything out of the ordinary. Besides, Rick will be in soon. He'll let me know if anything needs to be addressed, anything he can't handle himself, that is. I stand up and walk toward the door. Alex is right on my heels. I can feel her puppy dog eyes boring into my back.

"I'll tell you what," I say without turning. "If you help me make more coffee and clean up the breakfast plates from earlier, I'll *consider* telling you what it means."

Alex brushes past me and stops at the top of the staircase, her long dark ponytail swinging behind her.

"What if *I* make the coffee? Mom taught me how to make a

cappuccino. If I make you one, will you tell me?" Now her eyes look more like those of the little fox outside. Perhaps we should consider calling it Alex.

"Your mom lets you drink coffee?"

"Nope. She taught me how to make them so I can do it when they're in a hurry in the morning. She lets me put the extra steamed milk on my hot chocolate, though. Mom says no coffee until I'm sixteen. Which is fine. I don't really like the taste."

"So you *have* had coffee."

She shrugs. "Well, obviously I tasted it when I was making it. I needed to make sure it was the right temperature."

"If you can make me a cappuccino like your mom's, we have a deal. But you still have to help me with the dishes."

She starts to turn, then pauses. "If I make you a cappuccino like the ones Mom makes, *and* help you with the dishes, will you tell me what FCC means *and* give me a ride?"

I have to admit, the kid is good. There is no lack of confidence in her expression as she scans my face, looking for cracks in my resolve.

"Hmm," I mutter, trying to buy some time while I work on an answer that won't get me banned from future visits. I kind of like it here in Colorado. "How about when we're done in the kitchen, we head to a motorcycle shop I know of ..." her eyes light up, "... in your mom's car," I add, causing a bit of a pout. "We can go there and see if they have a jacket in your size for safety. I'll get it for you as an early birthday present. After all, thirteen's a pretty big deal. Then we can talk about maybe going for some short rides."

"Awesome! Thanks, Charlie." She does a little side hop and rides the banister down to the ground floor.

"Don't think I'm going to follow you down like that," I call out as she rounds the corner to the kitchen.

Smooth kid. She's got potential. I knit my brows and nod in agreement. She does have potential, just not in the way *he* would think if he were here ... in the flesh.

Chapter 19

Bonding

"How do you know about this place?" Alex asks as we walk past a shop window lined with helmets of every color.

She pauses to admire a sweet greenish gold motorcycle parked in front of the entrance, brushing the tips of her fingers along its shiny flank underlining the word *aprilia*. The bike looks like it jumped right out of one of those action thriller films I love dragging Becca to see.

"A friend of mine gave me a list of bike shops she knows spanning the entire trip here and in this area. She has connections. She's the one who restored the FCC and brought her back to life."

Alex giggles. "I still can't believe *that's* what it means."

"Uh uh uh," I say, wiggling a finger at her. "That's top secret information. Remember? You swore an oath. And we are only as good as our word."

She nods and pinches her pointer finger and her thumb together, running them across pinched lips.

We are only as good as our word, I repeat in my head. A phrase recycled from someone who applied it in a very different situation. Someone who used it only when it worked to his own advantage.

A young woman in jeans and a blue t-shirt with the shop's logo walks over to greet us when we enter the store. She's not much taller than Alex, but by the looks of her arms I'm fairly certain she could bench press us both.

"Hey there," I say. "I called about a jacket for my niece here, Alex."

"You must be Charlie," she says, offering a hand first to me, then to Alex, her grip as firm as I imagined it would be. "I'm Breanna. Any friend of Randy's is a friend of mine. Come with me."

Alex looks at me with wide eyes, clearly impressed by the exchange. A warmth blossoms from somewhere inside my chest. It's a new experience having another human being look at me with such unadulterated admiration. I like it. Obviously, Becca adores me, too, but this is different. Alex's is an expression of love, yes, but there's also an element of idolization. It's hard to explain. It looks like she not only enjoys being with me, but that she wants to be like me. I've noticed it in little things, like the way she changed her stride to match mine when we walked into the store. There's a certain feeling of power that comes with that kind of influence. Power laced with the pull of responsibility.

Breanna stops and waves a hand at a rack of jackets situated next to the smallest motorcycles I've ever seen.

"This is our youth selection," she says, sliding some of the jackets aside. "Alex's size is going to be right around here."

Alex runs her hand down the sleeve of the first jacket.

"Which one do you like?" I ask as she sifts through them.

"Pick out a few and you can try them on over there in front of the mirrors," says Breanna, pointing to the dressing room sign on the opposite side of the store.

Alex's eyes widen. She slides each jacket along the metal bar of the rack, carefully examining its colors and accessories before choosing four to try on. She's opted for the more adult motifs over fun and frilly. I also notice the jackets she has chosen strike a certain resemblance to my own in style, though she has opted for cooler colors, tone-wise. She's glowing as we stride over to the mirrors. Her excitement is contagious, lighting a spark of giddiness in me.

"Wow," I say when she tries the first one, a white bomber-style jacket with powder blue highlights on the shoulders running down its flanks and the top half of each sleeve. "I know we haven't seen the others yet, but that looks really good on you."

She somehow looks older than she did just yesterday. Anxiety at the thought of what Lindsey might think of this purchase creeps up on me. Then I see Alex's reflection as she admires herself in the trifold mirror ... her smile, her self-confidence. The jacket really does look amazing on her. And, I remind myself, she can wear it as a regular jacket when school starts. I'll bet it's great for hiking, too, with its cooling features and abrasion-resistant inserts.

"This one," she says, as if she's read my mind. "Can I get this one?"

I nod and brush her hand away when she reaches for the price tag.

"That's for me to know and for you to never find out. It's a birthday present, remember?"

She slips out of the jacket and hands it to me.

"Thank you," she says, her voice practically dancing with gratitude. "I love it. I can't wait to try it out." She winks.

I find Breanna and ask where the back inserts are. She throws in a couple maps when I pay, and despite a valiant protest on my part, gives me the employee discount.

"I owe Randy, big time," she explains without going into detail.

Alex and I thank her once more as we head out the door. As soon as we are outside, Alex reaches for the bag, eager to slip back into her new jacket.

"How about we take a little walk downtown and you can show me around?" I ask once we are back in the Range Rover. "Maybe we can get lunch and ice cream or something?"

"As long as you let me pay," she says, "Mom and Dad put money on my card to cover meals out."

She pulls a wallet from her back pocket, and slides out a credit card, before slipping it into one of the zippered pockets of her new jacket.

"Your parents gave you a *credit card*?"

Alex laughs. "I mean, it's not really a credit card. They load money onto it and they can see where I spend it. I think they get some kind of automatic alert when I use it. Dad says it's safer than carrying cash around. I can also get payments from the people I pet-sit for on it. Jimmy has one, too."

"Your little brother has a credit card? *I* didn't get one until I was in my thirties."

"Times have changed," she says, like a fifty-year-old in the body of a child. She gives a wink and pats her pocket.

"Dang. I guess they have," I say and even though I am kidding around with her, my mind is actually blown at the thought of my little niece and nephew walking around with credit or debit cards.

"Who knows. Maybe *my* kids, if I ever decide to have any, will be able to do some kind of retinal scan to pay for stuff," she says.

"Into sci-fi, are we?"

"Yeah, kinda. How about you? What kind of stuff do you read?"

My heart is warmed by the fact that she uses the word *read* as opposed to *watch*. Tom and Lindsey are doing a bang-up job with their kids, as far as I can tell. Of course, I can't tell Tom this. It might go to his head. I might mention it to Lindsey, though. If she's anything like my mom, compliments on parental savvy are the ones that almost always score the highest points. And I feel like I still have a ways to go as far as points with Lindsey.

I know for a fact she wasn't thrilled at the whole nasty *divorce* thing. She does seem to really like Becca, but Tom told me she's not too keen on the concept of divorce. Unless, of course, there's physical abuse. Maybe she just thinks I was too hasty getting married in the first place? I don't know, and I'm not planning to bring it up with her anytime soon ... or ever. How do you explain to someone in a happy marriage (at least I hope it's still happy), with a respectful partner, that not all cages have visible bars? Not all damage leaves bruises.

"Me?" I say. "I like thrillers, horror—but not slasher gore—and crime novels."

"I saw a Stephen King book on your nightstand. Is it any good? I haven't really read any horror. Mom would probably say I'm too young." Alex gives a knowing half-smirk, punctuated with an eye-roll.

"It's good so far. There's a reference to the hotel from The Shining in it, which I thought was pretty cool given that we did that tour at The Stanley."

I smile at the memory of the pic I took of the kids posing, their faces in the cutouts of a cardboard photo-op of the twins from the movie. When I recall Lindsey's reaction to my suggestion that it be this year's Christmas card, I think Alex is probably right in her assessment of her mom's opinion.

"It's not all that scary," I add, "if you want to read it when I'm done. You are going into high school next year, after all."

"Sick," Alex says, and shoots me a knowing look, observing my expression.

She's probably checking if I remember our *current youth expressions* lesson from my first days in town. It's true, I probably still have a lot to learn about her generation's linguistic choices. I still instinctively wonder *where* when she talks about *shipping* someone. But I know *sick* is a good thing.

"Want to drop your jacket off home before we head downtown? It's supposed to get hot later." I reach up and push the ignition, bringing the SUV to life.

"Nah, it's got its own cooling system," Alex says, lifting her arms and giving a wiggle. "Unless ..." She aims some industrial-sized puppy-dog eyes at me, and I know what's coming. "Unless we stop at home to drop off the car, so you can give me a ride on your motorcycle ... the FCC, I mean."

Chapter 20

The FCC and Alex

My phone buzzes and I see Becca's name flash across the screen. I don't have my cellphone paired to Lindsey's car, so I toss the phone to Alex and ask her to answer on speaker.

"Hi, Sunshine."

"Hey, babe!" I call out. "Gotcha on speaker phone. Alex is here."

Alex laughs, obviously on to my precautionary announcement. "Hi, Auntie Becca."

"Are you guys having fun?" Becca shifts into her *auntie* voice that all children adore and for a minute I worry that Alex might be a little insulted now that she's on the path to adulthood, or at least teenager-hood.

"Yes!" Alex answers without skipping a beat, scattering my worries to the wind. "Charlie and I went shopping and I got my birthday present early. It's awesome, Auntie Becca! It's a motorcycle jacket."

There's a pause on the line and I'm sure Becca will have a million questions ready for me the next time we speak in private.

"So, *Charlie* bought you a motorcycle jacket? Hmmm. Better

send me some pics." Thankfully, Becca has always been a quick study. "I'll bet it looks amazing."

I can hear her telepathically laughing and saying, *wait until Lindsey finds out.*

"It's *sick*!" I say, winking at Alex who is now rolling her eyes and giggling.

"Ooooh, someone's been teaching *Charlie* how to speak in teen." Now I'm rolling my eyes. Of course, Becca knows the lingo. Some of her therapy patients are teens. Now I just feel old.

"Well, I'm glad I got to talk to you both. We are going to take Dad to the lake for a few days. His doctor says some fresh air might do him some good."

"Doctor Charles," I say, the name souring my throat.

"Yup, Dr. Charles. Cell reception's not great out there, so I don't know if I'll be able to call or text. There's a landline, but only one jack ... in the master bedroom. Mom had it put in for emergencies. I might be able to get some service in the little town nearby, but I'm not sure, so I wanted to let you know."

"Rebecca, help me with the suitcase," her mother's stringent voice interrupts.

"Gotta go. Glad you guys are having fun. Wish I was there." She says the last part in a whisper, I'm guessing so her mother doesn't get offended.

"We wish you were here, too, Auntie Becca," says Alex.

"Yes, we do," I add. "Love you. Have fun at the lake and give hugs and kisses to your folks."

Becca laughs. "Love you, too."

"Why don't you like Dr. Charles?" Alex asks after the line goes dead.

"What do you mean? I don't even know him." I glance at her, then point forward. "Right turn here, right?"

"Yeah. Then follow the road all the way to the end and take a left."

I turn right and enjoy a few minutes of silence, hoping to have curbed her line of questioning.

"You made a face when you said the doctor's name, is all. It kind of looked like you swallowed a lemon." Alex shrugs.

Observant kid. She's got skills.

I take a deep breath and pop it out through my lips all at once.

"Well, I've honestly never met the man."

"Oh, and why did you guys laugh when you told Auntie Becca to give hugs and kisses to her parents?"

Ok, now I feel like I've accidentally walked into a therapy session. I remind myself that Alex is a kid, and kids are naturally curious—nosey even.

"Do they not like you?"

For a perceptive, observant kid, she's definitely not picking up on any of the body language I am currently throwing out there.

"Not really," I say. Then an idea. I point down at the shopping bag. "Why don't you get out the inserts so you can figure them out before we get home. If we're taking the FCC for a ride, you need to be geared up. Also, I want you wearing your thickest jeans. And do you have a pair of boots?"

"Will hiking boots work?"

"They should be fine."

Alex has pulled out the inserts and is reading the instructions. I release an inconspicuous sigh, having successfully changed the subject.

When we get to the house, Alex runs ahead and disappears inside. I park the Range Rover and approach the FCC.

"Hey there, girl," I say, resting a hand on the fuel cap. "Ready to take a little ride downtown? We're going to have an important passenger, so you'd better behave."

I collect my helmet and take it inside. Alex is already at the door ready to go. She has changed into a pair of thick stonewashed jeans and is wearing tan hiking boots with red laces. I knock on her back, my knuckles rapping against the impact foam insert she slipped inside her jacket. She has her borrowed powder-blue helmet tucked under one arm and a million-dollar smile pasted across her face.

"I'm ready to roll," she says.

"Gimme a sec. I'm gonna empty the saddle bags in case we buy something while we're out. You can help me pick out something for Auntie Becca."

Once the saddle bags are back on the FCC, I roll her out of the garage and wave Alex over.

"Do you have a spare opener for the garage?" I ask. She nods, hands me her helmet, and runs inside.

Lindsey has programmed a button on the rearview mirror in her SUV to act as the remote for the garage, something else I'll address when they get home. I'm not a fan of people having access to the house if they break into the car. I'm going to reset the system and get them a set of matching keychain openers to carry with them.

Alex pops back out through the garage door and lifts her hand over her shoulder, clicking the remote she's holding to send the garage door back down.

"Catch," she says, tossing it to me.

I grab it out of the air and push it into my pocket.

"Ok. Rules," I say after she slides her helmet on and clips it. I grab it with both hands, making sure it's snug on her head. "You mount and dismount from the left side of the bike and only when I tell you."

She nods, her brows knit in serious determination.

"If you want me to slow down, set a hand on my shoulder. If you want me to stop, tap my shoulder. When we turn, I need you to lean with me and look over the shoulder on the inside of the turn." I scan her face to make sure she's understanding exactly what I mean. "Got it?"

"Got it. Where should we go?"

"Just downtown. We can look at some shops and get lunch.

Give me the name of a restaurant you like and I'll put it into my GPS. Your helmet isn't mic'd up to mine, so it'll be hard to hear once we're on the road. I think I remember the way, but you won't be able to give me directions if I take a wrong turn."

She gives me a location and I plug it in before snapping my phone into its bracket on the FCC. Then I mount up and beckon her over with a wiggle of my index finger. She grins and approaches, her eyes sparkling with anticipation.

"After I start her up, I'll wave you over to hop on. Stay close and put your arms around my waist. Tuck your laces into your shoes and make sure you keep your feet on the passenger foot pegs," I say, giving them a tap with my foot so she can see where they are.

I start up the bike and she climbs on behind me. I can barely feel the difference, which makes me feel much more comfortable about our imminent ride. Alex is much lighter than Becca, my first passenger ever. I remember how nervous I was learning to compensate the first time I took her for a ride. This will be easier. I relax and give the engine a rev before heading down the driveway and out onto the road.

"That was sick," says Alex, biting into a cheese curd from our appetizer plate. "We need to ride up into the mountains. Maybe we can ride all the way to our cabin."

"Woah. Slow down. I can already feel your mom judging me from wherever they are right now over this little ride, and she doesn't even know about it yet." I laugh and reach out to ruffle her hair. She pulls back just in time to evade.

"What was the signal that biker was doing?" Alex asks. "You know, the guy we passed. He waved, then he was tapping on the top of his helmet."

"Oh, that," I say, chuckling. "He was letting me know there was a speed trap further down the road. Kind of like when a car flashes its headlights."

"Cool. I'll remember that for when I get my license. In a little over two years, I can get my permit, you know."

"Ugh. Thanks for making me feel old."

"Then, I just have to convince Dad and Mom to let me get a motorcycle license."

My phone pings. I reverse whistle a gulp of air, my face ending in a grimace when I see the text message.

"Dang. Do they have you wired? It's your mom. Your brother's all checked in at camp and they are headed to their hotel." I tap in a response, then show Alex the phone. "Anything you want to add?"

"Nah. I'm good," she says.

"They probably sent one to you, too. You may want to check."

A pink hue lights up Alex's cheeks and she focuses on her plate with much more interest than a tuna melt and fries would generally merit.

"Everything ok?" I ask, trying to catch her eye.

She shrugs and slowly looks up until she meets my stare. Then she reaches into one of the pockets of her new jacket and pulls out a little flip phone. She opens it and her fingers glide across the keyboard. Then, she slips it back into the pocket.

"Yeah," she says, her voice deflated. "She texted. I guess I'm not used to the alerts on this phone."

"Oh, you got a new phone?" I ask, not quite sure why her mood has soured.

She takes the phone out again and hands it to me. It's a little flip phone. Not much to it. I guess the kids would call it *retro* nowadays. I feel the skin bunching between my brows. I'm sure she was toting a pretty advanced smart phone the last time I saw her at Mom's house.

"What happened to your other phone?" I ask, not sure I want to know, judging by the expression on her face.

I watch her play with a french fry before popping it into her mouth. She reaches out without making eye contact and I hand her the phone. It disappears back into her pocket.

"I broke the other one," she says in a flat, matter-of-fact tone. She picks up her tuna melt and takes a large enough bite to end her half of this conversation, at least for the moment.

Not *it broke*, I note. But, *I broke*.

I consider a response, glad to have a few minutes while she chews.

"So ... you're using this one until it gets fixed?"

"It's unfixable."

"Until you get a new one?"

I decide this is my last attempt before moving onto another conversation. I can tell that she wants to talk about something, but this is going absolutely nowhere.

"I messed up," she says, just above a whisper. "I got upset and threw the phone. The screen smashed into a million tiny pieces and I don't even want a new one."

This is sounding a little serious for a lunch cafe conversation. I catch our waitress's eye and signal that we're ready for the check.

"Alex," I say in the most nurturing voice a completely child-oblivious adult like myself can muster. I reach out a hand and set it on the table near her, tapping gently with my index finger to get her attention. She sniffs and shifts her eyes up, meeting my gaze, then forces a half-smile.

"Why don't we hop back on the FCC and head home? We have plenty of time to go shopping another day. Let's just go back to the house, pull out the rest of that ice cream your dad brought home the other night and make some crazy sundaes. Later on, maybe we can walk along the path you were telling me about ... the gulch ... then we can finish up the day watching movies on the big screen in the basement. Sound good?"

"Yeah. That sounds good."

When she reaches for her wallet, I wave it back and pull out a wad of cash to cover what we ate, plus a generous tip. She regains a little of the hop in her step when the FCC comes into view and I see the beginnings of a smile blooming on her lips. On the ride home, her grip feels more like a hug than simply holding on. Her cheek is pressed against the back of my shoulder, and I suddenly feel protective, as if she were my cub.

AFTER TWO ENORMOUS sundaes with way too many toppings, we plop down on the recliners in the basement movie room and groan. I feel like a kid after a birthday party ... a kid who snuck into the kitchen while all the others were playing party games, and ate the entire cake. There's a little voice in my head telling me I'm too old to eat this much junk food. I tell it to shut up ...

"Hey Charlie," Alex says from her recliner. Her hands, folded over her stomach, rise and fall when she takes a deep breath. "Thanks for the ride today on The Flying Candy Cane ... and for the ice cream and stuff. Today was awesome."

"And it's not even over," I say. "We still have to take our walk—when I can stand up again without exploding—and watch movies until we fall asleep."

"Do you think we could just talk for a little bit first?"

"Of course." I push myself up in my seat. Could I be about to solve the mystery Tom asked me to investigate? The mystery of the sulky preteen? On day one? "What's up?"

Chapter 21

Alex's Story

"You know how I said I broke my phone?"

"Yeah."

"I was mad at my friend Chloe. I messed everything up. And now she's at camp and I'm not. I miss her even though I think she's being stupid."

"Though you do get to spend a fabulous two weeks with me," I say with a wink. She grins. "What happened?" I shift my weight and set my arm on the armrest, trying not to look too aggressive in my effort to coax out the issue.

"That's the thing. I swore I wouldn't tell anybody. You know, an oath like I did with you about the FCC. And, like you said, *we are only as good as our word* and all that."

Well, shit. I'll be damned if my words—borrowed perhaps, but uttered by these lips—didn't come back to bite me in the ass. I massage my jaw while I contemplate my next move. I've never been one to give up, even in the face of what might seem to be a checkmate.

"Have you guys been friends for a long time?" I ask.

"She was the very first person I met when I went to kindergarten. It's actually a really funny story." A spark lights up her eyes, inspiring a spontaneous grin. "We sat together at snack time. She had a bag of chips that just wouldn't open. So, we each grabbed a side of the bag and pulled."

"Oh no," I said.

"Oh yes. The bag exploded and chips rained down all over Mrs. Pritchard's classroom. We had to stay inside to clean up while the other kids went out to recess. We've been friends ever since." She pauses, her gaze wandering off over my head. "At least we were, until Camryn."

"Who's Camryn?"

Alex looks at me, her mouth a thin line. Her brows have wandered northward and the expression on her face is of someone who's said too much.

"Well, it sounds like Chloe is really important to you. And you guys have been friends for a really long time ... longer than this Camryn guy has been in the picture. I'm sure she'll come around."

Alex sighs and shrugs. "I don't know. We both said some pretty mean things."

"Well, any true friendship is going to have some bumps. I had a really good friend named Sarah when I was around your age. We had our fair share of arguments."

"Are you guys still friends?" There's a glimmer of hope in her eyes that immediately makes me regret my choice of an example.

"Well, no. I mean, we were still friends, but then she moved away. We didn't have all the ways you do now to keep in touch, and I'm not even sure where she ended up going. Tommy, your dad, had a huge crush on her ... which was weird for me because she was like a sister. Your grandmother practically adopted her."

This gets a big smile out of Alex, who leans in, obviously hungry for more ammo to annoy her dad.

"Anyhow," I say, "the point is when you're that close to someone, there are bound to be disagreements. Don't let a guy come between you. If he's a jerk, which, it sounds like given the way you said his name, she'll figure it out and she'll need her best friend to help pick up the pieces when that happens."

"He's a colossal jerk." Alex shakes her head and a mischievous grin sneaks across her lips. "A world class asshole."

I let my jaw drop and widen my eyes in exaggerated shock. The kid is almost a teenager, so I'm not really surprised at the colorful language. But, she's also my little niece. I do a quick inventory of the words I've been using just to make sure *I'm* not the bad influence. Nope. I think I've kept my tongue pretty well in check.

"Do tell?" I say and chuckle. "Tell you what. Let's make a deal. What is said in the movie room stays in the movie room. I know you swore an oath, and I don't want you to break it, but maybe you can talk up to and around it ... without actually breaking it."

Alex scrunches her brows in consideration. "What do you mean by *talk around* it?"

"Well, usually there's one part of the oath that is the real nugget—the secret that you promised to keep—the rest is kind of the background, or the setting of the situation at large. Usually, you can describe the more general part of what's going on, without revealing the secret you've been charged with keeping."

"Now you sound like my dad. Are you sure you aren't a lawyer, too?" She laughs.

"Never. I'm just good at finding ways around things. Heck, I might even guess what the problem is without you even having to tell me. I'll bet you'll feel better getting some things off your chest while still keeping your promise."

Alex nods. Her face has gone serious, a superhighway of creases and lines while she figures out what she is going to say.

"So," she starts, her voice low and wavering, "like I said, there's this guy named Camryn."

"A world class asshole," I add, eliciting a smile, a nod, and more confidence.

"Yes. Anyhow, Chloe met him on one of her online gaming

platforms. She likes to game a lot—something we do *not* have in common."

I nod in understanding, making sure my face is judgment-free and neutral.

"Anyway, she met this guy and she really liked him and wanted me to meet him, too. Like, *online* meet him. Not in person. He seemed really nice at first. Well, turns out he only lives like a couple towns over from us. I thought it would be a stupid idea to actually meet him in person. I mean, he could have been some creepy old guy pretending to be a teenager, right?"

A bad feeling is worming its way through my gut, but I suppress it, not wanting to spook her from continuing her story.

"Hmm mmm," I mumble.

"Anyway, she *really* wants to meet him. And I really want her to be safe about it. So, we decide I'll go, too, and we can meet up at the supermarket—y'know, because it's always pretty crowded. She asks what he'll be wearing so she'll be able to recognize him. Then, when he asks what she'll be wearing, I tell her to totally lie so we can sneak out without him noticing if he turns out to be a creep."

At least the kid has a good head on her shoulders. Still, this story is gnawing at the edges of my nerves, fraying them with each scenario it's setting loose in my overactive brain. I work in security and have heard some crazy shit. Hell, I've had to install entire systems for people who gave out a little too much info over the net to the wrong people.

"Did he turn out to be a creep?" I try to keep my voice calm and neutral, slow and steady. I feel the more I control my reactions, the more details she'll spill. Besides, so far, she's the one least deserving of judgment in this story.

"No. He was actually pretty honest in his description of himself. He's in high school— we saw his ID. He's a senior. Which, yeah, is a little bit older than we are. But," she says, a bit of defensiveness tingeing her tone, "Chloe is already fourteen. Her mom started her in school late because they moved overseas for a year when she was really little. Anyway, he's only a few years older than she is."

The fact she's going out of her way to justify their age difference makes me think she's not entirely comfortable with it herself, but I just nod and lean my chin on my palm. I lift a brow, urging her to continue.

"So, after they met, they started texting all the time. I complained about not hearing from her anymore. So, Chloe made a group text with the three of us, which was fine." Alex looks down at her thumb and starts worrying the cuticle with her other thumb and index finger. She takes a deep breath and holds it for a moment before puffing it out. I wait patiently.

"Anyway, things were fine until he started texting me. Just me. First, he asked what kinds of flowers Chloe liked because he wanted to surprise her. I thought that was really cool. But," she shoots me a furtive glance, "then he was just asking about me, which felt kind of weird. Wrong weird, y'know?"

I nod, eyes squinted. "Let me guess, you told her he was texting you?"

She looks down and gives a quick nod. Captive tears banned to the corners of her eyes, catch the light, broadcasting a deep hurt. Her mouth tightens into a thin line and squirms to the side. She clears her throat and swallows, steadying herself before continuing.

"She didn't believe me. She doesn't believe me. She thinks I'm jealous. I'm not. We yelled at each other. And ... I didn't go to camp because I don't want to be there if she does something stupid. But now I'm worried she'll do something stupid and I won't be there to stop her. And," she clears her throat again, "that's all I can say."

The last word comes out in a squeak before she clams her mouth shut, damming the flow of worry. She stares at me, gathering composure as the seconds pass. I have an idea of what she's worried about. It's pretty clear this guy, this world class asshole, intends to hang around the camp. If this is the case, I'm actually glad Alex didn't go. I don't know Chloe, but I can see Alex cares a great deal about her, and I know that caring deeply about people can create a kind of blind spot. Alex is only twelve. No match for a seventeen or eighteen-year-old guy, no matter what she may think.

"Well," I say, "I'm glad we get to spend this time together, if that helps. Also, I'm sure she'll be fine at camp. They have counselors and stuff, right?"

"Yeah," Alex says. "Each cabin has a resident counselor who does a head count every night and sleeps in the cabin. The younger kids like Jimmy actually have two. This is the first time I've missed camp since I was old enough to go. We always bunk together. She said she wouldn't miss me. She said she didn't care if I went or not."

The dam breaks, and a steady stream of tears flow down her cheeks. She wipes the back of her hand across her face, but not in time to stop some of them from landing on the arm of the leather recliner. I walk over to her, not sure how to help.

Alex jumps up and throws herself into my arms. Her body heaves with sobs and I can feel her warm tears soaking through my t-shirt. She sniffs, pulls her head back, and stares at the dark wet spot she's created on my front.

"Sorry," she says. "I got tears on you."

"And snot," I add, grinning.

Alex snorts and we both break into giggles.

"And snot," she agrees, blushing.

"Well, I was going to wash this shirt tomorrow anyway. You may as well give your nose a good blow."

"Ewwww," she squeals, falling back into the recliner and laughing. "No thanks. I'm not touching that slimy shirt."

"Ok. Let's go get changed. I'll burn the shirt and we can take a walk in the gulch. I want to see more of those cool-looking deer."

"No burning anything here. We're in wildfire country. People will lose their shit. And, you mean the pronghorns, right? The American antelope."

"Got it. Yeah, those. Oh, and I need to get some more pics of prairie dogs for Auntie Becca. She's fallen in love with the little critters."

"You know, there's a lot of people here who hate the prairie dogs. They think they're pests. I agree with Auntie Becca, though. They're adorable!"

"She actually suggested I buy a sidecar for the FCC so I can load it up with prairie dogs to bring home. Of course, I said no. I mean, how the hell would I get them to keep their little helmets on?"

As the two of us giggle our way up the stairs, memories of Sarah flood my mind like the waters of a swollen creek in a monsoon. And of course, floating along the stream of my past, the usual debris of guilt, inadequacy, and fears that I might not be the best influence on anyone, especially not my innocent little niece.

Chapter 22

Sarah

Sarah was the closest thing I had to a best friend, or a sister. I even invited her to my house every now and again. This was strictly against Bill's rules, but he never found out. She lived in an apartment with her mother, who worked most nights. Since her mother slept during the day, Sarah didn't have much of a family life. My mom was thrilled that I had made a friend and loved to dote on her when she came over. She had no idea that Sarah was so much older than I was. Neither did Tom, who had a pretty big crush on her.

When Tom graduated from high school and headed off to college, I was surprised by how much I missed him. We weren't really that close. I mean, how close could we be when he didn't know the real me? Still, I missed his teasing and his awkward attempts at brotherly advice. I was also a little jealous of his freedom, and new start in a new place hundreds of miles away. I had always fancied myself to be the more independent one, but was realizing there was a web of strings attached to my life, holding me tighter than I had imagined. I'd watched Sarah's hopes of moving to Colorado sink, and though she still kept in touch with Lucas, I could tell by the way she said his name and dodged questions, that she was giving up and letting go.

"It's fine," she told me in my room one evening. "My mom could really use my help around the apartment, anyway." She paused and sighed. "Oh, did I tell you I'm saving up for a car? That old lady who lives down the hall from us is thinking about selling hers. Her doctor told her she can't drive anymore, and it's just sitting there. She could use the cash. I go shopping for her sometimes, so she likes me and would give me a good deal."

"Cool," I said. My eyes widened and, without thinking, I ran my hand along the silver chain around my neck to its pendant. "Maybe we could go on a road trip. I've got cash hidden away. Together we probably have enough to drive across the country, maybe stop in Colorado." I stared into space, turning the glass tear over between my fingers, and imagined the two of us cruising down the highway, music so loud we could barely hear each other.

"Charlie, close your mouth." Sarah poked my arm. "You were doing that daydreaming thing again. You need to save your money for college. You're a smart kid. You get all A's. You could go anywhere, do anything."

I sighed and tucked the necklace back under my shirt. "Speaking of college, Tom wants Mom and Dad to fly me out to do some kind of sibling weekend thing at his school next month."

"Do it! That sounds amazing. Maybe I can hide in your suitcase."

"Wouldn't Tom love that?" I said, and we both laughed. We both knew the real reason she would love to come with me was because Tom's school wasn't far from the law firm in Colorado where Lucas was an intern.

"Bill doesn't want me to go. He says I might be tempted to leave and there are some perfectly fine schools nearby. He says he needs me to stay."

Sarah let out an audible puff of air. "Screw Bill. He doesn't own you."

We sat in silence, staring at the floor. "He is getting kind of old," I said, guilt tightening my throat. "He needs a little help getting around sometimes, now. Mom dropped me off at his place a few times to help when he was sick last month."

"What's his place like?" Sarah asked.

Bill told me that none of the others had ever been to his unremarkable little ranch home on the edge of town. He also made it clear that he didn't want me there, either. But he'd been sick as a dog with the flu, and my mom insisted on giving him a ride home when she saw him hacking and sneezing in the park. Then, after getting him settled, she volunteered me to drop in and help out until he felt better.

"It's what Mom calls organized chaos. Books, magazines, and newspapers stacked everywhere, but kept pretty neat. I got to see a picture of him with Esther. He spent most of the time I was there sleeping in a beat-up recliner in his office and yelling at me to stay out. I imagine that's where he keeps his files."

After a moment of contemplation, I added, "I don't think I want to stay here after graduation next year. Do you really think he'd release my file if I tried to leave?"

"I've seen him do it," said Sarah. "He's got stuff on all of us and he knows how to get it out and to all the wrong places. It's not pretty. What would your family think? Would you be able to get into college with a record? What about scholarships? Never mind that the *Bank of Bill* is holding most of our earnings, you know, 'to keep them safe for us' for severance pay."

My mom yelled upstairs, asking if we wanted some hot chocolate.

"Your mom rocks," said Sarah, before answering with an enthusiastic, "yes, please!"

We followed the tantalizing smell of brown sugar and chocolate downstairs and discovered there were also freshly baked cookies waiting for us.

"I need to spoil you before you leave for college like Tommy, and I become an empty nester," my mom said, laying the spread out before us on the kitchen table.

My dad peeked in from the family room. "I'll gain a hundred pounds if she keeps this up once you're gone."

We all laughed. Sarah and I exchanged nervous grins.

"Hey Mom. Do you think Sarah could sleep over tonight? Her mom said it would be ok, if it's ok with you."

Sarah kicked me under the table. There had been no discussion of her staying over, but I knew her mother was working and wouldn't miss her. And I had an idea I wanted to discuss.

"Does she have a change of clothes with her?"

"I have some sweats she can sleep in," I offered. Sarah scanned my face, obviously searching for signs of what I was planning.

"I guess that would be ok. You guys can crash in the family room if you want to stay up watching movies. There's popcorn in the pantry." She made to leave but stopped in her tracks. "Oh, Charlie, you can have the car tomorrow. I'll have Dad drop me off at work on his way to the office. You'll just need to pick me up."

"Great! Thanks, Mom. We're going to get ready upstairs, then we'll start our movie marathon. Come on, Sarah."

"Thank you, Mrs. Blake. And thanks for the cookies and hot chocolate."

"You are very welcome." My mom replied, and we rushed up the stairs.

"I have an idea," I told Sarah as soon as I shut my bedroom door. I opened some drawers and handed her a CU Boulder sweatshirt Tom had given me and some heather-gray joggers. "Go change into these and we can talk about it when you get back."

I changed into a pair of sweats while Sarah was gone. When she came back, she sat in the chair in front of my desk, her arms crossed.

"Well? What's this big plan of yours?"

I pulled out my chain, passing my thumb over the smooth, warm glass, and paced the floor.

"What if we break into Bill's house and find our files?"

Sarah sat back in the chair and leaned an elbow on my desk. "I'm listening."

Chapter 23

Alex's Business

When we step outside again, the sun is blazing. Though I'm not a huge fan of the heat, it feels different here than back home. Here, the shade brings respite. Back home, it's just a slightly darker version of oppressive.

There are many things I prefer about my change of venue, as much as I miss Becca. Here, I'm surrounded by wildlife that I've only seen in books, nature documentaries, or zoos (I'm determined to see a wild moose up in the Rockies before I leave). Here, mountains grace the western horizon, treating me to a colorful menagerie of oranges, yellows, and reds as they swallow up the sun each night. I'm also far from daily reminders of the mistakes I made when I was younger, though I do still carry them around for the occasional bout of self-flagellation.

I take a deep breath, pushing aside the memories of that day with Sarah so long ago. The one that changed everything.

"Oh, shit," says Alex, ducking back into the front doorway and pressing against the wall.

A sporty looking blue BMW passes the driveway. Once it's a ways down the road, Alex peeks around the corner and steps back out into the sun.

"What was that?" I ask, already deciding I won't address the language, which I take as a sign of trust. A sign she sees me as more of a friend, less as a babysitter.

"That was Mr. Benson. I didn't want him to see me."

"Yeah, I got that much, Captain Obvious. But *why* didn't you want Mr. Benson to see you?"

"Chloe and I have—or *had*, I guess—a pet sitting thing together. Y'know, like a business. He asked if one of us could pet and plant sit this week. I told him we were both going to be at camp." She rolls her lips in and bites them.

"And you're *not* at camp," I add, finishing the thought.

"Exactly. I was supposed to let him know I *could* do it, but with everything that was going on, I forgot. I guess he couldn't find anyone and had to change his plans."

"A business? Dang, my little entrepreneur niece."

"Yeah, I'm saving up for some stuff. We make pretty good money, but I'm not sure Chloe wants to do it with me anymore. The last couple times, she backed out to do stuff with Camryn instead. She got mad when I said he couldn't come along."

"Good call." I run a hand through my hair and scratch the back of my neck. "Well, when I'm dealing with clients, I find it's always best to be upfront. Maybe you should let him know your plans changed. He doesn't have to know *why* they changed or when. Then, if he still needs you, and if you're game, you can get the keys and make some extra cash. It's fine with me. But at least you won't have to go slinking around every time we go out, worrying about him spotting you."

Alex frowns in contemplation.

"Yeah, you're right. I'll go tell him this evening. No need for keys, though. He has a code on his door so we can enter. Anyway, I don't want to lose him as a client. He tips really well and I like hanging out with Thorn and Mr. Talon." She giggles at my confused stare. "Thorn is his big old Maine coon cat and Mr. Talon is a lovebird."

"Sounds like a dangerous combination, like Mr. Talon might end up becoming Mr. Snack."

"You'd be surprised. They're actually buddies. Thorn even lets Mr. Talon ride on his back and preen him sometimes."

An image of a bird riding a cat pops into mind. Becca may have shown me something like that on her phone once. She likes to find funny animal videos and send them to me. I think she's trying to get me used to the idea of having a pet.

"Anyway, I'm pretty sure Mr. Talon could take Thorn in a fight. Lovebirds have really strong beaks. Mr. Benson says he bit right through the vet's thumbnail once."

"Note to self," I say, pretending to write on an invisible pad, "never pet a lovebird."

Alex laughs and elbows me. "He's a really sweet bird. He sits on my shoulder while I water the plants and feed Thorn."

"I'll take your word for it. Speaking of birds, did you see those two up there eyeing us?"

I point to a large ponderosa pine across the road, where two large black and white birds are watching us, heads tilting to and fro. One flies down to the side of the road and snaps up a large insect I can't identify.

"Those are magpies," says Alex. "We have a lot of them. They're really curious."

"Cool, but kind of nosey, if you ask me. So, which way is this gulch trail you've been telling me about?"

"We need to cross the road where your new friends are and continue down that hill. You know that playground we pass when we go toward town? Well, on the other side of the playground, there's a path that leads to the gulch. If we're really quiet, we should see some mule deer on the way. Jimmy's also caught a few bull snakes and turtles on the path."

I pull out my phone, switch it to camera mode and snap a couple pics of the magpies. "Will there be any prairie dogs?"

"Maybe, further along the trail. We might even see some pronghorns if we're lucky."

"That would be awesome."

We trek toward the gulch, enjoying each other's company in relative silence. Once again I'm struck by how grown up my niece seems.

Chapter 24

Nature Walk

The walk along the gulch was amazing. Though, in a tragic twist, I completely forgot to apply sunscreen before heading out. I don't have Alex's dark complexion. She got that from her mom. My entire family is as pasty white as they come. I can already feel the burning heat emanating from the back of my neck. At least I wore a hat that shadowed my face. My nose is always the first thing to burn and I really would like to avoid looking like Rudolph.

Remember your sunscreen. You will be at a higher altitude and the sun is much stronger up there, more UV exposure. Becca's warning pings around in my brain. If only it had pinged earlier.

At least I got some awesome nature pics. Alex and I are oohing and aahing over them while enjoying drinks at a local coffee house. Well, I'm doing most of the oohing and aahing while Alex explains what I've captured on my phone so I can label my pics correctly when I text them to Becca.

"Oh, dang!" she exclaims when she scrolls to a shot I took of a bush with fern-like leaves peppered with tiny white flowers. "I didn't see you take this one. Do you know what this is?"

I bring the phone closer and stare at the image. "Is that baby's breath?" I don't know many flower names, but that one comes to mind. Alex looks like she's trying not to laugh. I look again. "I have absolutely no clue, which is why you're going to be the one caring for your mother's jungle."

Now she does laugh.

"Ok, I give up. What is it?" I ask, passing her the phone with a shrug.

"That's poison hemlock."

"Wait ... that's hemlock? The stuff that killed Socrates? What's it doing just growing out there on that cute little nature path?"

"Nature can be deadly," she says, sounding like a fifth-grade science teacher. "Did you know that some indigenous tribes used juice from hemlock to poison the tips of their arrows?"

"That I did not know. And here I thought the most dangerous thing we encountered today was that prickly pear cactus I almost walked into."

Of course, I know that nature can be dangerous. I guess I just expect it more from things that can come at me, like rattlesnakes or mountain lions, not pretty unassuming flowers that look like they should be in wedding bouquets.

"Do you remember where the hemlock was on the trail? I should shoot a text to the parks and rec guy. My mom has his number at home. Oh, and prickly pears actually taste really good. The fruits, that is. I would've grabbed one for you to try, but most of the fruits were either not ready yet or already harvested. Anyone's allowed to pick the ones that grow along the path."

"Cool," I say, making a mental note to taste prickly pear when I get the chance. Oh, and to stay away from little white flowers. The thought of prickly pears reminds me of a famous bear from a movie I loved as a kid. "Like Baloo," I add.

"Who?" Alex asks, brows raised.

"Never mind. It's from a movie I'm going to watch with you before I leave."

I take a sip of my iced coffee and go through my pictures again, picking out the best ones to send to Becca. Then I gather them into a text and hit send.

"Oh shoot. I guess she still doesn't have service," I say when my phone informs me that my texts could not be delivered. "I'll email them instead."

After doing just that, I redirect my attention away from my screen. The view is breathtaking, which is why we have opted to sit at one of the tables located outside the coffee house on its wraparound deck. A small windmill stands across the way near the path we walked to get here, its tail catching subtle bursts of air, positioning its wide, slender blades to better catch the wind. The sky is a brilliant blue canvas with white, fluffy clouds scattered here and there. It looks as if an otherworldly artist dipped his brush into a bucket of white paint and gave an absent-minded flick of the wrist.

I tap my niece's shoulder and point toward the horizon. The sun has begun its journey downward and is now floating over the mountains, threatening to jump behind their snowy peaks.

"We'd better get home if you're gonna drop by your neighbor's house."

"Yeah," she says, but the hesitation in her voice tells me she's a little nervous.

"Remember, you don't have to say anything about why you didn't go. You're here and available if he needs you. Keep it positive and he'll be happy to have the option. If you want, I can hang out at the end of the driveway for support. You could tell him you're stopping by on your way out to dinner or something."

She stands up and gathers her trash, shaking her head. "Thanks, Charlie, but I need to go over there by myself. I want to look responsible and independent, y'know? Besides, Mr. Benson is a really sweet guy. I'm not afraid or anything, just kind of mad at myself for not remembering ... maybe messing up his plans. His wife died a couple years ago from cancer. I don't think he has any kids, but he likes to visit his brother. He told me he wishes he could take Thorn and Mr. Talon with him on the plane, but he knows they're much happier hanging out here with me."

We are both quiet on the walk home. She's probably concentrating on what she's going to say to Mr. Benson. I am concentrating on catching my breath; this is the longest hike I've done so far in Colorado and I'm feeling the altitude. Between the thinner air and over-exposure, I feel like I can definitely take a nap when we get home. Maybe even just eat and call it a day. After all, we did have to wake up pretty early this morning.

We're walking up the driveway to the house when my phone rings. The rumble in my pocket gives me a bit of an adrenaline jolt. I'm hoping it's Becca. When I pull out the phone and examine the screen, Tom's name pops up. Of course. They must be at the airport getting ready to leave for their romantic (I hope) getaway.

"Hey, big bro. You and the missus getting ready to jump the pond?" I stop and do my best to hide the intermittent panting.

Alex turns and calls out a "hello," when she realizes who's on the other end of the line.

"We are at our gate and waiting for them to start boarding," says Tom. He sounds excited, giddy almost. "Everything ok? You sound a little out of breath. Feeling the altitude?"

So much for my efforts to hide the obvious. "Yeah. Alex took me for a walk along the gulch trail. I guess I didn't realize we were walking downhill most of the way until it was time to turn around and walk back uphill." I release a *whew*. "Apparently I'm not in the shape I thought I was." I pause and breathe deep through my nose. "You guys must be excited. Remember to take lots of pictures."

"Yeah, Dad. Take lots of pictures," Alex calls out from behind me.

"Ooooh. I'm Dad again! Working your magic already, I see. How's she doing?"

"Great," I say, trying not to let on to Alex that we are talking about her. I'm pretty sure the *Dad* thing was a slip on her part and don't want to remind her. "We're great on this end. Don't you worry about a thing. You and that pretty little wife of yours just head on over to the Old Country and leave the homestead to us." Alex rolls her eyes and makes a gagging gesture. Ok, perhaps I am laying it on a bit thick. I stick my tongue out at her before switching to a more earnest tone. "Seriously though, Tom. You don't have to worry about anything. Alex and I have everything under control here."

"I appreciate that, Charlie. Thank you. I'm not sure how my service will be over there, but I'll try to text you every now and then."

"Don't waste your time texting. Concentrate on just the two of you having a good time, big bro."

"They're starting to board the plane. Gotta go. Give the little munchkin a hug from us. Oh, and Lindsey says 'hi.'" I hear a voice somewhere near him call out a "hello" before the line goes dead.

I turn to Alex and wiggle my cell phone in my hand. "Looks like your folks are on their way."

"I hope they have fun. They've been arguing kind of a lot lately and I think it's because of me." She frowns and kicks a pebble, sending it rolling down the driveway.

"I'm sure it's not. That just happens sometimes with couples."

I'm not sure it's not, but it seems like the right thing to say. Whatever they are arguing about, even if it pertains to her, it's not Alex's fault. Besides, from what I saw in my short time with both of them before they left, there's plenty of love there. They probably just need some time away.

"Ok, I'll preheat the oven for a couple of those frozen pizzas I saw in the freezer. You head over to talk to the neighbor. When you come back, we can watch some tv while we eat. Then, I'll probably go to bed early. That hike really took a lot out of me."

"I'm going to hop in the shower before I go talk to Mr. Benson. I'm kind of sweaty from the hike," Alex says, picking up her pace. "I want to look professional."

She scoots up to the front door and punches in a code to

unlock it. I'm not a huge fan of wireless keypad locks. I've always preferred a good ole deadbolt and key myself. But, I get why they have it with kids forgetting their keys and all, something I myself don't have to take into consideration. So, when Tom asked about them, I made sure he bought the one least prone to hacking. On the upside, he didn't have to worry about giving me a key.

"I'll wait on preheating the oven until you are ready to leave," I call out as she ducks inside.

Instead of following her in, I sit on the front stoop to enjoy a little more fresh air and take in a view of which I could never tire. A storm is rolling in over the mountains now, though it's still too far away to hear any thunder. Flashes of lightning illuminate the inner sanctum of the dark clouds while stripes of gray reach down for the highest peaks, as if pulled by an artist's brush.

At the edge of the property, a small fox wanders out from the bushes, stopping cold when it sees me. We lock eyes. My jaw slacks.

Charlie, close your mouth.

The fox tilts its head and takes a tentative step toward me, stopping to pull up a dandelion and giving it a playful shake.

"Hey, buddy." It escapes my lips like a dry breeze, and for a moment I wonder if I spoke the words or simply thought them. "You must be Charlie."

The fox rolls onto its back, squirming in the dirt and making happy little laughing sounds.

"Man would Becca love you," I whisper, reaching for my phone. This moment deserves a video. No still shot could do it justice.

I almost have it out of my pocket when the sound of an approaching car spooks my little friend. The fox yips and ducks back into the brush.

"Shit," I say, jamming the phone back in and standing to stretch.

The engine gets louder and a sporty blue beamer appears in the distance, heading towards us. I walk to the end of the driveway as the car slows. The driver is an older gentleman with salt and pepper hair, which becomes more apparent when the passenger window descends. His outfit—a royal blue Lacoste polo and luxurious khakis with a sharp traveler's crease that looks like you could split wood on it—matches his ride. A pair of Dolce and Gabbana sunglasses rest on the bridge of his nose, hiding his eyes like a secret.

"Hello there," he says, aiming both a friendly smile and a wave in my direction.

"Mr. Benson, I presume?"

"Yes, indeed."

"I'm Charlie. Tom's my brother. I'm staying at his place for a few weeks. Though, I'm tempted to just pick up and move here. The views are gorgeous."

He nods and I get the feeling he's sizing me up behind those dark lenses. I stop short of saying that Alex is home with me, not wanting to spill the beans before she has a chance to talk to him. But at least now I can tell her he's home.

"Well, I'd better get inside," I say, glancing at my watch, which looks like it came out of a gumball machine compared to the Rolex he's sporting. "It's about time for dinner. It was nice meeting you, Mr. Benson."

"Nice to meet you, too, Charlie," he says before rolling up the window and continuing on his way.

I watch his car wind along the road until it reaches the drive leading to the house at the very end.

Whoa, I think, *I thought Tom's house was big.*

Wasteful, adds the voice. *I'll bet he sits on the board of some multinational ... jetting around, spreading their tentacles into every little hometown community like a cancer. You don't make that kind of money without compromise.*

"Right," I scoff, pushing back. "You're one to talk about compromises."

I have no idea how the guy made his money. What I do know is that Tom's whole house could fit inside Mr. Benson's and there would still be room for my little ranch. Though, I will concede that it seems a waste for a single person to be wandering about in all that square footage alone. Well, one person, a giant cat, and a bird that can punch through a fingernail with its beak.

I go inside and wait for Alex to come down. I remember my cell battery is almost dead, so I plug my phone into a charger sitting on one of the kitchen counters.

My mind returns to Mr. Benson. Alex was right, he seems like a nice enough guy. A little awkward maybe. Or perhaps I'm just not used to meeting someone of his caliber, money-wise. That's probably what has me a bit anxious now. I'm more used to the down-to-earth feel of the town Becca and I inhabit.

"You can start the oven," says Alex from behind, snapping me from my thoughts. "Sorry," she adds after I jump.

"No problem. I was lost in thought." I take off the hiking hat I borrowed from Tom, set it on one of the barstools, and comb a hand through my hair.

"What were you thinking about?"

"Nothing, really. Just daydreaming, I guess. Oh, I saw Mr. Benson drive by. He was heading home. That's one helluva home, by the way. I imagine it's pretty snazzy on the inside. Do Thorn and Mr. Talon have their own bedrooms with private baths? Or maybe a Jack and Jill?"

Alex laughs, one of those hearty laughs that animates her entire face and sets her ponytail swinging. It ends in a snort, which sets me laughing, too.

"Ok, I'd better get over there before it gets late," she says, her eyes resolute. She smoothes her long ponytail, gathering it with her hand and flips it back over her shoulder.

"Take your time, Ms. Entrepreneur. When you get home, I'll pop in the pizzas."

Alex gives me a thumbs-up.

"Go, get 'em," I say as she heads for the front door.

Chapter 25

A Thorny Question

While Alex is gone, I wander into the plant room—aka the jungle—wondering exactly how much vegetation actually resides in here. Sure it's intimidating, but upon closer examination, the variety of plants Lindsey has gathered is impressive. Everything looks like it's thriving, too. None of the brown spots I often see on my spider plant when I'm its key caregiver, before Becca inevitably swoops in to save the day and nurses it back to health. My thumb is the furthest color from green.

I sweep my gaze around the room, admiring the rainbow of flowers: pinks and reds, blues and whites, and even some in shades of black. Maybe it isn't so creepy after all. A deep breath treats my senses to a combination of sweet, musky, and citrusy aromas. There's an armchair nestled into one corner of the room, an excellent place to sit and contemplate all the work that went into perfecting this space. I peer suspiciously at the pot of tiny white blooms next to the chair. Nah, these don't have the ferny looking leaves. This could actually be baby's breath. A cynical chuckle escapes as a puff through my nose. Man, would that be a twist. My sweet, peppy sister-in-law some kind of serial killer growing hemlock in her house. I sink into the soft cushion of the armchair and drift off, my busy day under the burning sun getting the best of me.

When I open my eyes, the room is considerably darker, and, once again, creepy. I can barely see my watch under the gloom, which tells me I was out for a couple hours. I lace my hands behind my neck and stretch, tipping my head back and forth, creating a barrage of pops and crackles. I yawn and take a moment to orient myself, bring myself back into the present. Back to Tom's house. Back to the plant room. Back to the jungle.

A sudden thought strikes me: it's too quiet. Alex went to talk to the neighbor over two hours ago. Maybe she came back, saw me asleep, and decided to just go to bed. She's a pretty considerate kid.

I climb the stairs and find her bedroom door closed. I don't see any hints of light coming from the space around it. I knock gently. Then a little harder. When I open the door, the light from the full moon is flooding through her windows. Her bed is made, the room empty. She must still be talking to the neighbor. I decide to walk over to collect her for dinner. She probably got carried away playing with the cat and the bird.

I consider riding over on the FCC to pick her up. She'd love that. But I'm not sure where she put the helmet she borrowed. I don't see it anywhere in the room and certainly don't want to invade her privacy by nosing around. I wander down to look in the foyer closet.

No helmet.

What I *do* find is the key to the cabin. And, as I suspected it might, it shares its ring with a tag framed in bright blue plastic listing the address of the property.

Oh, Tom. All that's missing are directions and an occupancy schedule.

I pocket the keys so I'll remember to rectify the situation before hitting the hay later. I always empty my pockets on the night table before turning in. It drives Becca crazy. Though, in her defense, the fact that I keep doing this until she finally caves and clears the veritable mountains of receipts, cash, coins, and candy wrappers, is what really annoys her. The thought brings on a grin. I grab my jacket off a hanger in the closet, opting to walk to the neighbor's house. The night air will help wake me up so we can have a nice dinner together, maybe watch a movie.

When I step outside, a shadowy form scurries by. One of the foxes maybe. Or it could have been a skunk, raccoon, or any of the variety of creatures I've been told roam the property at night. The air is cool and crisp. This is another thing I love about my current location. Even on the hotter days during my visit thus far, the evenings and nights have always been cool. There's nothing worse than trying to sleep in hot, humid weather. The sheets get all bunched up and sticky, and the person you love, the one with whom you share your life and abode, transforms from someone you want to cuddle up to, into a lava-hot ball of fire that can only be avoided by performing a balancing act on the edge of the mattress ... feet out, of course.

I zip up my jacket and start my walk to the house at the end of the road. There are no streetlights anywhere along the way, only the occasional landing strip of driveway lights leading to neighboring homes washed in their own distant spotlights. But the moon is picking up the slack, bathing the world in its silvery gray light, giving my surroundings a bit of a surreal feel, like I'm walking though the negative of a photograph, or am the protagonist of an old black and white film.

At the edge of one of the driveways, another shadow shoots past me. This one ends up under a rather large bush that looks kind of like the blue spruces from Lindsay's Christmas portraits, but without its top half. I stop and lean forward to see if I can spot the owner of the shadow, taking care to listen to the portion of my brain currently reminding me there are skunks here.

Bright yellow eyes shine out at me from the depths of the bush. Do skunks have yellow eyes? What about foxes? Raccoons? I don't know. My thoughts are interrupted by a hiss. I don't think any of the animals I was considering hiss, but I can't be sure. I've never been much of a nature geek, having always fostered a preference for the manmade side of life—computers, vehicles, tech. You know, things I can control. Nobody really controls nature. Not that we don't try our very best. But nature's always waiting to reclaim what's hers. Just look at any sidewalk or road. As soon as man is distracted, BOOM, you've got little blades of grass, even flowers and roots popping through and tossing aside all our effort. Anyone who's seen the landscape in any post-apocalyptic movie knows who has the upper hand in Nature v Humans.

My game of solitaire twenty questions doesn't last for very long. When I squat down to get a better look, the largest feline I have ever seen outside a zoo struts out from under the evergreen. The cat's coloring is dark, though in the moonlight I can't tell whether its fur tends toward brown or dark gray.

"Thorn?" I ask, remembering Alex's description of Mr. Benson's cat even though I know that his cannot possibly be the only cat on the block.

The animal's ears flick back and forth when I say the name again, something I take as a passive aggressive affirmation. From what Becca has told me, cats don't let you know they're paying attention unless they want something. It's the kind of selective hearing skill that she sometimes insinuates I possess when she's teasing me.

I reach out a hand. "Thorn, is that you? Are you supposed to be out, or did you escape?"

The cat gives my fingertips a sniff before apparently deciding that I'm passable as a decent human and rubs against my hand. My fingers brush against something that is not fur. I look closer. It's wearing a collar.

"Do you mind?" I ask, reaching for the metal disk attached to it.

I glance around to make sure nobody has witnessed me asking the cat for its permission. The road is empty. I tip the disk toward a nearby landscaping light for a better look. Sure enough, the word *Thorn* is inscribed on the center of the tag in cursive script. A fancy collar with a fancy name tag for a fancy cat living in a fancy house with a fancy owner.

I give Thorn a scratch behind the ears and stand. He looks up at me with an expression of boredom and contempt that only a cat can muster. Then he winds his body around my feet. What is it about me that cats like? Do they not understand that I don't particularly like them back?

"Ok, buddy. I'm headed for your place to pick up my niece, Alex. You know her. She's been your babysitter on several occasions, if I understood correctly. You can hang out here or you can follow me back to your place. Your call."

Thorn meows, stands, and walks off toward his house.

Call me the reluctant cat whisperer, I think with a laugh before continuing my walk to Mr. Benson's place.

The house looks even more impressive up close than it did from down the hill. A combination of stucco and stone give it an almost castle-like appearance, a look accentuated by the central tower rising up from the front entrance, topped with a round terracotta roof, its tiles akin to the scales of a dragon curled up to rest on its peak. It looks like it could house a fairytale princess until the day she realizes she can let her hair down and escape.

The fact that the home is perched at the very top of the hill, with a rather dramatic decline on the other side, only adds to the illusion. When I wind down the driveway, I can see that the house is two stories in front, but three at the back. I imagine an impressive fully-finished basement that lets out onto the patio I can see from above. At the edge of the patio, a large Roman pool complete with detached pool house, which is large enough to serve as a guest house.

When I reach the front door, I hear a faint shriek from inside. The hairs on the back of my neck prickle, and my breath catches in my throat. I tilt my head to the side, leaning toward the door, but only silence follows. Then I remember Mr. Talon. Birds like to shriek, right? Maybe he's calling for his best buddy, Thorn, who has disappeared somewhere into the landscaping.

Paranoid much?

I ring the doorbell. It's one of those with the camera. Great, now there's a record of my paranoia. A glance over my shoulder reveals a motion activated camera up inside the entryway, as well. I recognize the model. It's a pretty reliable one, though I would expect something a little more upscale and high-tech for a residence of this caliber. If I end up moving here, I'll let good old Mr. Benson know that I could steer him toward a much better product and make sure his beautiful home is properly protected.

I hear faint footsteps approaching from inside the house. The door opens and Mr. Benson is standing in his foyer, a long smoking coat draped over a fancy pair of sweats. He rushes a hand up to his mouth to cover a yawn.

"I apologize," he says. "You've caught me on my way to bed. Charlie, right?"

"Yes, that's right. I'm sorry to bother you, but I'm looking for my niece, Alex." I crane my neck to peek into the house, which has exactly the classic posh look I expected.

"Oh, Alex left about half an hour ago. Said she was going to stop by to let some of her other clients know she's in town and available to pet sit if they need her."

"Oh. I really wish she'd told me."

"I'm certain I saw her send a text on her way out the door," says Mr. Benson, shrugging. "Seems you could have saved yourself a walk."

I nod and instinctively reach down to my pocket. No phone. I left it to charge. Shit. Well, that explains it.

"Sorry to bother you. Goodnight." I turn to leave until I remember the cat. "Oh, I'm not sure if he's supposed to be out or not, but I saw Thorn on my way here."

"Pardon?" Mr. Benson says, stopping the door before it closes. He is squinting at me, leaning his head through the opening.

I realize that this is the first time I've seen the man's eyes. They're dark enough that the dim light of the entryway blends pupil and iris into one black pool.

"Your cat, Thorn. I saw him on my way here. I think my niece said something about coyotes. You might want to call him in." Not that I care that much about Thorn, but he was well-groomed and plump. Not the kind of feline I could see coming out of a battle unscathed.

"Ah, yes. Thank you."

I head down the driveway, cursing myself for leaving the phone in the house. Even though Alex should have come right home. She knew I was making pizza. Well, she knew that I was supposed to be making pizza. She probably walked back and is wondering where the hell I am.

Thorn pokes his head out from behind a large landscaping boulder and meows. I stop and he trots over to me. He weaves between my legs, and I can feel the vibrations of a steady purr against my trousers.

"So, are we buddies now?" I ask, leaning down to scratch the top of his head.

I'm no fan of felines, but this guy is soft like a bunny rabbit, a far cry from the scraggly specimen Becca and the neighbors have been feeding back home. I hope he can defend himself. It's weird that someone who has obviously taken such wonderful care of his cat would leave him out like this. I run my hand down his back and he leans into the caress. Not a single burr or even the hint of a tangle in his long, soft coat.

"Well, you should get yourself back home," I say. "I have a niece to locate and pizza to eat."

Thorn meows and struts off toward his house. I watch until he is all the way down the driveway. Instead of going to the door, the cat parks himself in front of a detached garage with oversized wooden doors. I contemplate going back down to ring the doorbell again. I have no idea why the situation is bothering me so much. Since when am I this worried about a cat? Maybe Becca's tactics have been working.

I'm also a little upset with Alex. Text or no text, she should have come straight home. Maybe that's what's bothering me. It's definitely something we need to talk about when I get back to the house. I worry my lip with my teeth.

Something's tugging at my brain, asking it to stop and think, telling me to snap out of vacation mode for just a moment. I take a deep breath and calm my thoughts, close my eyes.

You've got skills, kid. Use them. What is bothering you?

"I don't know," I answer, but it's gnawing at me now.

His shoes, something inside me screams.

Yes, his shoes. He was on the way to bed. He'd been practically swimming in the sweats he was wearing under his smoking coat. The backs of his pants were dragging on his marble tile floor, and the wiseass in me had silently wondered if this saved him on housecleaning. But, I had caught a quick glimpse of his shoes when he stopped the door from closing. Quick enough that it registered somewhere in the back of my brain.

Not only was the man *on his way to bed* wearing hiking boots, but there was also dirt caked on them. I'd noticed some little chunks crumble off as he was turning to leave. Maybe there's more to Mr. Benson than the neighborly, grieving widower who employs Alex and her friend as pet sitters now and again. My interest is piqued. And when that happens, following up is so very hard to resist. Becca calls it *hyperfixation*. I call it a natural need to know, a healthy dose of curiosity. Besides, shouldn't I investigate a little further? I mean, for my niece's sake?

It's kind of a shameful justification, using Alex to cover for my curiosity. But it's all I got. I look at my watch. If Alex left about half an hour ago and is stopping to talk to the other neighbors, I should have plenty of time to give the Benson place a harmless little look-see ... from the outside, of course. I've only ever broken into a house once ...

And, look what that lead to. I squeeze my eyes shut and banish that gem of a memory back to its home in the darker recesses of my mind.

I walk a little further down the road in case Mr. Benson is watching me (why would he be?). Then I start down the drive of one of the neighboring homes and veer off into the tall grasses decorating the perimeter of their property. Keeping to the shadows, I ease my way toward Mr. Benson's place. The back patio is very well lit, up to and including the swimming pool, which looks like a giant, shimmering, blue jellyfish. There must be some pretty powerful lights along the rim and at its bottom.

Despite my best efforts to resist, the same compulsion to snoop on my brother's neighbor keeps dredging up the past. I only hope this time things work out differently.

Chapter 26

My Short Stint as a Cat Burglar

Sarah got up from my desk chair and flopped onto the bed, angling her body until she was facing me, elbows propped, the heel of each hand cradling her chin. Her expression, highlighted by the hint of a grin, spurred me on. She looked intrigued. And was that a touch of hope twinkling in her eyes? Of course. If we could find and eliminate our files, she'd be free.

"I've been in his house. I think I might know where they are. Maybe we can even find some of our severance pay," I said, my voice low but crisp. "We can grab the stuff and leave him a note saying that we're out ... done. If he doesn't have anything on us, he can't really do anything about it. You heard my mom. I've got the car tomorrow. We can go over there early before the sun rises. My dad's parked in the driveway, so they won't even notice the car's gone. And even if they do, we'll just tell them we went for coffee and donuts."

"What if we get caught, Charlie? What if Bill catches us? You've never seen him pissed-off. It's not good."

"Well, then let's not get caught."

She was wrong. I had seen him angry. I'd been to the counselor's office at school and she'd filled my head with all the possibilities out there just waiting for "a smart, conscientious student" like me. We scrolled through campus pictures and read about programs in criminal psychology, when I mentioned that might interest me. I started filling out paperwork, looked into campus tours, and researched scholarships. So, when my mom dropped me off at Bill's house to help him out, I was giddy with all my prospects and couldn't help but mention my excitement.

"Leave? You can't leave," he hollered, before a coughing fit forced him to sit for a moment. "We have good schools nearby. You can go to one of those."

I flashed my mom's smile. "I don't want to go to one of those. I want to move on. I want to start a normal life. This isn't fun anymore." I stopped talking when I saw his face turn a deep crimson red.

"Fun? You think this is about fun? We are taking back what is mine! These chains think they can just move in and shove everyone else out. We aren't done here. After everything I've done for you. Everything I've taught you. No. No, you can't leave, yet." He stood up and walked toward me. His hand came down on my shoulder with the same strong grip he'd had so many years ago in the pharmacy. "No. I won't let you. I have files on you, evidence of the things you've done. What would your counselor and those fancy schools think about those?"

I tried to shake free, but he reached over with his other hand and placed it on my other shoulder. He pushed me down into his recliner. "You sit right there and think about things for a bit. Think about what would happen if you tried to leave. I am going to make us some tea. You can join me when your head is clear."

I sat and fumed, trying not to let the anger boil over into tears. While I sat there, I scanned the room, as was my habit, as I had been taught.

Sarah and I didn't sleep that night. While movie after movie played on the family room television screen, we planned our very first—and hopefully last—home invasion. At around 3 a.m., we snuck out of the house and drove my mom's car to Bill's neighborhood. Sarah looked around at the houses, her brows furrowed.

"I thought Bill would live in a nicer neighborhood," she said.

I shrugged and parked the car amidst the line of cars already along the curb.

"That's his," I said, pointing down the street at a little white ranch about four doors down from where we were parked.

Getting into the house was easy. I still had the extra key he'd given my mom at her insistence, when he was at his worst with the flu.

"Somebody needs to be able to get in if you need help. It's just until you feel better," she'd said. He'd finally given her a key, which she then gave to me in case he didn't answer the door when I went to check on him. I never needed to use it, and I guess he forgot to ask for it back.

The house was dark, but not completely black. Little nightlights glowed along the walls like an airport landing strip, lending enough light for us to avoid tripping over furniture. The only sound we could hear, aside from our light breathing and soft footsteps, was the tinny clicking of the grandfather clock that stood sentry near the entrance. We did our best to time our footsteps to it. I pointed to a room at the end of a hallway and whispered "bedroom" into Sarah's ear. She nodded. I then indicated a door in the same hallway, but closer to us on the right wall, and whispered, "office."

With a finger to my lips, I signaled Sarah to wait at the edge of the foyer as per our plan. She would watch the bedroom door for movement while I searched the office. If he came out, Sarah would make a loud noise and escape out the front door. There was a large bay window in the office that I could use as an exit.

I made it to the office door, carefully cracked it open, then slipped inside. After letting my eyes adjust, I crept toward the bookshelf that occupied the entire back wall. My guess was that the cabinets on the bottom row of the built-in contained the files we wanted. A pale beam of moonlight shined through the bay window shears, supplementing the solitary nightlight beside the door.

I was about halfway to my destination when movement to my left caught my eye. My throat pinched, trapping a breath before it could reach my mouth. Bill was in the recliner in the center of the room. I tried to swallow my panic and assess whether he was awake or asleep. My lungs begged for air. I was unable to fill them for fear of being heard until the welcome sound of light snoring reached my ears. I contemplated turning back, but images of campus quads and laboratories filled my head. I had to push on.

I crouched down and opened one of the little doors under his extensive library, freezing when the hinges complained with a screech. Seconds passed, with the sound still echoing through my head, the volume magnified in my fearful mind. My joints ached with the tension of springs ready to snap at the slightest sign of movement from the recliner. For a moment, I was certain I felt his eyes on me, his rage drilling into my back. Yet, I dared not move. The hairs on my neck stood at attention, ready to feel the weight of his hand.

Run! The thought pushed at every fiber of my being, but I resisted. If it was over, it was over, but I refused to let fear dominate me.

A loud apneic snort caused my heart to skip, then relax into a rhythmic beat, if a little faster than before. Bill's respirations resumed slow and steady and I briefly squeezed my eyes shut before resuming my search with a probing hand through the half-opened cabinet.

I'd been correct in my guess regarding the bookshelf cabinets. Years of training and natural talent had clued me in when I was arguing with Bill. His subtle involuntary glance and body movements when he'd mentioned the files had spoken to me. I couldn't help but think that he'd be proud of my adroitness. After all, I was his magician, his master of illusion.

Sarah and I had decided that taking any of his money, even if it was meant for our severance pay, would anger him more than necessary. Besides, how could we start new lives and go straight with stolen money? No, we would just take our files and leave. I wanted to leave a note, but Sarah talked me out of it.

"That's just your need to show your skill, to show that you won. No notes. We don't have to say anything for him to know that we beat him."

I knew she was right, but there was something deep inside me, a primal instinct, that pushed me to take off my magnifying glass necklace and hang it on the desk lamp near the bay window. He would see it there before too long, and he would know that he didn't own me.

Chapter 27

Curiosity and the Cat

I run a finger along the silver chain tucked under the collar of my shirt. A nearby rustling sound brings me back to the here and now. Something presses against my side. Once again, I find myself face to face with Thorn, the giant house cat. This time it's truly a face to face, as I'm crouched down scoping out the best route to the house and back that avoids windows and cameras.

"Well, hello again," I whisper. "You don't mind if I take a little peek into your home, do you? I promise your daddy won't even know I'm there. Hell, maybe I can even crack a door and sneak you back in."

Thorn sits next to me and preens himself. It looks like permission to me. I map out the cameras in my mind. Honestly, they look more ornamental than functional. And why wouldn't they be? How many times did Tom and Lindsey mention how safe their neighborhood is? Their neighbor probably thinks the mere presence of cameras is enough of a deterrence. If I move here, I'll set him straight on the inadequacies of his current system. In the meantime, I plan on taking advantage of the clear blind spots to satisfy my burning curiosity.

The first building I encounter is the detached garage on the left side of the house. When I'm pressed up against its outer wall, I notice another steep drop. I give a nod to the architect when I see there's a secondary driveway leading from somewhere off the backside of the property to a lower level two-door garage. The only thing that could make this set-up any cooler would be a fireman's pole connecting the two garage levels. Sadly, there's no window on my side and I don't dare sneak a look in through the front windows that line the door. Not worth it. I can always ask Alex later.

I ease my way down the hill, pressed against the rough, cool stucco of the wall. Every now and then Thorn appears somewhere in the landscaping, his huge yellow eyes observing my every move. The rocks bordering the wall slide under my foot. I push my palms against the stucco, catching myself as pebbles bounce down the steep incline. Once I'm certain my slip has gone unnoticed, I continue my descent, turning to lower myself down the last drop. In contrast to the patio, the back of the house itself is fairly dark. The plantation blinds are closed and dark curtains span the length of the French doors connecting the home to the patio and pool.

A dim light shimmers inside the pool house, and shadows dance across its partially opened blinds. Multiple shadows. There are people in there. Is Mr. Benson's family visiting? I duck down into the grass, aware that I now have to avoid eyes on both sides. Perhaps I should just head back to Tom's place ... and Alex. This is already taking longer than I thought it would. But, that's now how hyperfixation works.

"Yeah, I said she left to go talk to the neighbors. That should buy us enough time to load up and move out."

"Matt called in. They should be here any minute. That Camryn kid was spot on with the codes."

"Great. Pack up the vans. We'll move out as soon as he gets here."

"What are we going to do with the kid, Mr. B?"

The voices are coming from somewhere above me. I recognize

the first as belonging to Mr. Benson, but the two people he's talking to are unknowns. They sound like youngish men. Obviously, it's the subject of their conversation that has captured my attention more than who they are for the moment. I hold my breath, trying to quash the icy chill working its way up my spine.

There's a balcony above me on the first floor of the house—the second floor from where I am. I furrow my brows and peer up from my hiding place among the ornamental grasses. Though the curtains are closed, the French doors at the back of the balcony are cracked open, allowing the gentle breeze to billow them inward. A light source somewhere behind the men casts their shadows on the curtains, which are something between darkening panels and sheers.

"We'll need to bring her along. When it's obvious she's not really talking to any neighbors, this'll be the first place the police come ... and they will. In the meantime, she's seen and heard too much to be out and about, thanks to this cretin," says Mr. Benson.

"What?" This voice sounds offended. "*He's* the one who let her into the house. Wasn't this neighborhood supposed to be practically empty?"

"*Let* her in?" the third voice scoffs. "The brat practically pushed her way through the door when she heard that stupid bird shrieking and you screaming like a pussy."

"Goddam parrot nearly took my finger off."

Lovebird, I think. *Point for Mr. Talon.*

"Well, you shouldn't have been fucking around with it."

"Fuck you. I hope it swoops down and pecks your goddamn eyes out."

I hear a scuffle.

"Knock it off." This is Mr. Benson again. "She comes with us. We can decide what to do with her later. Probably best if we release her there when we're on our way out. After delivery. No need to add any more reasons for more scrutiny."

"We could just leave her here. She doesn't know where we're going. By the time someone finds her, we'll be long gone."

"Maybe, but I don't want to chance it. If we let her go, I don't want her able to share her story until we're already halfway across the globe. Then we can tag out of this region and there'll be nothing to trace. Home invasions are a dime a dozen."

I head to the walk-out just below them, scrutinizing the pool house to make sure whoever is in there isn't coming out. Then, one of the younger voices says something that stops me dead and causes my heart to turn to cement in my chest.

"Yeah, she's cute, anyway. Thinks she's a little badass in her biker jacket. I wouldn't mind spending some more time with her."

Though I still don't know exactly what's going on, I need to find Alex, and fast. From what I have heard, she's somewhere on the property, but won't be for long. If I can't locate her, I'm going to have to find a way to be in one of those vans they mentioned. I can't let them take Alex when I have no way of tracking her. Obviously, sweet old Mr. Benson isn't what he seems. She must have walked in on something when she came to talk to him. Something *I* suggested she do.

Of course, if I hadn't left my phone at the house ...

I consider running back to get it. Calling the police. But they may already be gone by the time the police get here. I have no idea how far away the station is. Hell, they might leave before I even get a chance to grab my phone. No, I have to find Alex now. Then the two of us can make a run for it, and we'll figure out what to do from there.

A loud *meow* comes from somewhere above me. Thorn has worked his way up and onto the balcony and is apparently trying to get inside.

"Get the fuck out of here," yells one of the younger voices. The angry feline jumps back down by way of a decorative buttress.

Someone closes the French doors to the balcony and I can no longer make out what they're saying. I close my eyes and suck in deep breaths of the cool crisp air, trying to clear my head. Where do I start? This house is enormous. When I open my eyes, I focus in on the pool house. I saw shadows through the shades. Maybe they're holding her in there. It would make sense. She'd be less likely to hear their conversations from there. It seems like a good place to start.

I ease my way back, avoiding the light cast by the landscaping lanterns, and into the shadows, almost stepping on the cat. He jumps to the side, cursing me with a series of feline chattering sounds.

"What?" I hiss.

Thorn stands and trots to the pool house. I blow an angry puff of air out of my nose and follow. When I'm a few feet away from the building, I give it a better look to check for cameras. Once again, the cat is next to me, observing.

"The name Thorn fits you, you know?" I whisper to my feline shadow. "You're like a thorn in my side."

The cat tilts his head as if considering the insult. He regards me with something between boredom and superiority. Then he turns, hisses, and darts behind the pool house.

Was it something I said?

The door handle to the pool house clicks and turns. The cat must have heard someone approaching. I run to the side of the structure and press my back against it. I didn't see any cameras, but I was also distracted by the damn cat. I hope I didn't miss anything. I hold my breath and edge to the corner to take a peek. The building is angled in such a way that the side I'm currently pressed against is cast in shadows.

The door swings open, and my heart kicks like an angry mule at the sight of two people walking through the breech, carrying something. The object catches the light and I can now see it's a rug rolled into a tube.

Once the second figure is out the door, he, or she (I can see the one in front is a man, but the second figure is slender with a shape that insinuates a woman) kicks the door shut, but not before a dark, furry shadow slips past from the other side unnoticed. The rug is sagging in the middle and looks unusually heavy. My mind races, skirting possibilities I do not want to consider. For a moment I feel almost weightless, like I've been pushed off the edge of an abyss. Then a strained, shaky whisper comes from the pool house.

"Thorn, is that you? Are you ok?" The voice is Alex's.

I close my eyes and mouth a thank you to whatever God or spirits may be listening. My skin is tingling like I've just brushed against an electric fence—a familiar feeling having grown up near several cattle farms. A cool breeze tinged with the scent of chlorine tickles my nose.

I edge toward one of the windows, reminding myself that they wouldn't leave Alex alone in there. This isn't the movies where criminals tend to be buffoons. This is something studied and organized ... choreographed. Sure enough, I don't even make it to the window before a voice confirms my fears.

"What's that fucking cat doing in here?"

I crane my neck to glimpse through the slats of the plantation blinds.

"Fuck you," spits Alex.

This is followed by a sound that I never wish to hear again. Never for the rest of my days. I don't consider myself to be insensitive or callous, though those who don't know me well might think I am, at least borderline. What I am, in my own humble opinion (and I mean, who knows me better than me?), is distant. I feel the same emotions as any other red-blooded human being. Just as deeply, and maybe sometimes even more so. But, I have *skills* ... or so I have been told from a very young age. I'm observant. And to be this observant, it's important to remove myself from the emotional trappings of any given situation so that I may observe without bias, take true measurements using senses untempered and unfiltered. I'm also reactive and flexible. In order to react in the most efficient and productive way in situations that might be less than linear, one's mind must be clear and focused.

That sound I just heard breaks my concentration like nothing ever has. It clouds my judgment and strips my skills away in layers, until I feel like one raw, open nerve. I take a deep breath, my lips seized and trembling, and glare through the blinds.

Alex is sitting on the floor of the pool house, mildly illuminated by a series of small lamps, each arranged as a sort of perimeter around her. Her hands are bound behind her with a thick cord wound tightly around the leg of an ornate billiards table, the centerpiece of the room. She's wearing some sort of eye mask, pink and frilly, like the ones they sell in department stores. A trickle of blood runs from the corner of her mouth just under a bright red handprint freshly minted across her smooth young cheek. Her lips are pursed and I can tell by the way they squeeze, in rhythm with a slight heaving of her chest, that she is doing her best not to cry.

As my mind scrambles to reestablish order, to pull shut the door to my emotions, cracked open by the sound of a hand (one I now wish to break into a million pieces) against my niece's face, I'm struck by two thoughts. The first is how ridiculous and out-of-place the prissy sleep mask looks, like a porcelain teacup in a biker bar. This leads to my second thought, a good thought. Her eyes are covered. They don't want her to see them, or at least any more of them that she has already seen. A welcome confirmation that they really do intend to let her go.

Now that I'm thinking again, I let my gaze wander the room. A man who looks to be in his twenties is pacing around the table. Every few steps, he ducks his head down and peers under it. He's holding a gun.

He's looking for the cat. Stay hidden, buddy.

The far left corner of the room is draped in shadows. A ripple in the darkness like heat rising from an asphalt road catches my eye and causes my heart to race once again.

Chapter 28

Lettermen

A second man emerges from the shadows in the corner of the room. To say he's a large man would be like calling Cujo an *excitable pup*, or Mount Everest *quite a hill*. The handle of a large hunting knife protrudes from a sheath on his belt. He moves with confidence and awareness. A formidable foe.

"Knock it off, L," he says. "She's just a sassy fuckin' teenager. You don't have sassy fuckin' teenagers where you come from? I'll bet you were a sassy fuckin' teenager, what ... like last year? Don't let her get under your skin." He walks over to the younger man, who's now crouched by one of the armchairs, evidently still looking for the elusive Maine coon.

"Fuck you, Je—" The larger man grabs his shoulder and glares, prompting the gunman to reconsider his choice of words. "D," he says. "Fuck you, D. She needed a little lesson. Shooting her mouth off at me. Don't hear her shooting her fucking mouth off now, do you? Now where's that goddamn cat? Fucking thing's as big as a puma. I feel like doing some big game hunting."

They're using letters instead of names. Letters that don't correspond to their actual names, apparently. This is also good. Though, the younger guy's bravado and evident lack of control is worrisome. I continue my assessment of the room. There's a window on the back wall of the building. I can't tell if the blinds are open at all or not. That side of the pool house is deeper in the shadows, farther from the house, so there's no real backlight to clue me in. If the blinds are cracked, not only will I have better cover over there, I may also be able to get a better view of Alex from that angle. She's still now, her head bent forward and her shoulders squared.

"Knock it off." The older guy backhands the side of his partner's head. "You mess up again and you'll be the only thing around here being hunted. Get rid of that thing," he points to the gun. "We don't need another accident."

"That wasn't my fault," the one called L says, his voice kicking up an octave in a whiny plea that sounds like it's coming from an actual teenager. He tucks the weapon, which looks to be a member of the Glock family, into the back of his pants. "You know that wasn't my fault. He came right at me with it."

D holds a finger to his lips and points at Alex.

I slide along the outside of the pool house until I reach the back window. When both men are facing away, I position myself for a better view. The blinds are open a bit wider here and I'm much closer to Alex now. Her face catches the soft light of the lamp on the table in front of her. It looks like her lip has stopped bleeding. Her cheek still carries the mark of an open hand, though, which has begun to fade from an angry red to pink. She pulls in a sniffle and puckers her mouth into a determined pout as she wiggles her hands, working against her restraints.

The door opens and the two men who were carrying the rug come back inside. Just as the door is about to close, something zips past, causing one of them to jump like a sitcom housewife who's just spotted a mouse.

I can't help but spit out a chuckle *Wuss*.

"Fuck! What the fuck was that?"

The other occupants in the room are laughing so hard one of

them ends up bending over in a fit of coughs. L grabs for his gun again, but D slaps his hand away.

"Aww, come on. Just one quick shot. I can muffle it with a pillow. Pay back, y'know?"

He holds out his arm and I can see three long, thin, dark lines stretching up from his wrist.

"Aww, did the little kitty scratch you?" says Mr. Letter-less by the door, most likely desperate to shift attention from his recent sauté.

L lounges toward him, running into D's extended right arm and clotheslining himself. He lays, coughing and grasping at his throat for a minute, then scowls and allows D to help him up.

"That's enough," says D, who's looking more and more like the boss in here. He turns in clicks, staring at each man. "Don't be stupid. We're almost done and outta here. Don't be fucking stupid." Then he motions for the two letter-less men to approach and whispers something to them. They both nod, and I imagine he's asking about what they've done with the rug.

While all this is going on, Alex has been busy down on the floor. Quiet and busy. She hasn't made much progress on the knots around her wrists, but she has somehow worked the loop down the leg of the billiards table. Whoever secured the cord has tied it around the thickest, bulging part of the leg. If she can just slide it a little further, the loop will easily drop down the rest of the way.

Of course, the weight of the table will be a problem, if she's thinking of slipping the rope under the leg. Still, I can't help but feel a warm rush of pride swell through to my core.

The kid's got skills. Moxie and skills.

Now there's a word I haven't heard in quite some time. Bill used it all the time when he talked about the kids who worked for him.

You've got to have moxie to be on this team. Or *do you think he's got the moxie for this job?*

I remember laughing when I found the shelf in his cellar, lined with old empty glass bottles with the word *MOXIE* printed across their faded orange labels below the image of a middle-aged man with slicked back hair, wearing what looked like a doctor's lab coat, stabbing his finger into the air with a you'd-better-drink-this-if-you-know-what's-good-for-you expression on his face. I'd had a silly thought when I saw it. Something like *ah ha! This must be where Bill got his moxie.*

And now I find it's the perfect word for my niece. The kid's got moxie.

Mr. D reaches up and puts a finger against what I assume to be some kind of earpiece and nods.

"Yessir," he says. "Got it." He turns to the others. "We finish loading up and roll in about fifteen. Gather up your shit."

Chapter 29

Mr. B, I Presume

Fifteen minutes.

I press my back against the wall, trying to come up with some semblance of a plan to get Alex out of here. I don't even have a phone, never mind a weapon. I know there are at least seven men here ... armed men, I have to assume. Plus, however many arrived with *Matt*, per the conversation I'd overheard at the house.

The house, I think. Mr. Benson is an older man. I know a lot of families don't have landlines anymore. Tom doesn't. Becca and I don't. But Mom does. Becca's parents do, too. I'll bet Mr. Benson does ... especially if his wife had cancer. She probably had one of those things you press for help that's tied to the line, like the one Dad had. Not that I'm sure something like that would still be hooked up two years later. But ... maybe. I mean, the guy does live here alone.

All I need to find is a phone to call 911. Then I can leave the line open and hope the police come. This is a pretty nice house, the kind the police will haul ass to get to. And, sure, they'll leave once Mr. Benson tells them there must be a mistake. But in the meantime, their arrival will open a window ... one I'll be ready to swoop through to snatch my niece.

I step over to the ornamental grasses and work my way back toward the house. I only take a few steps before realizing I'm not alone.

"You need to stop doing that," I whisper to the large cat winding its way around me. "I mean, kudos for the claw marks you planted on that asshole's arm, but you're gonna give me a fucking heart attack."

I reach a hand down and Thorn ducks under it, arching his back up to meet my palm as he goes. His coat, rich brown with dark spots and stripes, is soft and soothing.

"We need to get moving. We don't have much time."

Once I'm close to the side of the house, I look to the doors leading into the walk-out basement. Bright lights illuminate the row of small, square windows along the top of the garage door, but there's no light coming from the walk-out, not even along the edges of the curtains across the French doors. I duck down and scoot past the garage, fighting a strong urge to look in one of the windows to see if there's a fireman's pole (thanks hyperfixation). A few steps from the house, but still under the cover of a floating deck off the main floor, there are two sets of patio furniture, one on each side of the entrance. Off to the side—my side—and closer to the back wall sits a large jacuzzi. When I'm as certain as I can be that nobody is watching, I dart over to the jacuzzi, which I now see is empty. Thorn hops up onto its edge and follows above me while I slip behind it and closer to the doors.

There's no way they'll be unlocked, I think. But they are.

I briefly wonder if it's a trap, but it's more likely that the doors were left unlocked because of the flurry of activity. Also, there's a whole lot of people who don't lock their doors in neighborhoods like these, making them easy targets for thieves. In this particular situation, the thought seems somewhat ironic.

I pull one of the doors open and slip into the dark basement. The plush carpet and the pleasant smells confirm my guess that it's fully finished even before my eyes adjust. I find one of those fancy dimmer switches just inside the door. I press a finger to the bottom of the panel and move it up the slightest bit until there's just enough light for me to get around without tripping over or bumping into anything.

I am in some kind of wide-open entertainment area, judging by the billiards table in the center—even more ornate than the one in the pool house. There's a ping pong table to my right and a line of full-sized arcade games along the wall behind it. Odd for the home of an older single man. Then again, from what I'm seeing, Mr. Benson must entertain quite a bit. A massive flatscreen television is mounted on the back wall. It's centered in front of two rows of cinema recliners, the back one raised for unimpeded viewing. A ceiling track runs around that area, outlining a room. When I look closer, I see a vertical stack of wall sections at the track's end.

Then there's the pièce de résistance: an impressive full-sized bar with a collection of spirits that would put the local joint back home to shame. A bottle of what looks like brandy sits open on the counter, next to an empty glass.

I hold my breath, close my eyes, and listen for signs of life. A gentle popping sound pulls my attention to the movie area, where I see Thorn stretched out, dragging his claws down the back of one of the recliners. I pull an airy reversed whistle through my teeth and shake my head.

"Your daddy is not gonna like that," I whisper.

Then, from the direction of the bar, I hear another sound. A soft muffled moan. I look over at the cat and bring a finger to my lips. He continues fine-tuning his claws, sparing me only a short, uninterested glance. I walk in the direction of the sound, scanning the room for something that I can use as a weapon, if necessary. On my way, I pass a decorative glass table. Its surface is cluttered with photographs. I pick up a thick silver frame with what looks like a family portrait and assess its weight.

Not the most effective weapon, I think, flipping it over to get a better look. *But it might help in a pinch.*

Another moan rises from the dark, and now I can hear that its source is low to the ground. I walk around a small desk and my foot catches something on the other side, causing me to stumble. I throw my hands out, letting the frame drop and land on something soft, but scratchy. The something emits an airy muffled cry, causing the hairs on the back of my neck to stand at attention.

When my frantic eyes adjust to this darker section of the basement, I see that I have tripped over a rolled-up rug: the same rug I saw the men carry from the pool house. I reach down and prod the bundled floor covering. It's lumpy ... and it's moaning. I push myself backwards, slamming a shoulder against the wall without even feeling it hit.

"Help. Please," the rug supplicates in a thin thread of a voice. "Please."

I scramble to my feet and look around. There's a small Tiffany lamp tipped over on a little table near where I smacked my shoulder. I right it and pull the tiny chain hanging down under the shade, grateful for the additional beams of light. The rug is moving ever so slightly, like a giant grub trying to inch its way back into the soil. I run my hands over the top of the roll until I find its edge. Taking a firm hold with both hands, I pull until it begins to unfurl and reveals the still form of a man.

His face is pale and frozen in an expression of horror and pain. I retrieve the frame I dropped when I fell and hold the glass under his nose, looking for signs of breath. Then I feel the cool, clammy skin at the side of his neck for a pulse. A faint *thump, thump, thump* taps at my fingertips. He's alive. Injured, but alive. I brush away the stringy hairs sticking to his face. He blinks, startling me. Despite his eyes being open, they're unfocused.

"Please, help," he says again, his voice raspy and desperate.

"Where are you hurt?"

"My head," he whispers. "My head. My chest."

That's when I notice the blood on the inside of the rug. So much blood. The carpet is drenched in it. He rolls his head toward me, revealing a nasty gash atop a swollen hill of flesh above his ear. It looks a little like a volcano.

And man, do heads like to bleed. I'd found that little tidbit out in elementary school when Tim Sullivan—aka Sully—slipped (though some say he was tripped. The incident was legendary among the K thru 4 group) and smacked his head on the corner of the teacher's desk. So much blood. Blood and fiery red hair.

"Oh, shit," I hiss. "Hang on."

I run around to the back of the bar. As I hoped, there's a stack of rags in one of the cabinets. The man's head is swaying back and forth, like he's politely refusing an offer. I press one of the rags against the gash to temper the bleeding, tying another around his head to secure it. Then, I try to find where his other injury is hiding. It doesn't take long. There's a dark circle, a badge of blood on the front of his dark button-down shirt, between his shoulder and neck. In the center of the badge, his shirt is torn.

I pull the shirt up. He's been shot, but I have no idea how serious the injury is, no idea what important organs might have been in the bullet's path. Remembering something from an action movie, maybe it was one of those super hero flicks, I gently tilt the man to take a look at the other side of him ... to see if there's an exit wound. He does, in fact, have a hole on the other side of him. I remember that being a good thing, but the amount of blood he is losing from both wounds is not good. I suspect that the pressure from the carpet was helping to mitigate the flow. But, now that I have unrolled him, I need to do something quick. I press rags against the wounds, doing my best to secure them.

When I've done everything I can think to help the stranger, I scan the room for a phone. There's got to be one somewhere. I stand and the man pleads for me to help him once again. I look down at him, ready to explain that I'm doing the best I can, then freeze at the sudden realization that this man looks familiar. I feel like I know him, but I cannot remember from where.

Then it hits me like a bag of wet sand. I pick up the photo

frame, and see the man looking back at me. There's much more color in his face and his hair is clean and coiffed in the photograph, but it is definitely him. He's standing in front of the house I've just invaded, his arm around the shoulder of a smiling companion. The couple is maybe in their seventies. Both have let their hair turn to a silky natural gray. Next to them, on either side, two more couples of a younger age, each with a brood of children in their teens or twenties.

I look at the man on the floor, then back at the photograph, thinking back to the day I met Mr. Benson ... in his sporty little BMW. Did he introduce himself? Or did I just presume it was him. Was Alex there with me? No, she was back in the house.

"Mr. Benson?" I ask, taking the man's hand. "Mr. Benson, is there a phone down here ... in the basement?"

The mention of the name seems to bring him to focus, clear a bit of the fog from his eyes. He looks up at me, staring as if trying to recall how we know each other. I look at my watch. I need to hurry. I need to get into one of the vans. I need to go wherever Alex is going. I cannot lose her.

"Mr. Benson ... a phone? Is there a phone? I need to go. The men who hurt you have my niece. My niece, Alex. The girl who pet sits for you. Your neighbor. If there's a phone, I will call 911, but then I have to go."

He locks his gaze on mine. Through the pain seared into his expression, I see lucid understanding.

He nods. "Phone's ... behind the bar. Go. Go help ... Alexandra."

I scamper over to the bar, my eyes flicking to and fro like that little white dot in advanced Pong levels. Where the bloody hell (no pun intended by this frantic brain) is the phone? The sound of a van engine is clouding my thoughts. Is that ... what's his name ... Matt? Or have they loaded everything up already? Only ten minutes have passed by my watch, though it seems like hours.

Then I spot it. It's on the fucking wall next to a bottle of Blanton's single barrel bourbon whiskey. A wall-mounted phone ... now there's a piece of nostalgia. I reach over the counter, yank the receiver off its cradle (is it still a *cradle* if it's vertical?) and dial 911 before setting it down and running to the door, a furry shadow by my side.

It's only after I have slipped out into the moonlight and head toward a dark cargo van that I realize something. Something important. I'm not sure I heard a dial tone.

Chapter 30

On the Road Again

When I sneak out of the basement and into the night, the lower garage door is open. I catch a quick glimpse of two black vans inside which, added to the one currently parked in the back driveway, makes three. It isn't going to be difficult to climb inside the one in the driveway. The back door is open.

I look to make sure nobody is watching and hop in. Thorn makes an attempt to join me, but I shoo him away. It takes a couple of tries, but he finally gets the picture and scrambles into the brush, grumbling little cat swears at me over his shoulder.

Your odds are much better here, buddy.

I watch him disappear before crawling deep into the belly of the van to look for a place to hide.

I tuck myself in among stacks of crates and a few pieces of expensive looking furniture and Persian rugs.

Pretty sure they won't be bringing the one from the basement. The resale value on that one is shot. I grimace. My thoughts are moving at a feverish pace, ricocheting between bouts of depleted desperation and giddy attempts at scheming. Every so often, my mind misfires stupid attempts at morbid humor.

There is a full partition between the cab and the cargo area, thank goodness. I have a similar van—though not a Mercedes. In mine, the cab is open to the back. That would've made it a helluva lot harder to stay concealed. The partition has a screen and a swinging door, but the vehicle is packed fairly tight, so I'm not worried about anyone accessing from up there. Just to be sure, I slide the deepest row of crates along so they are pressed right up against the door. Things do tend to shift, after all. With that thought in mind—not wanting to be pressed into a pancake at the first hard stop—I slide a few more boxes around and position myself under an oak desk. That should give me at least a little protection.

When I hear voices approaching, I duck back as far as I can and hold my breath.

"You got your number?" says a voice so deep and scratchy, I can almost smell cigarette smoke drifting off of it. It might be a woman's voice, but the gravelly tone makes it hard to tell. Still, in my mind's eye, it's a woman.

I close my eyes to better concentrate on what they are saying.

"Yeah, I'm bringing up the rear." There are two knocks on the side of the van like he's giving a good-boy pat. This one must be his. "We really taking that kid with us?" It's the voice of a guy who can't be much past his early twenties. It's smooth, but unsure, with a touch of forced bravado. I'm also detecting a hint of an accent, though I have no clue from where.

"Boss's orders. Got her loaded up in the garage, but we're just holding her until we're clear."

"What about the guy who lives here?"

My throat knots. If they go to get Mr. Benson, they'll know someone was there.

"Nah," says Mister or Missus Scratchy. "He's not a problem anymore."

They're leaving him for dead.

Did I hear a dial tone? I push the thought from my head.

When they move away from the van, I go back to breathing a

little easier. Then, a thought. How hard could it be to follow five Sprinters on a motorcycle? My keys are in my jacket pocket. I could run back to the house, grab my phone, and jump on the FCC. Then, follow the caravan from a distance. They have to drive past Tom's place to get to the main road, don't they?

The idea is so tempting, so rational, my body is already inching toward the back door of the van. That is until I remember the vans are parked in the back driveway and I have no idea where it leads. It could circle the property and end up somewhere along the road that goes past Tom's place ... or not. The only time I walked this high was to come looking for Alex. I know this road ends in a cul-de-sac at Mr. Benson's house, but I don't know how far back his property stretches. The only way I can be 100% sure to stay with Alex—something my mind and my gut both agree is paramount—is to be in one of these vans ... blind as to where we are heading ... and without a phone.

The back door of the van slams shut and there's movement in the cab. A door slams. Only one door, which means my guy's driving solo. A part of me is happy that the good guy-bad guy ratio is balanced within the universe of the van. The wavering young voice of my driver certainly gives me confidence that in a match-up, I'd have a pretty good shot (though a gun would put the slant squarely in his favor). Sadly, a solo driver also means no idle chitchat in the cab. The kind of chitchat that could provide me with some sorely needed details about my current situation and that of my niece.

The motor roars to life and after a few minutes I hear the driver say, "got it," (he must be wearing an earpiece) and the vehicle lurches forward, backing the crates away from the partition a little and momentarily trapping me under the table. This driveway seems to be a little less paved than the principal drive, and my tailbone takes a few painful knocks as the van bounces along. It feels like the driver is searching out every rut in a game of vehicular whack-a-mole.

We take a right turn and I welcome the transition onto an actual road, paved and maintained. Hallelujah. When I feel comfortable that making my way to the back of the van won't result in an unplanned trip to the ceiling or a permanent spot under a pile of crates, I ease out from under the table. It's pitch black in here, but I can still remember more or less where things were. There has been a general shift in the van's contents, resulting in some improv climbing, but I reach the back without too much trouble.

I run my hand up the inside of the door and feel that the windows are covered by magnetic covers. A sigh rushes through my lips. I was afraid the van might be one of the windowless models, like the one I use for my business. I slide two fingers behind the top corner of the right cover and ease it down. I know the guy said he'd be "bringing up the rear," but I'm not feeling particularly trusting or lucky at the moment. So, I squint out the tiny opening I've created to make sure there isn't another van right behind us.

No headlights. I look a moment longer in case the caravan has decided to exit the area sans illumination, a long black snake slithering along the back country roads. No movement other than the shadows of the trees lining our current path.

I peel the window cover down halfway and watch the world drop back. The last few trees of the little forest we are crossing disappear, and the night sky opens. To the left, the moon hovers over the peaks of the mountains I've been admiring since my arrival. The sky is dark, but the mountains are somehow darker, shadows framed by a slight reddish-orange aura. They loom like a row of teeth along the horizon, the razor sharp carnassial teeth of a wolf.

Chapter 31

When Those Who Wander Are Lost

I have no phone. I have no light. The fleeting glimpses of streetlights as we speed past only give me milliseconds to check my watch. We must be avoiding main roads and highways. I've barely seen a lick of traffic, and gave up on trying to keep track of landmarks or how many turns we make. I'm in a kind of limbo, the hum of the motor, the creaking of the crates, the sway of the van. A trance. My stomach is empty. My lips are dry.

I reposition the cover over the window and creep back to my spot under the table. Two Persian rugs, rolled tight for the journey, have worked their way under the edge of my shelter, so I curl up on the ends. My mind is spinning off somewhere in its own little wheel. Worry simmers just under my skin, unable to work its way down into my core. I am numb.

A rush of air flows through an open window up front, pushing me back through the years until I arrive at a moment of sheer joy. We did it! Sarah and I did it. I watch myself drift from Bill's house back out into the crisp morning air, files in hand. Watch like I would any miniseries or tv drama. Back to my past. Back to my *life of crime*.

After our little home invasion, Sarah and I spent the rest of the morning joy-riding in my mom's car. Our first stop was a donut shop, where we arrived just in time to buy a pair from the first batch out of the oven. The owner brewed some coffee for us, and we sat at the counter eating and chatting until daybreak. As soon as the sun cleared the horizon, we drove to a park outside of town with a fishing pond and picnic areas. It was a gorgeous day, not a cloud to be seen, and we felt like we were floating. We were free, starting our new lives.

A look through the files we took from Bill's house grounded us temporarily. A dog-eared sticky note on the very first page of mine caught my attention. There were notes scratched on it in Bill's distinct handwriting. I quickly folded it and slipped it into my pocket after making sure Sarah wasn't looking. My heart hiccupped in my chest when I looked through pictures he had of me shoplifting and detailed information about items I had stolen. I was ambushed by a feeling of disappointment in the person I had become. Sarah seemed less affected by the contents of her own file, which we had agreed not to share with each other, but her expression had sobered. With a few squirts of lighter fluid and a flick of a match, we cleared both our slates.

Once the records of our misdeeds burned beyond recognition, we laid on top of a picnic table to absorb the sun's brilliant rays. It was fitting that the first day of our new lives started with a perfect sunny day. Sarah talked about buying her neighbor's car and heading to Colorado to be with Lucas. I still had a year of high school, but was already dreaming of colleges in different states, countries even. Maybe I would meet someone one day, too, though I doubted anyone would ever really know me the way Sarah did. The sticky note felt both heavy and inconsequential in my pocket. I could burn it later.

I dropped Sarah off at her apartment a few hours after lunch and headed home to take a nap. Once the adrenaline wore off, the reality that we had not slept all night set in. When I arrived home, I decided not to maneuver the car into the garage, instead, abandoning it in the driveway to head inside and straight to bed.

Chapter 32

Elevation

A sharp knock of metal against the side of my head snatches me back from my trance. I open my eyes and see ... nothing. I blink hard, but it brings no change, no crack in the veil of darkness that surrounds me. My hand floats to the thin sleek chain resting against the back of my neck, a connection between past and present, a line to draw me back. Thumb and forefinger glide down to the treasure tucked under my shirt. The feel of the warm, smooth lens nudges me the rest of the way back to the present, to the van, to worry and anxiety.

An ache throbs behind my eyes. I rub my forehead, trying to work up enough saliva in my mouth to soothe my tight, scratchy throat, and relieve the pressure in my ears. In the end, I manage only a sad marble of mucous. I force it down with an exaggerated gulp, which helps release a bubble of air from my middle ears in a satisfying *pop*.

In the dark, cold confines of the van, my mind torments me with gadgets Becca and I researched together before I left. Backpacks with water bladders, their long clear straws waving like tentacles, beckoning me like disembodied index fingers. Travel mugs and little flasks filled with the crystal clear waters of springs whose names escape me. A memory jabs through the torturous show. I seize it like a drowning swimmer grabbing a rope.

I'm holding something in my right hand. Becca bats at me, tells me to put it back.

"That's for the trip, Sunshine. Not for now," she says, laughing, her nose crinkling up with a smile.

"But I love gummies, babe! Just one?"

"You know you won't just eat one, Charlie. And, those aren't candy! Put them away for when you actually need them ..."

Gummies. Gummies for the trip. Hydration gummies.

I unzip my jacket and work my fingers into a deep pocket. I scissor them shut when I feel the top of a packet, and I slide the gummies out of the opening, thanking Becca over and over in my head ... and maybe out loud, too.

I rip the top off the packet and carefully turn it over my cupped palm, giving it a slight shake to free some of the gummies into my hand. I snatch one and pop it into my mouth, then shovel the rest in straight after. Blueberry—or at least what candy companies have trained us to think is blueberry—washes over my taste buds like a salve.

My mouth floods with saliva and I tip the packet for more.

You know you won't eat just one ...

Put them away for when you actually need them.

I don't know how much longer I'll be trapped in here. Even if they pull over for gas, I can't just pop out of the back hollering "thanks for the ride, guys," grab my niece and run. I push aside the negative thoughts while I savor the remaining traces of blueberry with a hint of something salty that lines the inside of my mouth. I'm still thirsty and my stomach is rumbling gurgles of protest, but my mind is beginning to sharpen and my headache is easing. Sure, it's like putting a little bandaid on something that needs stitches. But it's better than nothing, and this particular bandaid is giving me a much needed boost.

The van lurches to a stop. We seem to be on an incline, but

without visual cues it's hard to be sure. The driver's door opens, and whispers reach for my ears like the playful currents of a summer breeze. Voices intertwine, words spinning like dust devils just beyond my reach. It takes total concentration, breath held, to catch a word, perhaps a phrase. They're not speaking English. Is it Spanish? Maybe, but it doesn't sound like the Spanish Ms. Gomez taught us in high school. Anyway, that was years ago and maybe what I'm hearing now is slang or something.

"What the fuck you whispering about? There's nobody around for miles." This voice is familiar. It's the voice of the guy who struck Alex. A sour taste pools in my mouth and invades my tongue. "Mr. B says he wants everyone speaking English, anyway. Draws less attention."

If there's nobody around for miles, whose attention are they going to draw, dumbass? I think, blowing a soft, sarcastic puff of air through my nose. My mouth curls into a sneer and my body tenses, squeezing my chest and pushing the steady *thump, thump, thump* of my heart into my ears. I shake my head, focus my resolve.

"We empty the vans?" This voice is young.

Geez, it sounds like a freaking kid. A kid with an accent I cannot place. Not that I'm any kind of world traveler or anything. I do watch my share of tv and movies, though, and I prefer subtitles over dubs, something Becca influenced quite a bit. She claims it helps build an ear for foreign languages. But, as much as I've been *building my ear* since we met, this one is beyond me.

"This your first tour, kid? The fences come in. You help if they ask you to help. Otherwise, stay out of the way. Keep your mouth shut and your head down. When they leave, we head to the next state, next base. You hit two states, go home, another team comes in. The end."

"When do we get our money? What we doing with the girl?" asks the voice that sounds like it's coming from a middle schooler.

Something slams against the van right next to where I have my ear pressed. I suck in a mouthful of air and rub the side of my head.

"The fuck you do that for?" asks another voice with the same accent as the boy. "He's a kid. He's new."

"Well then, maybe tell him to mind his business before he *really* gets himself hurt."

Silence follows, but it doesn't feel like the peaceful pause that comes at the natural conclusion of a conversation. The word that pops into mind for this particular type of silence is *ominous*.

"I thought I told you to get rid of that thing." A new voice breaks the silence. It also stirs up images of a face. A face attached to the body of a very large man. "And you ... get to the house and wait for instructions. You know, *instructionones* or however you say it. Wait for someone to tell you what to do. Get that kid a bandage or something. He's bleeding all over the place." I hear the shuffling of feet before the voice chimes in again. "You know the rules. No guns on the job. You got a pass because the old man came at you with it. You aren't getting another one."

"We aren't *on a job* right now. I'll get rid of it when we are. No rules about that. Besides, my *mistake* bought us more time."

"And more possible charges. Ones the police will take more seriously. Just keep that thing out of sight and don't do anything stupid. It's not that hard. When we move on, toss it in the stream or bury it somewhere in the woods. I don't care. Just get rid of it. I see that thing on you when we leave, I'll get rid of it myself, after I empty it into your face."

At the sound of fading footsteps, I close my eyes, processing the information I have. For every *where is Alex* running through my mind like ticker tape, I squeeze my lids tighter and remind myself I need distance. Distance to plan. Distance for calm. Distance to use my *skills*.

You need a weapon. These people are organized. They are connected. And, the one you're going to kill has a gun ...

My eyelids fly open at this declaration by the voice in my

head... his voice. I don't want to kill anyone. I just want my niece back. I've never killed anyone and don't plan on starting now.

Really? Is that what you tell yourself? You've never killed anyone? Not that you didn't have your reasons.

"That was an accident," I whisper into the dark, resuming my breaths, now shallow, distant relatives of the deep, centering pulls of cool, calming air from before.

An accident. I can almost hear the sneer contorting his mouth. *Keep telling yourself it was an accident. I think we both know what your intentions were ... in your heart.*

My mind drifts back to that day. The one Sarah and I were celebrating. The one that was supposed to be the first day of the rest of our happy lives. Slate cleared, I was flying high like an eagle, oblivious to the fact that I was more like a housefly heading directly from one spider's web to the next. Did I want him dead? No, I was just upset. Name me a teenager that doesn't get upset. Did I think it ... ever? Was I relieved after?

I bite the inside of my bottom lip, drawing a trickle of blood into my mouth. I don't have time for this. I don't have time for him to drag me back to yesteryear with his misplaced accusations. I need to find Alex. I need to get out of the van and look around, get my bearings. I can't just stay here waiting for some fence to come in and discover me. I grab the tear drop lens dangling at the end of my necklace and push it back under my shirt.

The profound silence around me creates a vacuum, which my body fills with the whooshing of blood and crackling of joints. I make my way to the back of the van, doing my best not to shift the vehicle, cringing at each creak that joins the chorus in my head. To me, they sound like banshee screams. My rational mind assures me they will be indistinguishable from the sounds caused by random gusts of wind outside.

My outstretched hand brushes one of the window covers, and I slide it aside, allowing a beam of moon-kissed night to stream into the van. I pause for a moment before leaning closer to peek outside. Ten feet away, a squadron of pine trees stand watch, their shadows stretching toward the van. It's the only movement distinguishable through my peephole. I widen the gap, sweeping the area through squinted eyes.

Once I'm as certain as I can be that I'm alone, I feel for the door latch. Before trying it, I hold my breath, listening once more for any signs that someone might be nearby. Nothing. At least, nothing obvious. The latch clicks, once more kicking my pulse a few beats faster. I remind myself that the noise is minimal. Surely, the gentle winds rocking the pines and other sounds of the night have covered any sign of it.

When the door is open just enough, I slip out into the night. The moment my feet hit the ground—a combination of dirt and patches of compressed grass, victims of the van's tires—I'm overwhelmed by the fragrant waves of forest air that brush over me. The intoxicating scents embrace me, pulling memories of camping trips to Hocking Hills with Tommy and Dad from deep, forgotten stashes of the happier events of my childhood. Memories from before I began turning down opportunities to head out of town to explore with them.

I'll stay home with Mom, I'd say. *Bill needs help with some stuff, and I can just hang out and catch up with homework while Mom's at work.* They trusted me ... and, they trusted Bill.

Hocking Hills is my point of reference, but it's not exact. Here, there's a sweet, comforting smell mitigating the chill trying to work its way under my jacket. It reminds me of hot butterscotch cookies fresh from the oven. A smell that evokes images of Mom, with her collection of aprons, some passed down from her mom. Together with the strong scent of pine, it somehow takes the edge off my anxiety and uncertainty.

I press myself against the back of the van and cock my head, listening once again for footsteps and whispers. A quick glance around the van doesn't reveal anyone, but I do see the silhouette of a rather large home just up the road, its windows a warm glowing yellow. They must be in there getting ready for the fences. Alex must be in there too.

I'm a little surprised that nobody is guarding the vans, but after giving it a thought, I decide it must mean we really are in the middle of nowhere. A place where they have absolutely no concern about being discovered. The upside being ... well, if they aren't worried about being discovered, they won't be expecting me. The downside is we're likely pretty far from civilization and thus salvation. Unless I can get my hands on a vehicle of some sorts, Alex and I are going to have a rather long hike ahead of us. And the element of surprise isn't going to last very long once they discover her missing. Of course, I have to find out where she is first.

I make my way up the road, ducking behind the vans as I go, attempting to get a better idea of my surroundings. With a certain amount of healthy skepticism, I peek into the driver sides of each vehicle and give their doors a quick tug as I pass them. It would be stupid not to, after all. I've already decided that not everyone in this group is—how can I say it—a sharp tool. There is the possibility, as minute as it may be, that one of them left their keys inside. No luck.

When I hear what sounds like a stream somewhere nearby, I decide to make a quick detour to take a look. Don't they say you need to follow flowing water downstream to get to roads and towns? Given the popping of my ears, and the fact that I feel out of breath after only a short walk up the road, my assumption is we're somewhere up in the mountains. If this is true, I need to figure out how we're going to get out of here without jumping from one dangerous situation to another. Being lost in the mountains without food or shelter isn't exactly appealing to me either.

I follow the sound of the stream to the edge of the trees, noting the deep darkness beyond them, only to realize that it's not water I'm hearing, but the wind rustling through the leaves of a copse of aspens standing among the pines.

So much for this episode of The Naturalist.

The line of a poem pops into my mind. Is it "go forth, under the open sky, and listen to Nature's teachings," or "list to Nature's teachings?" I can't quite remember, but I do know the name of the poem: *Thanatopsis*, by William Cullen Bryant. I had to recite part of it in front of my English class in tenth ... or maybe eleventh ... grade.

Something about the poem had spoken to me, though that's the only line that still lingers in my brain, hanging out in there with remnants of jingles and other snippets of poems committed to memory in my youth. I thought about using it as my senior quote in the yearbook, but opted for something a little more flippant and positive when I had a better grasp on the meaning of the poem and how it was a contemplation of death. I had done enough contemplating on the meaning of death by that time.

Chapter 33

Discovered

The trek up to the house is more exhausting than I expected. Despite my brain pressing me to hurry, my body isn't complying, and several stops are necessary to slow my shallow breaths. Each inhalation feels like pulling a pillow through a keyhole. I can't help Alex if I pass out on the way, or alert someone to my presence with a wheeze or a cough, so I pause to regroup when necessary.

On what I hope will be my final rest stop, I see five shadowy figures posted outside the house. They look more like they're lounging than guarding anything. Two of them are smoking, their hands moving to their faces at regular intervals, the cigarettes glowing orange in the dim light. Three more are speaking in low voices, laughing, and bumping shoulders. None see me crouched in the brush next to one of the many boulders speckling the property.

The house isn't as big as it seemed from below, but it's still impressive. A considerable part of what I originally thought was house is actually the rock-laden hillside supporting the structure. A large. tilted slab of rock juts up, flanking the home on one side. From here, I can see that the front of the house sits high atop a ridge, while the back is supported by a foundation of large stones, increasing in height as the slope descends.

Two spacious decks shoot out from the back of what must be the main floor. A majestic Christmas-tree-shaped pine stands between them, obscuring the view from one to the other. Thankfully, the only light is coming from inside the house, though I can see the silhouettes of sconces mounted high on the exterior. An aura of fading moonlight washes over the outside of the home and the land around it. Fortunately, there are plenty of shadows to mask my approach thanks to the lack of landscaping. Grasses, shrubs, and aspens pepper the land behind the home, left to thrive, I imagine, after the original clearing was forged for construction.

There's no light coming from under the decks, so I decide this will be a good place to approach. The night is alive with the sounds of rustling brush, and the clicking and stridulating of invisible creatures. As long as I'm careful with my steps, it'll be easy to approach without being heard.

Under the larger of the two decks, the ground is comprised of loose dirt scattered with the occasional stone. The rest of the path I walked on was pounded down by foot-traffic, but this looks undisturbed, like a fresh blanket of snow—earthy, brown snow. As I make my way up and under, I sweep a hand through the soft cool earth, tossing bits here and there to mask my footprints in the unpalatable event I've not left with Alex by dawn.

A rustling deep in the shadows, closer to the house, sends a shiver through my bones. I catch my breath and stare in the direction from which I think it came, trying to make sense of the dark canvas before me. What kinds of animals might be under here? My imagination starts at chipmunks and marmots, works its way through raccoons and skunks, and up to mountain lions and black bears.

The rustling sounds again, this time a little closer. I'm trying to decide between fight and flight, my heart pounding like a timpani under my ribs, when a voice whispers from the darkness.

"Mateo?"

I recognize the youthful voice I heard from inside the van. Shit. This kid is one of them. I need to get out of here. I need to find Alex and get out of here.

No, you need to grab this kid. Shut him up before he realizes you are not Mateo and yells for the others. He's already injured. Finish him. ... coming here to steal from us.

The vehemence of this thought runs through me like a shudder. He's one of them, but still ... he's so young. My morals may not be saintly, but they're screaming over that it's not ok to attack a kid, even if it's to save my niece. I retreat, hoping the shadows will conceal me, that he'll think I was an animal spooked by his voice.

There's a group of boulders next to the giant Christmas tree between the decks. I hurry toward it, pressing against the cold, rough, stone surface. I wait, straining to hear movements above the soft natural chorus of the night. The eerie call of an owl sounds from somewhere nearby, three *whos* followed by two more.

The sixth *who* comes from the lips of a young boy, now staring at me from around the side of my hiding place.

"Who are you?" he asks in a whisper, his voice barely audible above the sound of the wind. "English?"

I nod and put my hands in front of me to show that, despite what the voice in my head demands, I'm not a threat. He doesn't look worried about me at all, which I find odd given the circumstances. His head is cocked and his brows are furrowed below a shock of short, dark hair shaved to a length that gives it a fuzzy appearance. One side of his mouth is curved slightly into an expression of amused curiosity, and his eyes, which appear even darker than the shadows around us, hold me in a steady gaze.

He looks even younger than he sounded, but I know appearances can be deceiving when it comes to age and adolescents. Bill had Sarah playing the part of a young kid well into her early twenties, after all (she was weird about her age, and I'm not sure to this day how old she was). She also looked the part—when she wasn't wearing her *going out* make-up, that is. Still, there's an air of naiveté about him that I can't quite pinpoint. One he suppresses, puffing out his chest and intensifying his gaze, as if he has read my evaluation of him in my eyes.

In my head, I hear a clock ticking the seconds away, underscoring the quiet tension as we size each other up. I decide I have nothing to lose. There's no way I can get ahold of this kid if he decides to run and call out for the others. No way I can stop him. But for some reason he hasn't, yet. So, I take a chance.

"I'm looking for my niece," I say.

His eyes drift to his left before locking onto mine once again. He shakes his head, lifting his shoulders in a slight shrug. I dig into my brain for some ... any ... of the Spanish I learned in high school. The word niece is nowhere to be found.

Perhaps your praise was a little hasty, Ms. Gomez. I do remember some words for family members, so I give it a shot.

"My niece ... *la hija de mi hermano*. Her name, *nombre*, is Alex, and your friends have her."

"Your ... niece," he says, like he's participating in an English lesson, committing the new word to memory. "Alex."

He nods, but his gaze drops and his shoulders slouch with a sigh. This makes him look even younger, like a child who's just found his presents from Santa in his parents' closet on Christmas Eve.

"They have her," he says. "But, not my friends." He turns his head to the side and gently touches a bandage close to the back of his head. I think of the impact I heard from the inside of the van and dip my head in acknowledgment.

"Do you know where she is?"

The boy shrugs, then points up at the house behind us. I briefly contemplate my options. I'm not concerned about him giving me up anymore, but he's just a kid and he's obviously out of the loop. *Could I use him to find Alex?*

It's while I'm in the midst of contemplating this new conundrum that my stomach cramps, releasing a grumble loud enough to scare off any mountain lions in the area. I cringe, firming the muscles around my gut in an effort to quiet things down. The boy stifles a grin.

"Hungry. You are hungry," he says, with an exaggerated *h*.

I wince and nod. "And thirsty."

He holds up a hand, a smile lighting his face. With his other hand, he reaches into his jacket pocket and pulls out a small, clear plastic bottle of water. When he offers it to me, I just stare at first, like I'm witnessing water being turned into wine. He presses it closer and I take it, scrambling to open the cap. The gummies were good, but this is absolute bliss. I try to temper my greedy gulps, but the cool liquid slides so pleasantly down my parched, scratchy throat. I close my eyes for a moment to savor the last few drops, and sigh.

"Thank you," I say, not sure if my tone can possibly relay the gratitude in my heart.

"Welcome," he says. "I get food for you and come back."

My lips tighten, and I run my hand through my hair, briefly grabbing hold of a large clump at the back. Sure, we've established a modicum of trust between us, but this makes me nervous. After all, wouldn't it be in his best interest to rat me out and get rewarded, maybe get some kind of bonus for his efforts? It's not like he owes me anything, quite the opposite actually.

You can't trust him. He's not one of us. Don't let him go. He'll rat you out.

Ironically, it's this hateful voice in my head that pushes me toward trusting him. When he reaches out and touches my hand, the voice is banished back into the recesses of my darker mind.

"I not tell anyone," he says. He gives me a deep nod and turns to leave.

"Wait," I call out, just loud enough to get his attention. "What's your name?"

A guileless smile graces his lips. "Sebastián," he says, his tone that of a schoolboy making a new friend on the playground. "Or ... Tatán." He extends a hand, squaring his shoulders like a gentleman. "Nice to meet you."

"Charlie," I say, giving his hand a shake. "Nice to meet you, too." The kid, Tatán, has a nice firm handshake. I'll give him that. "Tatán, can you find me a flashlight?" I roll one hand like I'm holding a flashlight and put the other hand in front of it, flaring my finger out to signify light.

His forehead wrinkles with consideration, then he nods. "Charlie," he says, his *ch* sounding like a soft *sh*. "I get food. I get light."

He turns and disappears into the shadows, leaving me alone with my grumbling gut.

Chapter 34

The Ask

Left alone, I consider scooting back under the deck, but the thought of ending up cornered against the house's foundations, if I have misplaced my trust in Tatán, leads me to stay where I am for now. I have a better line of vision here, peeking around the boulders and through the pine branches, and more than one path away from the house to the cover of the woods.

I sit on the hard, cold dirt and listen for approaching footsteps, praying that when the time comes, I will hear only one set of feet. My gurgling stomach makes it hard to make out Bill's spiteful voice telling me I'm making a huge mistake trusting some *illegal* with my life, that he taught me better than this and I'm a stupid, naïve child ... not the *magician* he knew when he was alive. But it's there all the same, working my anxiety like a baker kneading dough.

No, I think, placing a hand against the front of my jacket where my pendant lies tucked against my chest. *You don't get to tell me what to think and what to do anymore. You are gone.*

And why is that? the voice counters. *If you've forgotten, I will remind you.*

No! I wince. *You're gone. Stay gone.*

Gone, yet you carry me with you wherever you go ... carry me with you for the very reason I am gone from this earth. You are responsible, Charlie.

I squeeze my eyes shut and bite down on the swollen bulge inside of my lip, once again freeing a rivulet of warm coppery blood.

"Shut up," I whisper over the roaring of blood through my ears. "Shut up."

"Charlie?" The call wisps through the branches, brushing away the voice in my head.

It's Tatán, and thankfully *only* Tatán, given my inattention. I shake my head, scolding myself for letting down my guard, for letting that voice get the better of me. I need to be more careful, more focused. I need to save Alex. In the moment, I wonder if I really did kill Bill, because right now I'm glad he's dead.

"Here," I whisper, waving my hand from behind the rocks. "Still here."

Tatán slides past the prickly branches protruding from the tree and sits next to me. He's carrying something wrapped in crinkled, well-used foil. He holds it out to me.

"For you, Charlie," he says, emphasizing my name in a way that reminds me of Alex and her recent attempts to annoy her parents. I sigh, bringing a slight pout to his face. "Ok?" he asks.

"Yeah, yeah. Thank you," I say. "It's just ... something you said reminded me of Alex."

He squints at me, his head tipped. Then, pushes the foil at me again. "Is very good, Charlie."

My stomach gurgles its approval, making us both laugh, and I accept the packet of food from him. When I pull the foil aside, I close my eyes and breathe in the redolence of exotic, enticing flavors rising from its contents. Two large pockets of golden dough that kind of remind me of giant dumplings or small calzones sit in the center of the foil. They're warm and inviting, and my stomach cries out for me to stop messing around, to take a bite already.

"*Empanadas de pino*," says Tatán, pointing at them. "Mateo make them."

"Thank you, Tatán," I say, not quite certain if I am pronouncing his name right. "And, thank you, Mateo."

I take a bite, the size of which my mom and Becca would most definitely consider rude, and quickly lean forward when warm, savory juices stream down both sides of my chin, eliciting yet another chuckle from my new friend.

"Wow," I say through the delicious mix of beef, onions, and I'm not sure what else. "These are amazing." I'm about to clarify with *muy bueno*, but stop short when I realize that *very good* would not be enough of a compliment. I lack adequate words in Spanish. Anyway, I can tell by his obvious delight that he understands.

I gobble down the first empanada and reach for the second, when it suddenly occurs to me that I might be eating Tatán's portion of food. I look over at him, licking the juices from my lips, and extend the foil with the remaining empanada toward him. He shakes his head, then pats his stomach.

"I am no hungry. Is for you," he says, to my delight. I bite into the crisp, salty crust, making short work of the second warm bundle of flavor.

As I solemnly push the last bit into my mouth, he pulls another small bottle of water from his pocket and hands it to me.

"I almost forget," he says, retrieving a small flashlight from his other pocket.

I press the business end of the flashlight to the ground and flip it on, smiling at the glowing halo that appears. Then I thank him, open the water, and bring the bottle to my lips, careful this time not to empty its contents completely. I pocket the light and bottle before contemplating my host. Despite his docile, naïve appearance, he is what can only be described as an international thief. I wonder how many houses this kid has burgled in his time here, his *tour*.

I've read stories about this kind of thing online: South American gangs. Burglary rings that the headlines call *crime tourists*. A cute, catchy name most likely bestowed by the press to make the issue more digestible and a sure read. Some of my clients back home called me after our local news channel ran a story on the issue, wondering if they should add cameras or sensors. At the time, I told them to relax, that it was probably exaggerated by the press to get views. Now, I'm not so sure, though there haven't yet been any incidents that I know of in my little home town. From what I read, they tend to hit more affluent areas than ours.

Never would I have guessed that I'd find myself right in the middle of one of their operations. Without my cameras, my sensors and sirens. Without even my cellphone. A situation I can only compare to Yo-Yo Ma arriving at his dream performance, one he's been preparing for his whole life ... without his cello.

I stare at the kid sitting next to me, the kid with the face of a cherub, searching for any ill intent. After all, one of my supposed *skills* has always been reading people. This kid, though, is an enigma. I wonder how old the other *tourists* are. Obviously, the men I saw at Mr. Benson's place were more of an upper-management group: American contacts—handlers, if you will. The ones I heard didn't even seem to speak Spanish. Though, I'm willing to bet Mr. B does. He seems like upper upper-management. Someone to be afraid of.

"You speak pretty good English," I say, breaking the silence. "Did you study it in school?"

"Yes, but the brother of my mother teach me more," he says, a note of pride in his voice.

"Your *uncle*? *Tío*," I add, surprised at the ease with which the word popped into mind. "The brother of your mother, your *tío*, is your uncle."

He considers this for a moment, his index finger and thumb holding his chin, then nods. "Yes. Uncle. My uncle teach me more English when he lives with us. Now, he is here."

"Here with you?" I ask, leaning forward and pointing at the

ground. I shake my head, already judging this man, this uncle, for getting his nephew involved in something so dangerous.

"No here." He shakes his head, also pointing to the ground. Judging by his scowl, I'd say I have upset him quite a bit. "Here," he hisses, raising both hands. "In USA. He's live in California."

"Ah, ok." I nod, a little embarrassed at how quickly I jumped to conclusions. "What town?"

His shoulders relax a bit, though his eyes are still set, like he understands I had bad thoughts about this uncle of his, who he obviously admires.

"Robin," he says. "Robin, California. You know?"

I shake my head. My knowledge of California is limited to Sacramento (thanks to my fourth-grade social studies class and our State Capital Bee), Los Angeles, Hollywood, San Francisco ... and that's about it. I might be able to think of a couple more places if I put my mind to it, which I don't.

"After this, I leaving to go to California," Tatán whispers. His brows furrow, crinkling the bridge of his nose, and his mouth cinches into a thin line of determination. "I find my uncle."

"Do you know his address? The place where he lives in *Robin*?"

I'm not sure if I'm just making conversation or if I'm starting to grow concerned for this kid. California is a hell of a long way from here without transportation, money ... or documents, and I don't know which way the group is headed after this. I don't even care. I just want to find Alex and get her home. Yet I suspect *upper management* is going to give any money due to this kid and the others to someone higher up to distribute. I don't imagine they want any of the crew getting crazy ideas about staying in the States where they could be arrested and interrogated.

He reaches into his pocket and pulls out a crumpled piece of paper. Then, with the care of a medieval monk unrolling a sacred scroll, he spreads it open onto his knees and hands it to me. There's an address scribbled in barely legible, smudged, black ink.

It is a street address, though the paper doesn't name the town. I imagine this was done as a precaution, in case it falls into the wrong hands. Anyhow, even if I knew the name of the town, I'd still have no clue where it is. California is a big state.

I smile and give it back to him. He carefully folds the paper and returns it to his pocket. He gives it a gentle pat, as if to make sure his treasure is secure. When his gaze meets mine again, there's something new in his eyes. Despite the dry mountain air, a shimmer catches the fading moonlight. The right corner of his lower lip is tucked firmly between his teeth and a deep breath raises his shoulders, suspending them there for a moment.

"Charlie," he says, in a soft steady voice. It sounds like he's trying the name out, and I suddenly feel like I'm interviewing for an important job, a position of trust. "Charlie. I don't know where is your ... *niece*."

The kid's a quick study, I think, and wait for him to continue, suppressing the urge to release the torrent of questions damned up inside. I can see he has more to say and don't want to spook him to silence with the intensity of the emotions burning through me.

He looks at the ground and runs a finger along the dirt, making and erasing squiggles in quick succession. I force a smile and relax my frame in an attempt to project an air of patience to prepare for the moment he engages again.

"I try to hear, but the *tourists* cannot go inside the house. Only the place for automobiles."

"The garage," I say. Makes sense. The less they see and hear, the better.

"Garage," he says, committing the new word to memory. He sniffs and passes the back of his hand under his nose.

He's trying to decide whether or not to say something. He's weighing his words in a way that isn't just English-is-my-second-language. The thought further commits me to my strategy of patience, despite the passage of each second pressing its weight on me like bricks being stacked upon my soul. I lean in, nudging him with my thoughts.

"I try again to know where is Alex. I sneak inside the house. When I know, I come back. When I know, we get Alex and I come with you."

There it is: the ask, the trade. He finds Alex for me, and I take him with us when we leave. Both propositions increase the element of danger. The first for him and the second for me, and for Alex. I know they won't be happy about Alex getting away and will surely make an effort to find her. But I'm also certain they're keeping her away from the action, making sure she doesn't know anything about who they are or the operation as a whole. So, if they don't find her fairly quickly, they're more likely to move on than to risk everything going after her. They may even think she'll stay lost in the forest.

Tatán is a part of their operation, even if a small one. He's been around them, studying them. And, though the less intelligent among them may see him as just a kid, anyone with a brain can tell he is crazy smart. The fact that he speaks English as well as he does may be an asset for him in the long run, but it makes him a dangerous liability for them if he suddenly disappears. They *will* hunt this kid down until they know he is no longer a problem.

On the other hand, he's willing to risk his life to find out where Alex is, despite working on his own plan to disappear after his tour is over. Sure, he has a better shot of getting to his uncle with help, but he'd be faster and harder to find on his own.

A deep sigh fills my lungs with the cool butterscotch-pine air around me. I run a hand through hair and sharpen my focus on him. He, too, is playing the false patience game. He's starting to remind me of myself at that age. Though perhaps on a grander, more international scale, Tatán now finds himself held captive by circumstances similar to mine when I was younger.

No! The zealousness of the voice hits me like a migraine. *It is not the same! These people are invading our homes, stealing from us.*

We were protecting our town. Punishing those heartless chains for the things THEY stole. For the pain THEY caused.

I wince and push back. *From YOU. The things you think they stole from you. You and your Esther.*

From EVERYONE. They come to our towns and kill everything local. They pillage the community with their false discounts and cheap junk. You can keep your new little pet if you wish, but don't you DARE compare what he and his friends are to us.

Tatán studies me with deep, pensive eyes. I fake a quiet cough, a fist to my mouth.

"Sorry," I whisper. It's so dry here. I pull out my water and take a sip, peering at him over the bottle.

He's studying me, a hint of skepticism in his gaze. I don't know what led him here, but something tells me this kid has more valid reasons than most to be skeptical, cynical even. He sighs and cinches one corner of his mouth. I perceive a slight wobble of his head from side to side.

"I know, Charlie ..." The words stutter through his lips, like he is forcing them out against his better judgment. He is done with caution, ready to roll the dice, all or nothing. "I know is hard to believe someone like me: *un criminal*."

I wince at his raw candor, at the wound I feel inflicted by the sharp accuracy of his intuition. My mouth opens to spill words of denial, but he raises a hand.

"I know. Is ok. My mother was hide from my father with me. He is a very bad man. My uncle, he helps us hide. Then, he get a chance to come here to work and he send us money. He want to bring us here to live." The boy pauses, casting his gaze to the ground. "But, my mother, she die in a accident. She's give me my uncle address. In hospital, she's tell me place where he is. But, I no can come here alone and no can get the monies from my uncle. My friend say he know how to go to United States. He say there is jobs." He shakes his head again, and I see shame in his eyes, but it is tempered by determination. "When I come here, the mens say we only go to the home with so much, too much. And, nobody's home, nobody's get hurt."

A tingle runs through my body like static pushing up the hairs on both arms. At the same time, a lump works its way up my throat. I feel ashamed. Ashamed for thinking of this child as some kind of international criminal. Ashamed of my own past choices. Ashamed of advantages I took for granted. This kid has read me like a book, despite any cultural hurdles. He isn't like I was. He's in it for his very survival. I was feeding my adrenaline, high on the rush I felt after each job. As much as I told myself that Bill was right and we were somehow protecting our town, I was in it for me … until I realized I had trapped myself, a realization that spurred a reaction akin to that of an animal caught in a snare. And now, years after freeing myself, I still carry that snare with me.

"Ok, we will all leave together. And I will help you find your uncle," I say, surprised when Tatán throws his arms around me and squeezes.

"Thank you," he whispers. He lays a hand on each of my shoulders and we lock eyes. "I go look and listen in the house. When I find Alex, I come back."

I nod and look around. "I'm going to walk to the woods … the trees," I say when he cocks his head.

"The woods?"

"Yes. I'm going to explore the area, try to figure out where we go after we get Alex. We cannot walk the road. We'd be too easy to find. If I'm not here when you come back, wait behind the tree. Stay down next to the rocks." With each statement, I gesture to underline my meaning. His eyes are sharp and focused and he drinks in every detail, punctuating each with a nod.

When I finish talking, the boy I had labeled an international thief extends his right hand. I take ahold of it with my own and the deal is sealed.

Chapter 35

The Naturalist, Part II

When I wander back over to the forest, I'm once again greeted by the sound of the wind rustling through the aspen trees.

Not water, I remind myself, focusing on the chorus of other sounds surrounding me. Branches scratching and creaking above, those fallen in days past snapping under my feet, and sounds of unknown creatures in the night. Insects sing and a lone owl hoots his woeful plea. I place a hand against the first tree I meet, a lonesome sentry standing apart from the rest, and pause to look back over my shoulder.

The house is still visible at the top of the hill, which means I am to its occupants, as well. I need to wait until I'm deeper into the woods, hidden by the canopy of its majestic trees and the brush and rock formations, to turn on the flashlight. In the meantime, I move steady and slow from trunk to trunk, leaving the last beams of the setting moon in my wake. Before venturing too deep into the forest, I lean close to the ground and turn the flashlight on. I brush old needles and leaves away until I find a sharp rock about the size of a golf ball.

"Sorry," I say, giving the tree next to me a pat. Then I scratch a small x into its trunk just below eye-level. I have no intention of getting lost in the forest, especially not at night.

I continue marking trunks as I ease through the trees and brush, sweeping the ground with the light for any signs of a path. Nothing. Once we have Alex, we'll have to head downhill and hope for the best. I spot a small clearing and decide to investigate before returning to the house. The ground hardens, and a turn of the flashlight reveals a large slab of rock beneath my feet. It continues for a few yards before the ground disappears beyond it. A sigh of relief brushes through my lips when I see that it's only a short drop, and the incline isn't too steep.

I sit on the edge of the rock and close my eyes to take in the sounds of the night. The only movements I hear are of the small variety, which is comforting. I don't feel like a flashlight, a water bottle, and a half-empty package of gummies would be very effective weapons, or even deterrents should I come across a bear or mountain lion. The fact these small creatures are skittering about suggests they're not aware of any predators in the immediate area. They know the place a lot better than I do, so for now, I trust their instincts.

I push myself to my feet, brush off my jeans and prepare to head back, but a sound catches my attention. There's rushing water nearby. I'm certain of it this time. It sounds like it's coming from the bottom of the incline. Sliding down to investigate wouldn't be terribly difficult, but climbing back up would take too long. I have to get back to the house to wait for news of Alex.

I shine the light toward the opposite edge of the clearing onto a cluster of boulders. Though the area is devoid of trees, the underbrush becomes thicker as I approach the rock formation. Sure enough, just on the other side, the ground slants downward and there is a void between clusters of bushes and ferns. A void filled by the slow-flowing waters of a small mountain stream, which sparkles against the beam of my flashlight.

"Yes," I hiss. I've found our guide down the mountain. I follow it with my light until I can't see any further, then sweep the beam back to the section in front of me. The banks of the stream are thick with vegetation, lined with ferns, grasses, and bushes. Some of the bushes look rather uninviting with their burrs and prickers, others greet the beam of light with blossoms in blues, pinks, whites, and yellows.

Whites, I think. *Little white flowers that look like baby's breath or queen Anne's lace, with ferny leaves. Could it be?*

I approach one of the bushes, and, if I'm not mistaken, I'm once again admiring the notorious killer of Socrates himself: poison hemlock. I don't have my phone, so I cannot be one hundred percent certain, but my gut is telling me this is it.

"Hey there," I whisper, careful not to get too close to this beautiful assassin. "Look at you, just sitting out here in the forest, mingling with the pretty little flowers and ferns. I hope you don't mind, but I am going to snip off a few pieces of you to have with me just in case …"

Just in case, what? I think, covering my hand with my sleeve and breaking off a stem of snow-white blooms.

I tuck my new treasure into my only empty pocket: a sealed, water-proof pocket on the inside of my jacket. It wouldn't do to stash it with my gummies, after all. Then I walk back to the place where I entered the clearing, tuck my marking rock in with my water bottle, and search for the first tree with an X. Once I find it, I go from one to the next, tracing my steps back to the road. Maybe I'm not Sir David Attenborough, but I'm channeling Dave Canterbury. Marking my path will be the perfect way to find the stream once we have Alex.

A smile tugs at the corners of my mouth. It's funny how I'm already thinking in terms of *we* now when plotting Alex's rescue. Something about Tatán has touched my heart. Something about this brave little kid demands respect.

Chapter 36

Realization

When I get back to my hiding place behind the giant spruce, Tatán isn't there. But something else is waiting for me. I sit and catch my breath, gathering the small foil package at the base of the tree. Thank goodness I was paying attention to where I stepped. The moon has set, and when I extinguished the flashlight at the edge of the forest, all I had to guide me was the soft glow filtering through the window sheers in the house. Above me, the sky has exploded into a million tiny sparks of light. Some shimmer, dancing like the open flame of a campfire, celebrating their originality. Others stay fixed in their luminosity, as if set as points of reference, stoic and steady, unchanging and dependable.

I unwrap the foil and revel in the fragrant vapors that rise up to greet my senses. I have no idea what the dish is, but am betting that Tatán's Mateo made it. How I would love to invite him to one of the potlucks Becca is always trying to convince me to attend. There would be no need for convincing in that case.

I raise the foil to my mouth and bite into a corner. The top layer is some kind of sweet corn, and underneath, a mixture of cheese and beef ... and is that a raisin? I'm not a fan of raisins, per se, but I now know they have a purpose in life, as a part of this magical concoction. I'm going to have to ask what this is called, and find out where I can get more when this is over.

I suddenly realize that I don't even know where Tatán is from. Sure, I read that the *tourist criminals* were coming from South America, but that's a pretty big place. I'm more than a little embarrassed at my lack of geographical knowledge. I've always been so focused on my own little world.

As you should be, Charlie. We are stewards of our town, our way of life. You need to keep fighting. Protect your town. You have seen with your own eyes what happens when nearby towns are invaded by big corporate chains, gutted and devalued. Flooded with outsiders, flowing through town to pick away at its remains like vultures, pushing out the good folk.

I squeeze my eyes shut, pushing the voice away. Sure, I have seen the dilapidated towns on the outskirts of ours. Sure, these are ... were ... places worth fighting for. They were quaint towns like my own, that flourished in different times. But, it takes a village to fight. And that village needs to know what it's fighting for, or it's simply a dog chasing its own tail. Nobody can fight progress, keep it away forever. So, maybe we were fighting the wrong battle, ignoring the war looming around us. Maybe there was ... is ... a way to incorporate the new without forgetting the old.

No! We were fighting exactly the right battle, the battle for preservation! Some things should NEVER change. We had a life. We had a home. Neighbors that all knew each other and cared. And they took it away ... killed Esther.

Only now that I know love, do I truly understand the pain Bill must have felt at the loss of his Esther. Only now do I understand the depth of the rancor poisoning his heart, strangling his empathy and blinding him to the beauty that can be found in the new and unknown. Grief and pity writhe through my soul, combining into a new understanding of an old friend and mentor.

Don't you pity me. Don't you dare, you ungrateful wisp of a child.

I take another bite of the offering Tatán left, proof of the vastness of the world I do not yet know, and silence the venomous voice.

When I finish, I take a measured swig from the bottle of water. I'm ready to end this, to get my niece and Tatán and get the hell out of here. I'm ready to move on with my life, to leave my ghosts behind, to rejoin my family and future. And I'm ready to forgive myself for past transgressions and the time wasted living in their shadows.

I have lost all concept of time, but it is beginning to feel like an eternity. Maybe I should get off my ass and take a look around. Tatán might need help locating Alex. He obviously came back to tell me something, maybe to ask for my assistance. I'm sure it wasn't just to leave the tasty treat in the foil. He may be much more of a master at entering homes than I am, but I have one big advantage over him for now: I'm an unknown. I'm invisible, because nobody is expecting to see me.

Back in the day, my task was to change the perception of who I was, before performing my magic and helping myself to that which wasn't mine. Here I'm a ghost. And as long as I can remain a ghost, there will be no need for redirection.

I push the last bit of food into my mouth, taking a moment to enjoy it before the metallic taste of adrenaline takes over. A taste I used to crave, to thrive on when I was younger, before a job, right after a job, even just thinking about certain jobs. A taste now tainted by possible consequences, by the involvement of people I actually care about.

The lights in the home are extinguished, and I wonder if the fences are coming tonight or maybe tomorrow. I was never involved with that part of Bill's operation, but I did occasionally hear him grumbling about how finicky and unreliable his own were, how they lacked moxie. Though Bill tended to slap those labels on just about anyone who didn't see and do things his way and on his timeline.

I ease my way out from behind the tree, careful to stay in its shadows while I assess my position. I could climb the pine to access one of the porches jutting out next to it, but this option is unappealing. I was a tree-climber as a kid, and avoided anything in the conifer family after an unfortunate climb in the park left me covered in sap, or pine tar, and sticking to anything I touched. Tommy had thought it endlessly funny to hand me tissues that day, telling me I could simply wipe it off. I swear I can still feel the fibers clinging to my skin like little white leeches. I had to wait until we got home from our family picnic to fully remove it. To this day, the scent of rubbing alcohol makes me nauseous.

Climbing is still an option if it turns out to be the safest way to scout the place out, but I'm going to try my darnedest to find another before I commit. From the curve of the access road around the left side of the residence, I can tell I'm not currently at the back of the house. It's angled so the front entrance is on the side of the slope, leveled specifically for the driveway and entrance to the home and the garage. The left side is also the most likely path for any traffic down to the vans, to meet the fences or check the goods. My best bet is to slide around under the deck to my right and to the back of the house, toward the jutting boulders I first thought were part of the house. That side also sits close to a grove of aspen trees which, with the constant flicking movements of their finely toothed, heart-shaped leaves, will offer me cover from anyone looking out the windows above. Hopefully there will be some kind of door to the lower floor at the back of the house ... if it isn't a daylight basement.

All these thoughts and doubts are simply keeping me from doing what I need to do. I cannot wait for Tatán any longer. I want to be on the way down the mountain before daylight. The more time we have to put distance between us and them in the dark, the better. I take a deep breath, trapping it in my chest for the count of three before letting it escape through my mouth in a thin, wispy cloud. I'm ready, but there's one more thing I need to do before I proceed.

Chapter 37

Release

"*I will* get Alex," I whisper, my eyes still closed. "I will get Alex and I will move on with my life when we are through this. I will let go."

Once more, an image of my last happy day with Sarah floats to the top of my thoughts like a soap bubble. This beginning will be different. It will be a true fresh start. I see my younger self riding home in my parents' car after dropping her off, after a morning spent laughing and dreaming. My mind floats back, ready to relive and release.

I opened the front door and was surprised to see my mother sitting in the living room. She was supposed to be at work. Instead, she was on the sofa with her face in her hands. She lifted her head when she heard me walk in.

"What are you doing here?" I asked. "What happened? Is Dad ok? Tom?" She stood up and came over to hug me, which had the exact opposite effect of the comfort she was obviously going for.

"Mom, what happened?"

"Oh, sweetie. It's so terrible. It's Bill. They found my phone number on his fridge, so they called me. He didn't have anyone. They didn't know who to call."

She was not making any sense. I tried to calm her down to get her focused. The sound of Bill's rhythmic snores as he dozed in his chair still echoed through me.

"Who called? What are you talking about?"

My mother took both of my hands in hers. "There was a fire, sweetie. They said it started in his office. One of those necklaces his wife used to make was hanging near the window and the sun caught the magnifying glass. It set fire to the papers on his desk. I told him I would tidy it for him. Remember, I told him? He wouldn't let me." I nodded, and pulled one hand away, pressing it to the front of my shirt, against the bare spot where my necklace should have been. I couldn't speak.

"All those books and papers. He was asleep in that old recliner. They said it was the smoke that killed him. I'm so sorry, sweetie."

Close your mouth, Charlie, I heard him say in my head when I realized it was open. *How's your life of crime going now?*

I OPEN my eyes and slide my index finger under the chain resting against my skin. It loops and gathers until it's trapped like a mouse in the clutches of a boa constrictor. I pull it from the grip of the silver chain and let my fingers glide down to the teardrop magnifying glass.

It's no longer the clear, shiny object that fascinated me as a child. The lens was warped by the heat of the fire, and a smokey gray film grips it like ivy round a tree. Not only that, but it looks like a wisp of smoke has somehow worked its way into the center of the lens itself.

I had told my mother I wanted to wear this one instead of my own. She never knew they were one and the same, and thought it was morbid of me to hold on to it. My therapist told her that everyone mourned differently and she had dropped it, providing me a list of different cleaning solutions she'd found on the internet that were supposed to help remedy smoke damage. She even offered to bring it to a jeweler to see if it could be professionally cleaned. But I didn't want to clean it, to fix it. The smoke served as a reminder, and its presence felt like comfort, support—or maybe it was some kind of self-punishment.

When this is over, I will get it cleaned. I can't quite bring myself to say I'll get rid of it, but I will get it cleaned.

Chapter 38

The Search

I can't wait any longer. Even if it's somehow strategically advantageous to hang on, I can't do it. As much as I've tried to distance myself from the situation, to evaluate my options in a neutral, objective manner, I simply cannot fully reach that state of mind. The image of Alex confiding in me, Alex looking up to me, Alex trusting me, is stamped in my mind. It's a lens I cannot help but look through, a decal stuck indefinitely on the window of perspective.

I jump up, then sit down just as fast when flashing dots pepper my vision. The altitude. Remember the altitude difference. I was fighting the effects when I first arrived at Tom and Lindsey's house. Now, I'm higher up. I don't know how high, of course, because, like an idiot, I forgot my phone. But my surroundings and physical hints—like the fuzziness wrapping my thoughts, and the feeling that a bison has taken a permanent seat on my chest—are indications that the change in elevation was not insignificant.

I stand again, but this time with more caution. The warm, flavorful mélange of Tatán's thoughtful gift is now a fond memory. My heartbeat shifts from sluggish to strong and steady, as if a clot has been thrown, clearing the way for the adrenaline essential for my success. I edge along the stone foundation, palms sliding around each rough, convex surface they encounter.

My brain has engaged, each gear catching the tooth of the next and picking up speed. The old familiar feeling of being *on* washes over me. Every sound, every smell, every sensation is now filtered through the lens of purpose. I'm ultra-aware, a raw nerve flexing at every stimulation. The night has grown quiet, with the exception of the aspen leaves quaking in the breeze.

There's a glass door on the back side of the house. It's not a sliding door as I had hoped, but a single French door. Its wooden frame is scratched and peeling, a victim of time and the harsh mountain elements. There's no curtain on the door that I can see, but it's completely dark. My gut tells me this is not a finished basement, rather some kind of storage. A glance upward reveals two levels of windows. The window just above me glows a soft yellow, and is obscured by a curtain or sheer. The one above that is darker, but not completely black.

Probably a bedroom, I think, running a hand along the frame of the door in front of me before trying the knob.

Of course, it's locked. But an examination of the frame reveals that the door is not only weathered, but warped. It won't be difficult to breach it and enter the basement even if I can't jimmy the lock, which looks older than I am.

Bill trained me on all sorts of locks, not that I used that particular skill while working with—for—him. I think he just got off on the fact that I picked it up so quickly. It amused him. It's come in handy a few times when demonstrating to my clients why they may want to upgrade their door locks and add some cameras.

There's a significant space between the door and frame where the latch bolt meets the strike plate. I wiggle the tip of my finger into the space, fairly certain my fingernail is clicking against the edge of the bolt. I jiggle the door, careful not to make too much noise. The bolt has caught, but isn't deep. I stand with my shoulder against the door and take a firm hold of the knob, one hand over the other. Pulling back with the full force of my body weight, I lean into the door. It takes me two tries, but I'm able to free the bolt. The door swings into the dark, dank cellar with a moan, dumping me onto the concrete.

I lay still, willing my heart to slow so that I can hear if my activity has alerted anyone. In here, the soft mumble of distant voices flows like a draft echoing through a cave. The sound is uninterrupted, its tone unaltered. Though I cannot make out the words, it sounds like a fluid conversation, not something one would hear if the sources of the voices were alarmed.

I am still a ghost.

Without a source of light, my eyes struggle to adjust to the darkness, and I find myself taking a step at a time, arms outstretched, in search of a wall or, better yet, a banister. I retrieve Tatán's flashlight and tuck it under my shirt before turning it on, limiting both its potency and its potential to give away my position.

There are two sets of stairs on opposite sides of the space, which is, in fact, being used for storage. I wonder if any of the boxes and crates around me contain stolen goods, or if the gang is simply *borrowing* an empty vacation home. I look back at the door I came through, trying to orient myself and decide that the staircase on my left must lead up to the garage.

I head to the stairs on my right, dousing the light when I begin to ascend. After a creaky first step, I shift my feet to one side, closer to where the tread is fastened to the stringer. This limits the play in each board and allows me to continue with minimal noise. Still, when I reach the door at the top, I pause to listen.

I still cannot make out what's being said, which is good because it means the occupants are not directly on the other side of the door. But the tone has changed. It sounds more animated, perhaps even a bit contentious. There's a small gap at the bottom of the door, but no light sneaking under from the other side. I probe with a flattened hand and discover some kind of draft blocker on the other side of the door. What is it my mom calls them? A snake? Yes, a draft snake. I can feel its fuzzy felt skin against my fingertips. I give it a gentle poke, pushing the beans, or rice, or whatever the filling is aside and allowing a small beam of light to creep in.

I press my ear against the doorjamb where the light has appeared. It sounds like the voices are about a room away, and they're arguing about when the fences are going to get there, the lack of snacks—especially beer—in the house (a push in the direction of the *borrowed* vacation home theory), and the fact that the *tourists* have requested use of the bathroom more than once.

"Can't they just piss in the woods?" says the voice I recognize as belonging to L, the one that most grates on my nerves.

"What if they need to take a shit?" This one I don't associate with a face.

"What, they can't shit in the woods? There's a pretty endless supply of nature's toilet paper out there, too. Not much left in here and I ain't wiping *my* ass with no leaves."

"What was that?" the other voice asks and the room falls silent.

My throat seizes, trapping my most recent breath inside. My eyes widen, though they cannot see anything other than the grayness around me. Did they hear me? I'm almost certain I didn't make any noise in the seconds leading up to the question. Did they see the dent in the draft snake?

I ease back against the hinge side of the door, readying myself for some kind of attack. If I stay low, I might be able to ram the door and knock them off balance. Then I could roll into the room and play whatever cards I may be dealt to the best of my ability, a ghost revealed.

The door doesn't open and I'm left straining to hear, to understand what is happening.

"Hey, what are you doing in here? Stop!"

Malaise rises from deep within, pushing acid up into my throat. The voices are still far enough away that I chance cracking the door. The light is filtering in through the frosted pane of a glass door, with the room before me some kind of empty mudroom. I slip out of the cellar and quietly close the door behind me, taking care to slide the draft snake back into place.

There's another door on the far side of the room with a small, clear glass window divided into four squares on its top portion. A lit sconce outside helps to illuminate the space. Thick weather mats lay just inside, home to an array of boots, of the hiking and ski persuasion. To the side of the door, a long plank with sturdy wooden pegs runs the length of the wall. Some are empty, but most hold coats or jackets of various sizes.

A commotion on the other side of the frosted-glass door relieves any concern I may have about being heard.

"He said stop!" yells L. "Fucking stop!"

Feet scuffle and something falls and shatters. A vase, maybe? Then the sound of footsteps running and a door opens.

"Fucking grab him," screams L, among the sounds of shifting feet and panting. "Move!"

I run to the door leading outside and press against the wall, keeping my body in the shadows as I gaze outside.

"Let go. *Liberame!*"

It's Tatán. He's trying to free himself from the clutches of the man called D. Several other members of the US-based group are milling about just inside the front door. For a moment, it looks like Tatán has seen me through the window. I shrink back, but keep my gaze fixed on him, mentally sending my support. He spins around and rakes the side of his shoe down his captor's shin.

I wince, my own shins tightening in an involuntary, empathetic response. D yelps and Tatán drops to the ground, rolling once before taking off toward the forest. I turn, ready to make for the cellar door and run outside after him. Then I hear the shot.

My heart stops. My jaw slacks, pulling against the dried saliva sealing my lips. My mind replays the phantom whistle of a bullet, followed by a sickening thump.

"Why you do that?" a voice screams. "Why? Eez a kid!"

Time slows to a crawl. I force my body to turn back to the door, command reluctant eyes to focus on the scene outside. I already know what I will see, yet the sight of it cuts through me like a blade, severing my nerves, numbing me through to the bone.

Tatán is splayed out on the driveway, face down. His small body is bathed in the crossbeams of light stretching out through the open door at the front of the house. I will him to move ... to get up and sprint in a surprise-I-fooled-you flight ... but he remains motionless. A group of his fellow *tourists* stand beside him, staring at the man with the gun, L.

One dares to crouch down and cradle the boy, defiantly ignoring L's instructions to step away. Even after receiving a staunch kick to the ribs. Even when the gun is trained down on him, its muzzle brushing the hair at the top of his head. Instead of backing away, the man slowly looks up until the muzzle is resting on the bridge of his nose, his expressionless gaze aimed into the killer's eyes, drilling through them. L flinches and takes a step back, steadying the weapon with his free hand.

"Drop it," says a voice behind him, gentle but firm. It's the man I thought was Mr. Benson and though he seems calm, there's a definite air of anger in his pitch.

"He was going for the girl," says L, a nervous shimmer giving the word *girl* a slight hiccup in the middle.

L lowers the gun and Mr. B nods, surveying the scene. He makes a point of looking each and every person in the eye, ending his rounds by laying a hand on the shoulder of the man cradling the boy.

"*Condolencias*, Mateo," he says with what sounds like it might be genuine regret. He gives the man a final pat and motions for his crew to return inside.

"I had to," squeaks L, shoving the gun into the back of his waistband. "He was going for the girl."

Mr. B brings a finger to his lips, silencing the man, and walks inside, followed by the others. When L lags behind, D grabs his arm and leads him along.

"You've done it now," he whispers.

The front door closes, limiting the light to that cast by the solitary sconce. I watch, immobile, my heart frozen in the depths of my chest, like some ancient, obsolete creature trapped in a glacier. Two of the men outside crouch next to Mateo and help lift the limp body of the boy I admired, the child who wanted to find his uncle, to live happily ever after in Robin, CA. They walk slowly toward the garage, disappearing from view. A door slams and I sink to the floor.

I sit hugging my legs for a moment, chin resting upon my knees, and I cry. Long, painful breaths push up from my lungs and out through dry lips parted in a prolonged grimace. Tears flood my cheeks, soaking my face and assaulting my tongue with the salty taste of devastation. I cry until my chest hurts, until my head pulsates, until my brain screams, telling me to pull myself together. More than ever now, I need to focus and get my niece out of here.

Chapter 39

Revelation

I fumble with my bottle of water and force a sip past the lump in my throat. My cheeks are warming and the cold sting of grief is transitioning into something darker, more primal. Something I can use to my advantage. I take a deep breath, temporarily banishing tender thoughts of Tatán to a mental compartment I know I will revisit. I allow the heat of resentment to flow through my veins, careful not to lose control of it, not to let it blossom into blinding rage.

When the tremors have subsided and my thoughts are sharp, I creep over to the door with the frosted pane. I wrap my fingers around the knob, but stop short of turning it at the sound of approaching footsteps.

"I thought I told you to make him get rid of that gun." It's the voice of Mr. B, though it now sounds more annoyed than angry.

"I did, sir," says D in a voice that screams reverence and fear. "He said he'll ditch it before we leave. He thought it might come in handy if something goes south with the fences. That kid was trying to get to the girl ... maybe help her get away."

After a prolonged moment of silence, Mr. B speaks again.

"That gun is a liability. Make sure the body is taken care of and the gun is scrubbed and destroyed. Bury them both, but not anywhere near each other. And keep L out of trouble. This is strike two, and he only gets that because he's your sister's kid. There is no strike three."

"Yes, sir. Understood."

"And, D?" says Mr. B, interrupting the sound of retreating footsteps.

"Yes, sir?"

"Fetch Mateo and tell him I'm hungry. Make sure he cleans himself up, then have him make one of his salads, the one with all the tomatoes and onions. I'll take it in my room."

The rapidity with which this man swings from annoyed and angry to calm and hungry concerns me more than a little. His apparent lack of humanity makes him someone I wish to completely avoid if at all possible.

I wait for a moment after the room falls silent before slowly turning the knob and cracking open the mudroom door. The room I'm entering is a large gourmet kitchen, fancier than I expected, given the log cabin look of the home's exterior. It's empty, though voices float into the space from somewhere just beyond the passage into what I imagine must be a dining room.

To my immediate right, there's a small cove with a partial wall concealing it from the cooking area. It houses a work station cluttered with papers and envelopes. The wall in front of the built-in desk is covered in a colorful display of sticky notes, the bottom halves of which curve away from the surface, as if about to take flight. It resembles a kaleidoscope of butterflies resting before migration.

I push a few papers aside and pick up a torn envelope with wavy blue postal lines dancing across a stamp of the American flag. I examine the address printed in its center, then fold and pocket it. Honestly, the address doesn't give me even the slightest clue of where I am, but it could come in handy later on.

A light comes on in the main part of the kitchen, causing my breath to catch. I lean back against the wall separating me from whoever has entered. The refrigerator door opens with a signature fridge *pop*, breaking the seal between its frosty interior and the outside world. Someone is rifling through its contents, pushing things here and there, perhaps lifting them to examine labels before depositing them once again.

I risk a peek around the corner, comforted by the sounds of deep refrigerator exploration. The appliance is located on the opposite wall, meaning whoever is in there looking around will be facing away from me. Sure enough, my sweeping gaze brushes across the back of a head of black hair positioned in front of the gaping fridge doors.

My gaze also reveals that with minimal exposure I can observe the activities in the kitchen reflected in the doors of the double oven, which sits at an angle in the corner of the room.

"Hey ... Matty, right? You almost done with Mr. B's salad? *Finito*? *Salado*?"

My body goes rigid, glare fixed on the oven doors. It's L and his flippant voice hits my ears like an icepick. He walks over to the man, Mateo, and gestures at the ingredients laid out on the counter next to the refrigerator.

"I speak English," says Mateo, pronouncing each word with a tone that clearly says *fuck you*.

"That's great, Matty," says L reaching out to bump the stoic man's shoulder. "Hey, sorry about your little friend ... your *amigo*."

Mateo's eyes narrow, but the rest of his face remains neutral.

"Had to be done, Matty. He was taking off. Deserting."

My tongue brushes against the back of my bottom lip, pausing at the metallic taste of blood seeping from a fresh bite. I take a measured breath, holding it for a moment when my lungs feel full. When I release it, I imagine my muscles relaxing with the controlled flow of air. It's a technique Becca taught my father to help deal with his pain. The pain I'm currently experiencing is of a different kind, but it does seem to help.

"Anyhow, the boss man's waiting for his salad. Better get to it. Oh, and whip me up a little sandwich while you're at it. We still have some of that ham we grabbed from the last place. Dress it up with some of that shit you made this morning. Maybe throw in some salad. I'll be back in ten minutes to pick it all up. Got it?"

He leans toward Mateo's face and, for a moment, it looks like Mateo is going to bite off his nose like a rabid pit bull. Instead, he smiles politely and nods.

"Yessir," he says and turns back to the task at hand, gathering an armful of tomatoes and onions to place next to some other ingredients he has arranged on the counter.

When L leaves the room, Mateo's shoulders slump. He pinches his mouth over gritted teeth and shakes his head. For a moment, I think he might cry, but his face quickly tightens into a reddening scowl. He sets to work slicing up tomatoes and onions with the grace and skill of a master chef, the fluidity and accuracy of his movements holding my attention like the dangling pocket watch of a hypnotist.

Once he has added everything into a large metal bowl, including a dash of this and a splash of that (I'm no cook), he mixes it all together and sets it aside. He puts both palms against the edge of the counter and leans, dropping his head briefly and turning it side to side.

Shaking out the kinks, I think. That's what Bill used to call it, and man did his spine crackle.

He grabs a plate and pulls a roll out of a nearby grocery bag. When he picks up his knife again, he jabs it into the bread, splitting it open in a manner that makes me think he's imagining it is L's chest. He stacks on some ham and adds a few pieces of the tomato and onion salad from the bowl. Then he opens the fridge and pulls out a fistful of greens, separating them into bunches before cutting them up and arranging them on the sandwich like an artist laying down paint. Before closing the sandwich, he curls his lips into a sneer and spits on it.

I feel ya, buddy. If only spit could kill.

My eyes widen. No, spit cannot kill ... but I know something that can, and it just so happens to look like the frilly lettuce in the sandwich. I reach into my jacket and unzip a pocket. With my shirt sleeve over my hand, I withdraw the little bunch of hemlock, twirling it back and forth in front of my face ... but not too close.

Lucky for L, there's no way for me to get this into his little sandwich, I think. *And, lucky for him, I'm not a killer.* As much as I hate this man, I don't think I have it in me. I don't think I could.

Sure you could. Bill's amused voice invades my thoughts. *You have.*

Go away! I fling the thought at him like David releasing the stone that killed Goliath. *I need you to go away. I need to get Alex, to have a clear head. Please, go away.*

Have you ever thought that maybe I AM your clearer head? We are linked, Charlie. I knew it the moment I saw you lift that necklace at the pharmacy. That was the moment I chose you. Esther thought it would be Sarah. She insisted Sarah would be less trouble, that she had less baggage. Sarah didn't have much of a family, after all. But I knew it would be you.

What would be me? What are you talking about? I close my eyes and lean against the partition wall, massaging my temples. The sensation of falling washes over me like a rogue wave, falling deeper into myself.

Thomas Campbell said, "to live in hearts we leave behind is not to die." Just as Esther is in mine, I am now in yours.

I don't think that's what that means.

My world is spinning. I'm floating. Reality flies high above me, a tiny window out of reach. *You're not in my heart, anyway. Not anymore. Not after everything you did. I trusted you and you were keeping files on me!*

You needed guidance, Charlie. All young folks need guidance now and again. You needed a strong hand to guide you. To shape you. I chose you because we connected from the very first moment we met. You were my new Sarah.

I smack the heels of my hands against my temples. This last statement has opened a window, jarred my mind back. I grab my wallet, tucked snug into my back pocket, and slide a finger inside. I pull out the small yellow sticky note, folded down to the size of a postage stamp. The sticky note I found years ago attached to the top of the file Bill had created of my misdeeds.

I open the note, taking care not to tear the paper at the folds, where time has thinned it to fine vellum. Bill's bold, loopy handwriting greets me when I finally press the paper flat against the wall. Of course, I know what it says, though I've not gazed upon it for more years than I can remember. I know, but it still strikes me like an open-handed slap. He wrote it down the day we met. Jotted it on a sticky note which he fastened to a folder he never knew he'd fill. Or maybe he did. Maybe it's like he said and we connected that day and my fate was sealed. I don't know.

I stare at the paper, trying to connect my thoughts, corral them so that I can focus. My lips form each word as I pronounce them without sound.

Met a kid with skills. Little girl named Charlie. Charlotte? Only five! My next Sarah? My next me?

Chapter 40

Recovery

I return the paper to its home, slide my wallet back, force myself into the present. I can deal with this shit later. Alex needs me. Now that my mind is focused on the here and now, I realize the kitchen has fallen silent. There are no people reflected in the oven doors. A bowl and a plate with a sandwich sit on the kitchen counter.

Yes, the man named Mateo made them. I saw him make them. He must have left the room while I was caught in my own head. He must have gone to let them know the food was ready. How much time has passed? I think back to the last moments I remember, the last ones that are clear. L said something about being back in ten minutes, didn't he?

Footsteps approach and I tuck myself back a little further, flustered at my break in attention. I conjure up some choice profanities for Bill, and aim them at whatever part of him has attached itself to me.

"Well, would you look at that?" says L from the kitchen. "What a sweet-looking sandwich. You've outdone yourself, Mateo."

The oven doors mirror him leaning over to inspect Mateo's

work. Directly behind him, Mateo nods once and reaches around to lift the plate and the bowl, offering both to L.

"Oh no. You take the salad up to Mr. B," says L, grabbing the plate with the sandwich. "I'm taking this up to my new assignment. Thanks to your little friend, I now have to babysit until we leave." He turns and walks out, taking a large bite of his sandwich and humming approval as he goes.

Mateo lingers in the kitchen, fluffing the salad with a fork. Then he turns and looks into the oven doors. He's grinning.

My heart quickens and my throat feels like I've just swallowed a cup of sand. Is he looking at me? If I can see his reflection, he can see mine, right? But how does he know I'm here? And if he does see me, why isn't he sounding the alarm? He does a slight bow with his head before turning and leaving the room, salad in hand.

In the foggy portion of my mind, the part filled with echoes of Bill's voice and wisps of my past, I see myself walking into the kitchen, placing something into the meals Mateo has prepared. Surely it's a dream, a vision of unfulfilled intentions. A way to satisfy my anger without tarnishing my soul.

I look down at my hands, following up on a sudden revelation. They're empty. I reach into the inner pocket of my jacket, still unzipped from before. I look to the ground, but the hemlock is nowhere to be seen.

I must have dropped it when I was daydreaming. Perhaps it slid under the desk, but now isn't the time to look. Alex is upstairs and that psycho is with her. Does he still have the gun? I don't know. Even if his uncle already made him get rid of it, he may have a knife or something else. I need to make sure I don't accidentally enter the wrong room. I know Mr. B is somewhere up there, too. I'm still a ghost ... mostly. I can still do this.

Three loud knocks echo from somewhere upstairs. I follow the sound, stealing from shadow to shadow until I see a staircase.

"Sir, the salad." The voice is Mateo's. It's abnormally loud. Is it for my benefit? Is he trying to let me know where not to wander?

Whether or not it's intentional, the result is the same. His voice is coming from the left side of the upstairs area. I'll go to the right to search for Alex.

A door opens and closes. Has Mateo entered the room or only handed over his offering? I slide up the steps, my body low and tight to the banister. If anyone enters the room below me or the hallway above, I will surrender my advantage, my invisibility.

But nobody does. I crawl up the last few steps, peeking through the balusters before moving into the hallway at the top. Mateo must have entered the room through the only door I see down the left hall. I scurry to the right where there are three closed doors.

The first door I encounter is narrower than the other two. I briefly lean my ear against it before cracking it open. As I imagined, it's a linen closet. When I press my ear to the second door, I'm greeted by the rhythmic sound of snoring combined with some not so rhythmic complaining.

"Would one of you please shut him up? He sounds like a fucking chainsaw."

"Why don't you do it yourself? *I'm* not waking him up. Dude could snap my head off with one of those big-ass hands."

"Maybe just roll him on his side. I heard that can stop snoring."

"Fuck off. If it's bothering you, you roll him. I'd like to continue living, thank you very much. Here, take my earbuds and shut up. They're supposed to be noise canceling or something."

Door number three it is, then, I think, grateful that said door is on the opposite side of the hall. The two bedrooms don't share a wall, and I can hear water running behind the wall at the end of the hall, so it must be one of those jack-and-jill bathroom set-ups.

I lower myself onto the floor, hoping neither of the doors down this hall suddenly swing open. The one on the other side of the staircase doesn't concern me as much. If someone exits that door, I'll hear it and have time to duck into the linen closet thanks to the curve of the hallway. I look through the dimly lit space between the door and the wooden panels of the floor, holding my breath at the close passage of a foot, then two. The boards creak under their weight, heightening my awareness of their proximity.

They pass by once again, shadows of movement mere inches from my face. Then again, before heading toward the other side of the room. Three rapid knocks, *pop, pop, pop,* from inside.

"Fucking hell, would you get out of the goddam bathroom already," says L, a slight tremor in his voice. "Come on, man. I need to get in there."

The sound of running water stops and a door opens and closes in rapid succession.

"Oh, man. Fuck," L's voice is muffled now, but the sentiment is clear.

Somebody has a tummy ache. The left corner of my mouth pinches into a sneer at the thought. *Karma and altitude sickness sure are a bitch, my friend.*

The moaning and other unpleasant sounds I now hear signal an opportunity. I get up and crack the door open, careful not to make any noise. When I don't see anyone moving about, I give the door another controlled push and slide into the room.

A single cottage lamp illuminates the space, which looks more like an office than a bedroom. The walls are lined with bookshelves, filled to the brim—and in some cases overflowing—with horizontal stacks of books. There's a large, old-fashioned looking, wooden desk with a wooden wheeled chair set in front of it under a window on the far side. Letters and papers jut from its abundant slots, both horizontal and vertical.

The space looks like a writer's haven, but for a small cot in the corner of the room, tucked into the shadow thrown by the desk which sits between it and the only light currently switched on. Something shifts in the dark, causing the wooden cross-legs of the cot to creak and my heart to skip.

"Alex," I whisper, approaching what I now see is a shivering bundle of fabric atop the cot with long, dark hair flowing out from one extreme.

The bundle goes still, then twists in a way that reels the dark hair up and under. It rises with the sound of a deep breath and a sniffle.

"Charlie?" The voice is faint, spent, but there's no mistaking the word it has uttered. "Auntie C?" This time a little louder, as if questioning the reality of what she heard.

I sigh, easing the tension that's been building steadily at each turn of my imagination as to her condition. Her voice is weak, but she sounds ok. I lay a hand on the sleeping bag wrapping her like a cocoon.

"Yes, it's me. It's Auntie C." The use of the old familiar name, the one she, herself, bestowed upon me when she was a toddler and couldn't manage a proper *ch*, lights a warmth in my heart that spreads through me like a fire through kindling. It stirs memories of her, a little spitfire of a child, gripping my arm and pulling me here and there to show me each new amazing discovery. *Auntie, see? Auntie, see?* she'd exclaimed until Auntie C naturally became her special name for me.

As much as I enjoy the new level of maturity our relationship has reached, and respect her wish to refer to me as Charlie, shedding her childhood habits like a butterfly leaving its chrysalis, hearing the words *Auntie C* from her now feels like balm on a wound.

"Yes, it's me. Shhhh. Let's get you out of here," I say, pushing the sleeping bag away from her.

A blindfold covers the upper half of her face and by the positioning of her shoulders, I can see that her hands are bound behind her. I push the cloth up and over her head. She squeezes her eyelids shut several times, squinting at me and smiling. I smile back, bringing a finger to my lips before leaning over her to work on the cloth strips used to tie her hands.

The knots are compact and tight, a situation that was surely worsened by attempts she made to free herself. I scan the room for something I can use to help free her from her bonds, which I now see are also around her ankles.

I settle on a letter opener set out on the writer's desk. Its side isn't sharp, but the pointed end will help loosen the knots. I rush back to the cot, and start on the restraint around Alex's ankles. If I can remove that one, we can get out of here. I can free her of the rest when we're safely away from the house.

I work it enough to slide a finger into the center of the knot, set the opener down and wiggle both sides until I'm able to widen the loop. It'll be faster to slide the cloth down past her feet than to untie it. Whoever did this must've been an Eagle Scout in another life.

"Auntie," Alex hisses, as I ease the loop past her left heel.

I shift my gaze to hers, registering a look of panic before I'm grabbed from behind, and a cold blade is pressed against my throat.

L has managed to reenter the room without alerting me. I curse myself for underestimating him, for pegging him as a hapless idiot with a tummy ache.

"What do we have here?" he whispers in my ear, pressing his body against the back of mine and moving me away from Alex.

I wince as the edge of the knife slips along my neck. He isn't applying pressure, but I feel the sting of a cut all the same. I slow my breathing, which hiccuped into frantic pants when he grabbed me. He tilts the knife to the side and turns me toward him with deliberate slowness, making sure to slide his hand over my breast and giving it a squeeze.

Before I turn away from Alex, I offer her a reassuring nod. It's not alright. Nothing is alright. But she's already been through so much, and I want to at least appear to have a modicum of control so that she won't lose it. I'm terrified of what this man might do if that happens. She nods back and sinks back against the sleeping bag.

"Well, hello there, *Auntie*," L whispers when I'm facing him.

I shift my body, trying to distance my face from his. He slides his free hand down to my buttocks and yanks me closer, leaning his face in to smell my hair.

I realize that if he's whispering, and hasn't called out to his friends, he may have plans of his own for me. He may not want to share. Whatever these plans are, I don't want him to try anything in front of my niece. Nor do I want her to see what I mean to do to him in return.

"Let's take this into the other room," I whisper, directing a pleading gaze toward him. I relax the tension in my body to make him think he's in control.

"Not sure you really want to go in there," he says, chuckling through a malicious sneer.

I shrug and force a sheepish look. I can play this game. I played it for years with my ex, Paul. The game of survival over venomous masculinity. The one that involves dimming my light and playing the role of the weak, shy, thankful female. I can play the shit out of this game.

For years, I swallowed my pride, second-guessing my worth all the while. I'd met Paul while working for Bill. We dated for a couple years after Bill passed away, then got married. Looking back, I realize I was jumping from the comfort of one toxic relationship of dependency to another. My guilt over Bill's death threw me right into Paul's arms, a place where I could hold on to the past while pretending to make a future. It somehow felt like a union to which Bill would lend his blessing.

I thought Paul was the steady hand you needed. I thought he could steer you the way I did, with Esther, too. I apologize for not realizing that you, yourself, were the steady hand. You can't blame me for that. You can't blame an old man for being old-fashioned. Turns out we have more in common than I could imagine.

His condescending laugh reverberates through my brain, ceasing only when I'm jolted back into the world where a slimy psychopath is squeezing my ass and pressing his crotch into me.

"Hey," he hisses, spittle flying from his mouth. "Did you hear what I said?"

It takes all of my self-control to quell the fire in my eyes before looking at him. I shake my head, taking care not to move my neck against his blade.

"Sorry," I say in my best meek, frightened voice. "I didn't." I bat my eyelids and widen them into the round helpless orbs of a baby harp seal.

"I said, let's go." He slides his hand up from my ass to the back of my head and pushes me in the direction of the bathroom door. "Let's go before one of the assholes in the other room decides he needs to take a piss. And," he grabs a fistful of my hair, turns my head, and presses his cheek against mine, his lips brushing my earlobe, "keep quiet or your niece will be next. Right now, I'm pretty sure we're going to let her go. If you cooperate, give me a little happy time, I'll make sure we do."

His eyes say otherwise, but it's not in my interest to point this out, so I nod with compliance. Once we are out of this room, out of Alex's view, I can try to find a way to deal with this asshole. The less I struggle now, the better chance I have of taking him by surprise when his dick takes over from his brain.

"Open the door," he says when we reach the bathroom, spraying the nape of my neck with spit. "Try anything stupid and I will flay you like a trout and finish my business with your niece."

I turn the nob and ease the door open. He pushes me inside and rushes to lock the opposite door. Then he turns and motions for me to shut the door, bringing a finger to his lips.

"Shhhh," he says, brandishing the knife while his other hand reaches down to undo his jeans.

I back into the door, closing it with my body, not daring to turn my back on him. He's having trouble with his zipper and his knife wielding hand is beginning to tremor with what I guess to be excitement, frustration, and anticipation all at once.

"Fuck," he mumbles under his breath as he tries, once again, to get a good grip on the reluctant zipper. "Fuuuck." Certainly, the bulge in his crotch is not helping. "You open it," he hisses through a mouthful of drool. "Fuggin opn it."

I approach slowly, palms out, eyes on the blade, which is now shaking in his fist. When I grab the zipper, he pushes his crotch toward me in a half stumble.

"Hurry," he whispers, his breathing now labored.

I pull down the zipper and he reaches in to free himself. "Now, take off your goddam pants," he commands through rapid breaths. "Takem down n commeere."

It's getting harder to understand his slurred speech. I tilt my head and he motions with the blade for me to come over. Just as he's reaching for the front of my pants, he lurches toward the sink and vomits, all but missing his target. His whole body is shaking now. When he looks up and locks his gaze on mine, I can see that his eyes are dilated.

"What da fuuu?" he asks, glaring at me like I might have an answer. His breathing sounds shallow, and his free hand is pressed against his stomach.

He takes a step toward me and stumbles to the floor. I jump back, avoiding the blade of the hunting knife at the last second. A dark circle widens in the crotch of his jeans. He rests his cheek against the checkered tile floor, drool pooling beside him, and moans.

I stare for a moment before reason kicks in and propels me back to the door. A heavy mournful sound rises from the man on the floor.

"Damn, he's in there again with the shits," says a voice from behind the other side of the Jack-and-Jill, the side containing an unknown number of thugs armed with who knows what. "The fuck did he eat?" A round of stifled laughter filters in and L's eyes roll back toward the sound. His lips tremble and his mouth opens and closes like that of a fish pulled from the water onto a riverbank.

I rush into the room where Alex is huddled on the cot, her back against the wall. The fear that greets me when I look into her eyes shifts to confusion, then joy when it's obvious that I'm alone. She opens her mouth to talk, but stops when I raise my index finger. We can talk after we get the hell out of here.

While I was gone, she was able to work the cloth binding her ankles the rest of the way off. She turns her body to show me the letter opener clasped between her fingers. She's been trying to work at the remaining knot behind her back.

"Hang onto that," I whisper into her ear as I help her off the cot. "We may need it."

"Where's that man?" she asks in a trembling hiss.

"Shhh. Don't worry about him. We need to get out of here." *Before someone needs to use the bathroom.*

"Where are your shoes?" I ask once she's back on her feet.

Alex shrugs and I remember the boots lined up on the mat in the mudroom. Looks like we are going to have to make a little stop. Before we exit the room, I look around for anything that might be useful for our escape. The knife in the bathroom comes to mind, but I decide against it on the off chance that the slime ball called L is starting to feel any better.

An object set on the edge of one of the bookshelves catches my eye. It's a plate with the remnants of a sandwich on it. I walk over and take a closer look at the scattered mix of crumbs and bits of sandwich innards.

Is that? I push aside an onion bit to examine a small fern-like frond.

"What is it, Charlie?" Alex whispers, looking over my shoulder. The fact she's back to calling me Charlie is reassuring. She's moved from fright to calculated flight.

"Nothing," I say, emptying the plate into a nearby trash bin and sliding it under the cot. I'm thinking of Mateo when I do this ... just in case. "Let's get out of here."

We creep down the hallway in single file. I take a final look back to make sure that all doors are shut. Alex follows close behind and I occasionally feel her forehead touch the center of my back. Her breaths are getting stronger and more regular, her grip more firm. Adrenaline is kicking in and doing its job.

Once we reach the empty kitchen, I grab the knife Mateo was using. I show it to Alex, and she turns her back to me, raising her arms. I cut the cloth ties around her wrists and grab a dishcloth off the counter, wrapping it around the knife like a sheathe, then tying the ends around one of my belt loops. Alex gives each of her wrists a quick rub, then envelops me into a bear hug.

"Thank you, Charlie," she says. "Thank you for finding me."

I give her a squeeze, then take her hands in mine. Deep blue bruises flower around the two red stripes circling her wrists.

"I'm fine," she whispers. "Now let's get the fuck out of here." A quick puff of laughter shoots from her nose at the sight of my faux indignation.

"Good idea," I say. "Follow me."

Chapter 41

Out into the Open Sky

I lead Alex into the mudroom and point to the row of boots on the floor. She's trying on a second pair when a door slams and a voice calls out from somewhere in the house.

"Wake up, Jesse," a man yells in a frantic voice.

"You mean D," says another. "You know the rules."

"Whatever! Wake him up. There's something wrong with Mi ... L. There's something wrong with L."

"What do you mean there's—"

"Just wake him the fuck up! And someone get Mr. B. We have a serious problem."

My eyes widen and I direct my attention to Alex, whose absence I imagine is the *serious problem*. I motion for her to hurry. She throws the second pair of boots to the side, apparently too small, and grabs a noticeably bigger pair. She slides them on. They are huge on her feet, but we don't have time to be picky.

She reaches for the door handle beside her, the one that leads out to the front of the house.

"Wait," I hiss.

Confusion has turned to panic on the next level of the house.

Cries of "where the fuck is she?" and, "how did she kill him?" and "where's Mr. B?" fly to and fro.

"Mr. B doesn't look so good," says one of the men, panting.

"What the fuck is going on here?" asks the only voice I recognize. The one that belongs to the hulk of a man I now know to be L's uncle. A door opens, then slams. "We need to find that little bitch now."

"What does Mr. B want us to do?" A door opens, followed by a sharp *crack!* I imagine the large man's fist punching through drywall, and shudder.

"Mr. B isn't available for comment. I'm in charge for now and I say we need to find that little bitch and whoever helped her." He's lowered his voice, but it simmers with rage. "You three, come with me. You stay with Mr. B. See if you can get him on his feet."

Heavy footsteps scramble down the stairs.

"This way, Alex," I whisper, waving her toward the door to the cellar. "We need to go down there."

When the door is closed behind us, I put an arm out to stop Alex while I pull out the flashlight and shine it at the steps. This would be the worst time to stumble down a flight of stairs, and I can see Alex is already having trouble getting around in the boots she chose.

"Was that blood out there on the ground?" she asks, eyes wide. "It looked like blood."

"We need to go, Alex. Focus and watch your step."

When we get to the bottom, I point to the old door across the cellar and douse the light. Now they're looking for her, for us. They may be anywhere out there and I won't make the mistake of underestimating anyone again.

"No flashlight from here on out. Take a minute to let your eyes adjust and grab onto my waist," I tell Alex, and we slide our feet along the cement floor, easing our way toward the faint light visible through the glass door.

When we reach the door, I press my forehead against the glass, straining my eyes in search of movement. The world outside is still, so I open the door just enough for both of us to exit, not bothering to close it again. I can hear voices in the distance, on the other side of the house. When we get to the corner of the house that leads to the space under the first deck, I peek around, ducking back when I catch sight of a flashlight beam sweeping by on the other side.

"We need to get into the woods," I say, pulling her toward the grove of aspens behind the house.

There's an open area between the aspens and the next opportunity for cover. The only other possibility to distance ourselves without crossing in front of the house would involve scaling the boulders set next to the house, and I don't see that happening. I'm not a particularly agile climber anymore, and only scaled trees when I was younger. Besides, the boots Alex has on must be at least two sizes too big.

We crouch at the edge of the aspen grove and wait for an opportunity to dart into the tall clumps of grass growing alongside the driveway. I turn to Alex, who's gulping air in little hiccups trying to stay calm.

"Hey," I whisper, taking her hands. "We've got this. Try breathing in through your nose and releasing each breath through your mouth, like this." I pull in a deep breath of cool mountain air, not stopping until my chest is fully extended, then release it. She mimics me, a little too quickly for the first two breaths, then gains more control. When this happens, I feel the muscles in her hands relax.

"Ok, when I tap your knee, we're going to scoot over to the grass over there."

Another flashlight beam slides by, and I bring a finger to my lips, motioning with my other hand for her to stay low.

"Where the fuck is Mateo? *Donde es* ... oh, fuck it. You know what I'm asking. Where is he?"

The voice is close, too close. I turn my head to see if I can pinpoint its exact location ... somewhere in front of the decks.

Somewhere near the giant Christmas tree. My chest tightens, spreading tension up through my shoulders.

They're blaming Mateo. Of course, they're blaming him. They think he helped Alex.

A bolt of guilt shoots through me, and concern for this man I don't even know. *Tatán knew him.* Grief takes a stab at my heart now, but I fend it off and push the visions of what happened back into their compartment in my mind.

"Who's Mateo?" asks Alex. I shrug my shoulders in a little white lie. We don't have time for this now.

"Where's Mateo?" asks a calmer voice. One laced with contempt.

A shadowy figure stumbles into sight and falls to the ground. Alex and I both catch our breath and duck lower to the ground. A man with a flashlight walks over and jerks the fallen man to his feet. He yanks the man's hands behind him and holds him still, while the hulking shadow of the man named Jesse approaches.

The restrained man tries to back away, but is shoved forward by his captor.

"Easy question," Jesse says, shrugging. "Where. Is. Mateo?"

"*No sé*. No know."

Obviously not the answer Jesse was looking for. His fist shoots out like a jackhammer and catches his target under the chin, dropping him to the ground. The man who was holding his hands looks down and gives him a kick, shrugging at the lack of reaction.

"Get as many flashlights as you can find. We're going to search the woods. They can't have gotten too far in the dark. The little bitch doesn't have any shoes either."

"What about the fences? They're supposed to come tonight."

"J's staying behind to deal with that. Hopefully, Mr. B will be back on his feet, too."

"I don't know, man. He really didn't look so good."

Jesse grabs his shoulder and gives him a shake. "Get more flashlights, then get your ass back out here."

As soon as they are out of sight, I tap Alex's knee and we bolt for the tall grass, using them as cover to make our way down the drive and past the vans. Though I'm certain any noise we make is covered by the confusion happening back at the house and the cool breeze rustling the leaves around us, I find myself holding my breath more than once.

Outside the front of the house, at the end of the driveway, the lights are getting brighter. Flashlights are passed out to the search party, their beams fanning the sky like spotlights. The outer sconces, which were off when I arrived, are coming on one by one, illuminating the landscaping around the house.

Seems we moved out of range just in time. Now we need to get across the road and into the forest before the group of men start down the drive.

"We need to get across now," I tell Alex, pointing to the area of the woods where I've marked a path to the stream. "There's a stream that we can follow down the mountain."

Alex nods, glancing back at the group with the lights, eyes wide.

I take hold of her hand. "On three," I whisper. "One, two, three."

The last number has barely left my lips when we bolt across the street, knees bent and heads low. We're almost across when the headlights of an oncoming car light us up as if we were on a Broadway stage. The driver hits the horn, leans out the window and cusses at us as we slide past, attracting the attention of the group starting down the drive from the house.

"Shit! They just ducked into the woods! Go get them!" Jesse's voice booms through the night.

The driver of the car opens his door and calls up the road. "I'll come back. Too much shit going on here. My boss doesn't like attention." He closes the door and backs the car up, jamming on the brakes and swinging it around.

"No, wait!" Jesse calls out to the taillights as they fade away down the road. "Fuck."

My first few attempts at locating the x's I carved in the trees are unsuccessful and we don't have time to stand around. Without my markings or a flashlight, we'll have to navigate blind, try to continue heading downhill as fast as we can from tree to tree.

The men with the flashlights will be here soon. The ground is uneven and littered with branches and rocks. We're moving much too slowly, but a twisted ankle or broken bone would end our flight completely. When we're deep enough in not to see the lights behind us, I quickly light the flashlight to take a look around, taking care to keep the beam low, then turn it off again.

"Over there!" a voice calls out.

"Shit," I whisper and pocket the light.

In the brief moment of light, I did see a way ahead, but now they know where we're going. This isn't going to work. We are going to be caught.

I don't even want to think about what the guy will do after what you did to his nephew. I ignore the voice and lead Alex around the wide base of a ponderosa pine, then over to some rocks I saw reaching up from the ground.

I place her hands against the closest rock and point ahead to the tops of the trees, which fall off suddenly up ahead, revealing a sky full of stars. She nods with understanding. The ground drops off not too far ahead of where we are. Without a flashlight, we cannot see how steep the drop is, so we need to proceed at a snail's pace.

Alex leans closer, knocking the flashlight from my hand. I scoop it from the forest floor, a fresh idea blooming in my mind. I motion for her to continue around to the other side of the rocks to hide, then press my body against the rough surface of the boulder behind me and wait, my ear angled like a satellite dish scanning for UFO activity.

Though my jacket is faring well against the cold, an icy chill is seeping in from the rock. I try to ignore it, shifting position and pulling my jacket down as far as it will go in the back. The snapping of twigs and thumping of feet is getting closer. I gather a rock the size of a softball from the ground in one hand and grip the flashlight in the other, sliding my thumb up along its side until it is snug against the switch.

Now or never, I think, and launch the rock toward the drop as hard as I can, switching on the flashlight and launching it in the same direction. The light spins for a moment, then disappears over the side.

"There! That way. The light just flicked on over there. Hurry." The sound of steps comes quicker. They're breaking into a run.

I duck around the rocks to join Alex, and we wait, huddled against each other at the base of the formation.

"Shit!" a voice calls out, followed by the sound of something, someone ... maybe more than one someone ... sliding and rolling down the incline. The noise stops with a sickening crack and the footsteps stop.

"Goddamit, watch where you're walking," Jesse says. "One of you climb down there and see if those two are ok. The other comes with me to where the light was."

Was, I think. *Good. The flashlight must have broken when it hit the ground.*

This will keep up the illusion we're still on the move, unless they find the flashlight, of course. But what are the odds of that happening?

Beams of light reveal parts of the forest around us, dimming as their owners move further away into the woods. Until we are once again alone in the dark.

"Where do we go now?" Alex asks, her voice a soft breeze in the night.

"Well, we've bought some time. But I don't really see how we can go any further without getting hopelessly lost out here. With no flashlight, we'd also be risking a nasty fall or an encounter with something that sees much better in the dark than we do. Our best bet is finding somewhere nearby to hunker down until morning." I hope my efforts to filter most of my doubts and fears from my voice were successful.

"We can try to squeeze into the space between these two boulders," Alex says, pulling me gently toward the base of the rocks a little further down the incline. "I saw it when you threw the light."

Sure enough, where the two rocks meet, there's an opening. It takes a little doing, but we both squeeze through and into a cozy little pocket lined with a carpet of pine needles that has accumulated over the years.

In a matter of minutes, Alex is asleep, her soft rhythmic breathing interrupted by the occasional whimper. Poor kid was exhausted. Shit, she's not even a teenager yet, and she's been through more than most people go through in an entire lifetime. I lay my head against my elbow and begin to drift off. Before succumbing to the weight of my own exhaustion, my mind wanders to thoughts of another kid who went through a lot. A kid who won't have the chance to experience anything else, one who isn't going to get to live happily ever after in the good old US of A.

Chapter 42

Going With the Flow

Something brushes against my cheek, pulling me from a pleasant dream in which Becca and I sit picnicking by the side of a clear mountain stream. The sound of gurgling water over smooth, shiny stones fades and I awake to the now familiar sound of the wind gently winding through the leaves of the aspens around me.

I open my eyes and roll my head to the side where Alex sits tickling my cheek with a heart-shaped leaf.

"Good morning, Charlie," she whispers. She wears a jaded smile much too old for her young lips and in her eyes I see a maturity forced upon her by circumstance.

"Good morning, Alex. Ready to get moving?" I reach over and ruffle her needle-filled hair. "Planning on taking the forest home with you?" I pull a few of the closer pine needles off her head and let them fall to the ground.

"Where's your phone?" Alex asks, brushing a few more of them out of her hair. "We should check to see if you have service."

"Wise words, my dear. But sadly, my cellphone is sitting cozy on a table in your house charging. Pretty sure it's done by now, too. Yours?"

"The asshole that was in the room with me snapped mine in half after I told him he was an asshole. The other guy got pissed. Said they could have used it to find me if I got away. So, I guess it was a good thing he broke it. I mean, it was just a flip phone anyway." She grins after watching to see if I'll say anything about the language she's using.

Kid, after what you've been through, you're welcome to cuss like a sailor if it makes you feel better.

"Charlie?"

"Yeah?"

"What happened to that guy, anyway? The one who was in the room."

I run my hand over my mouth and along my chin, buying some time to decide on an answer. Then I flare my brows and shrug. "I guess he got sick."

"Was it..?" She tilts her head and gives the corner of her bottom lip a nibble. "Was it something he ate?"

Her line of questioning is making me uneasy. I shrug again, pinching up the corner of my mouth and shaking my head.

I don't want to go there, sweetie. I really don't want to go there.

"I'm going to peek out and make sure nobody is nearby. I imagine they went back to the house to wait for people to come buy the stuff they stole so they can get the hell out of town. It would be stupid for them to stay too long and risk being caught. Still ... stay here while I look." I edge my way to the opening between the boulders, as happy to get out of our tiny hideout as I am to get out of answering any more questions.

I slide through the gap on my stomach, brushing off my jacket once I'm out and on my feet. Leaves rustle somewhere to my left. The sound is coming from the clearing on the other side of the rocks. I hold my breath and ease around the rocks, craning my neck, cheek to the stone, to see the source of the noise.

When I've had a good look, I hurry back to summon Alex out of the tiny cave. I motion for her to lead the way and follow with my hands on her shoulders. She looks around into the clearing and lets out a whispery gasp. She turns and looks at me, mouth agape, then smiles her before smile. The one she's supposed to have for at least a few more years before the depths of puberty and the trials and tribulations of adulthood rob her of her childhood wonder.

We gaze into the clearing together at the enormous creature nibbling on the leaves of an aspen less than twenty feet away. It turns and nuzzles the calf at its side, then reaches up to pull down a branch of the tree it has chosen as a snack. I've never seen a moose before, and the sheer size of her sends a staticky shiver through me that lightens my heart, makes me feel like I'm floating in a dream. Sunlight filters through the trees, casting a shadow that looks like the fluttering wings of a million butterflies, adding beauty to the already magical scene.

The calf gives a series of whimpers, pleading for its mother's attention. She snaps off the branch and drops it down to him. The calf trots around her, kicking up its back legs in a kind of happy jig, then grabs the branch and munches on mouthfuls of leaves, making content little *hoots* as it eats.

At the sound of a high-pitched motor echoing in the distance, the mother moose flattens her ears. She takes one last nibble and nudges her baby forward with her head. When the motor revs, and gives a long, sustained scream, the two pick up their pace and wander off into the woods.

"That sounded like a motorcycle," says Alex, looking up at me.

"It kind of did. There must be a road down that way." I point to what I think was the direction of the sound.

"I think it was more from that direction," she says, pointing a bit more to the right.

"Well, let's start walking, see if we can find it."

For the first twenty minutes or so, we walk in relative silence, with only a "watch your step" here or a "hold up a sec" there. We both have dreamy half-grins pasted across our faces, thanks to mamma moose and her adorable offspring, and I'm grateful for the lifting effect it's had on my soul.

Alex stops and leans forward, her grin temporarily turning to a grimace.

"My feet hurt," she says, sitting on the trunk of an old fallen tree and pulling off the oversized boots.

I sit down beside her. "Let's take a look,"

The skin on her heel is an angry red around a large blister where the boot has been rubbing with each and every step. Another blister protrudes from the dorsum. This one is oozing a milky white puss. I cringe, scrunching my nose at the sight of them. I imagine the other foot will look about the same. We aren't going to get very far if the situation worsens.

"Ouch." It's all I can think to say at the moment. She nods in agreement.

I take out my water bottle and give her a swig. It's down to the last third of the bottle. We've been trying to conserve our resources. I still have some gummies left, too. Those will be our emergency back-up.

"I think I have an idea," I say, removing my jacket. I'm wearing a t-shirt underneath and a tank top under that. *Dress in layers!* That's what everyone told me about visiting Colorado. And I listened.

Alex turns and I strip down to my bra, then slip back into my t-shirt and jacket. I pull at the tank, rubbing the bottom of the seam against the splintered tree bark next to me to get a tear started. When it is in two pieces, I pick up Alex's bare foot and fashion a bandage around it with one, taking care to wrap it tight enough not to slide but not too tight so as to cause her too much pain. I tuck the end into the wrap and stretch her sock back over it. I repeat the process with her other foot, which I'm happy to see is in a little better condition.

"Now," I say, sliding off my shoes, "we're going to trade shoes. Mine are still too big for you, but the wrap should help."

I hand her my shoes and she slides her feet in one at a time, wincing when she does. Then she stands and wobbles forward a couple steps.

"How's that?"

"Better," she says. "Still hurts a little, but better."

"Good," I say, picking up one of the boots she was wearing. I slide it on and wiggle my toes. It feels like I've stepped into a cavern. "Dang, how the hell were you able to walk at all in these?"

Alex shrugs and shoots me a smirk. I remove the boot and stuff some leaves into the toe. After repeating this with the second half of the pair, I put them both on and walk around in a circle. Alex watches and waits for a verdict.

"Not the most comfortable things, but they'll work. Ready to roll?"

A couple hours later, we've still not found a road or even a path. Our progress has been a little slower than I would like, but it's better to be slow and steady than to destroy our feet completely or trip and fall. The terrain has been uneven at best, and downright treacherous in some places. We've been traveling downhill the entire time, stopping occasionally to listen for the sounds of a stream or river, or better yet, traffic.

The vegetation looks thicker in the distance, which Alex tells me is a sign of a possible water source. But both of us agree we need to rest for a few minutes before continuing on. We sit on another fallen tree and I pull out the bag of gummies, taking out one for each of us.

"You have *candy*?" Alex says, eyes wide. She licks her lips, then lets her mouth gape open.

I laugh and hand her a gummy. "It's not really candy. At least that's what Auntie Becca said to keep me from gobbling up the whole bag when she gave them to me. Seriously, though, these are hydration gummies with electrolytes. I still have a few in here, but we need to save them for later."

She rolls the little green blob around in her hand for a

moment, then pops it into her mouth. "Well, it sure tastes like candy," she says, raising a brow. "Hey, Charlie?"

Uh oh, I think. *More questions.*

"Yes?"

"How do you think those guys got into Mr. Benson's house? I mean, they even had his car. Do you think he's ok?"

I shrug, pushing back an image of the elderly man in a Persian rug, bleeding. Once again I'm unable to remember whether or not I heard a dial tone ...

"I heard shots when I was there and at the mountain house, too. Did those guys shoot at you?"

"No." Well, this is an honest answer, at least. I leave it at that, and Alex drops it, most likely taking the cues I am frantically throwing out with my expression.

Sticks snap somewhere in the woods, startling us to attention. We've been keeping our voices down, but not to the point where I'm one hundred percent sure we haven't been heard. I point behind the stump, crawling over and behind it to demonstrate my intent. Alex crawls over next to me, snuggling in under my arm.

"Breathe nice and slow," I whisper. "I'm sure it's nothing, but let's wait a few minutes, just in case."

She nods up at me, and by her eyes I can tell she's not at all convinced that it's *nothing*. The forest is quiet and, apart from our encounter with the moose and her calf, we really haven't seen more than the occasional squirrel or tiny bird during our trek. The lack of wildlife has taken me by surprise.

We lock gazes when the unmistakable sound of voices reaches our ears, though it's impossible to hear what's being said. We are not far enough away from the house to trust that anyone out here would simply be a hiker or camper. I hug my niece closer and huddle down to wait for whoever is out there to move along.

When the steps move away and I'm fairly certain we're alone again, I poke my head over the trunk and scan our surroundings.

"I think they're gone," I whisper. "Let's get moving. Do you really think there's water over there?" I nod toward the area Alex was excited about.

"I'm not sure, but usually the vegetation gets a lot thicker when there is. I go with Mom a lot when she's out doing her botanist thing."

I nod and raise a hand with crossed fingers before we continue toward the thick green line of plants visible in the distance. There must be a break in the trees there, because bright, golden sunlight shines over the lush green patch, giving it an even more inviting appearance. The going gets a little harder the closer we get to our goal. Thick bushy shrubs scratch at our clothes and a few times we have to stop to free each other from some unfriendly looking plants with grabby thorns or burrs.

"Look, Charlie," Alex exclaims in a squeaky whisper. "Thimbleberries."

"What-le-berries?"

Alex holds up a few bright red, fuzzy little berries and pops them in her mouth. "Thimbleberries," she says, between chews. She picks another and hands it to me.

"Looks like a raspberry," I say, well aware of my complete lack of knowledge when it comes to the leafier inhabitants of our planet.

I pop it into my mouth and, after a quick burst of sweet-tart flavor, a slight honey-like after-taste remains. Not bad. Even if my stomach wasn't growling like an angry badger, I'd probably enjoy these tasty, crunchy little berries.

"What do you think?" She wipes a trickle of juice from her chin.

"Pretty good. Though I'm not sure I like the company they keep. Isn't that ...?" I point to a bush popping with bunches of little white flowers

"Yup, that's hemlock, for sure."

"Maybe we shouldn't be eating this if they're so close to those ..."

"Don't worry about it, Charlie. They aren't *that* close. Besides, hemlock isn't dangerous unless you touch it with an open wound or eat it."

I nod, instinctively reaching up to touch the outside of the pocket that recently housed what I have now confirmed to be poison hemlock.

After tossing down a few more berries, we continue through the tangle of green.

"Shhh," says Alex, snapping me out of some rather dark thoughts. "Hear that?"

I tilt my head and concentrate. Yes, I do hear it. It's the sound of water. Not a roaring stream, but a steady trickle coming from somewhere nearby. We take a few more steps and push aside some grass to reveal a tiny brook running through the weeds.

"Ok then, let's follow it and see where it leads us," I say, thinking that this kid might yet make a naturalist of me.

Chapter 43

Back on Track

After another couple hours of walking—what I guess to be around midday by the position of the sun—our stream, which has been steadily widening, leads us to a small log cabin with a detached shed and garage. There are no cars in the drive and the shades are drawn in every window.

Alex and I linger in the woods, hidden behind the thick, sweet-smelling trunk of a ponderosa pine, while we look it over, scanning for signs of life.

"I really don't think anyone's in there," I say, breaking the heavy silence. "Besides, if there is someone home, there's no way they're involved."

Alex furrows her brow and looks over at me as if to say, *how would you know?* A sentiment that remains unspoken.

"Let's do this, then." I lay a hand on her shoulder. "You stay here and I'll go ring the doorbell or knock or whatever." Panic flashes in her eyes, reminding me that this kid is going to need a lot of support when all of this is over. "I'll be careful. If anything looks at all suspicious, we're outta here. You take off down the stream and I'll meet you as soon as I can."

Alex rolls her lips in between her teeth and nods. I give her a pat on the shoulder and head down to the cabin, looking back when I'm close to confirm she's well-hidden.

Before knocking, I press my forehead against one of the front windows, cupping my hands around my eyes to limit reflections. Through the curtain, I can make out the shapes of several pieces of furniture. There's no movement that I can see. I ball my hand into a fist, knock three times, and listen for any kind of response.

Nothing. I turn toward the spot where I left Alex and shrug, palms up. After a few more seconds of waiting, I decide that nobody's home and wave her down to the house.

"What do we do now?" she asks, joining me in front of the door.

We walk around the side of the house where we find a large gas generator that has definitely seen better days. Judging by the amount of dust blanketing the appliance, I'm guessing it hasn't been used in quite a while. Perhaps they just come here during the day. There are no sconces or cameras anywhere on the outside of the house. This may be their only source of power. Maybe it's some kind of rustic hunting cabin, or something that was passed down to kids that were not interested in *roughing it*. Whatever the case, it doesn't look like we're going to get anything out of this stop. I certainly don't expect there to be any food inside and even if there is, it probably isn't edible.

"I guess we can check the garage," I say, not expecting much. "The shed looks like it's about to fall over, so I'd rather avoid it."

Alex nods and tails me to the one-car garage. The doors are the kind that swing out—carriage doors—and they're in dire need of some TLC. Time and weather have worn away much of the original white paint, leaving only flecks, and caused both doors to sag, misaligning the bolts and strike plate. There's a bicycle chain looped through the rusty pull handles, securing the doors.

"Tell me you don't want to go in without telling me you don't want to go in," I mutter, causing Alex to giggle.

I give the doors a tug. The chain holds fast, but one of handles comes right off the door, startling Alex. I hold it up in wonder, which pushes her into a full-belly laugh.

"They don't make 'em like they used to," I say. "Which is not always a bad thing."

I give the freed handle a tug, pulling the other door open with a long *creeeeaaak*, then let it drop and swing until it comes to rest under its companion. A cloud of dust puffs up off the floor as the door swings open. It hangs in the air for a moment, swirling through the beams of sunlight filtering in through dirt-caked windows, then settles.

Most of the items inside are as useless as I suspected they would be. Most. The thing that's catching my eye is a blanket-covered object sitting dead center. Alex runs over and grabs the top of the blanket. I motion for her to pull it off, stepping back when she kicks up another round of dust.

"Would you look at that," I say, walking around the motorcycle, running a hand along the sleek yellow gas tank. It looks like it's only built for one rider, but I remember a trick that Randy showed me. The bit of plastic on the back flips off, revealing the rest of the seat ... and a key.

Does no one take security seriously anymore? I think, shaking my head.

"Cool," says Alex, wiping away some dust that was able to work its way under the blanket. "What's a *Ducati*?"

I think back to the waiter that served me on my way to Colorado ... saving for his, what was it? *Scramble*? No, *Scrambler*. Not sure if this is one of those, but it's a beautiful machine.

"Think it works?"

"I do not know," I say. "It looks like it's in pretty good condition. Whoever owns this place has let everything else go to shit, but must really love this bike. I'm sure they won't mind us borrowing it, though. I mean ... it is kind of an emergency. As soon as we figure out where we are, we can drop it at the nearest police station."

Alex looks up at me, seeming to consider the situation. She runs a hand through her long dark hair, scrutinizing the motorcycle. Finally, she turns and nods. "Definitely an emergency."

"First things first." I turn and find exactly what I'm looking for, a red five gallon gas container. It's about half full.

I'm rethinking the cabin now. There may actually be edible food in there. But if I can get this motorcycle running, we won't need it. The Ducati isn't like the FCC, but after hearing Randy constantly talk about how much easier it is to start "more modern" bikes, I finally allowed her to demonstrate. So, after a moment or two of examining the bike, and trying to remember exactly what I saw her do, I pour the remainder of the gas into the tank and try to start our best way out of here.

It only takes a couple attempts before I have it purring like a panther, another sign that this motorcycle is loved. Alex runs over holding a black helmet with a skull painted on it in one hand, while brushing dust off of it with the other.

"It was hanging on the wall," she says, handing it to me. "I could only find one, though."

I hand it right back to her. "Let's see how it looks on you, then."

She pulls it over her head and fastens the strap under her chin. It's a little bit big on her, even after some adjustments, but beggars can't be choosers. I pat the top of it and give her a thumbs up.

"Hop on," I say after taking a seat and familiarizing myself with our new ride. "Let's see what she's got."

"What should we call her, Charlie?"

I honestly hadn't even thought about it. After all, it's not my bike. But, I'll go along if it makes her feel better. "How about we call her Bev?" I say, laughing.

"What?"

"Borrowed Escape Vehicle," I say. "Bev!"

"Bev it is," she agrees, wrapping her arms around my waist and readying herself.

This is *not* the FCC and I'm absolutely terrified that I'm going to lose control of the powerful machine, which seems to want to take off like a rocket. The fact that we're riding on a dirt driveway, then a dirt road, isn't helping my anxiety.

Just get down the mountain. Just get down the mountain, I chant in my head. *No need to rush. Just get down the mountain.*

Another half hour goes by before we reach an actual town. I pull into the first parking lot I see and stop the bike. It's the lot of a touristy looking diner with a killer view of the mountains. Alex climbs off the bike and looks around. She pulls off the helmet and sets it on the seat. An older couple exits the restaurant and walks past us on their way to an old Subaru Forester parked a few spots over. The man rushes to open the door for his wife, dropping his wallet as he goes. He sees it fall and grumbles.

Alex runs over, picks it up, and hands it to him.

"Why, thank you, sweetie," he says, pushing it back into his pocket. He looks at me and smiles. "You've got yourself a very sweet little girl there."

"Young lady, honey," his wife corrects.

"Looks like you're raising her right, too. Have a blessed day."

I thank him and watch as he helps his wife into the car, giving her a peck on the cheek before closing her door.

It's what I had with Esther, a faint voice whispers in my head, but I can barely hear it. I'm ready to move on from the past.

Chapter 44

The Bill Comes Due

The waitress in the diner gives me directions to the nearest police station, just a few more miles down the road, and insists that we try a piece of cherry pie before we get on our way. She seats us at the front window and comes back a few minutes later with a cup of coffee for me and hot chocolate for Alex.

"You two look like you've had quite the day," she says. Alex nods, looking up at her through bleary eyes set above dark puffy circles. "Well, this is on the house. When you've got some food in you, you can head over to the police station. It isn't going anywhere."

"Thank you," I say, realizing how small-minded I've been, believing I had to stay in my little corner of the world, purporting to protect something that isn't limited to one little place. Something that's in the people, not the place.

At the station, I pull out the envelope I took from the writing desk in the mountain home and hand it to the officer manning the front desk, explaining that they might want to drive up there and take a look at this address. He has us take a seat next to one of the desks in the back and we recount our story, first to one detective, then repeating bits for the others that wander over when they hear what we're saying. They've heard of *tourist criminals* and, though, incredulous at first, a quick call to the station in Alex's town is all they need to verify the first part of our story.

Mr. Benson was found in his home shortly after we left. There must have been a dial tone, but sadly, it was too late. There was no way they could know what had happened, except that he'd been burglarized. His family would be flying in to make arrangements.

The mess they find at the mountain house brings on additional questions which we answer as best we can. No, we don't know the names of the men found dead in the house. No, we have no idea how they died (I bite the inside of my lip to shreds at this question, but I'm pretty sure they chalk it up to nerves after such a terrifying experience).

Those are the only bodies they find up there, and there's no trace of the gang, though the officers tell me they might have a few leads thanks to the information we have given them. They were also able to grab Camryn and are hopeful that information found on his phone could help. Turns out he was just some local jerk trying to make an extra buck by scamming teens into giving him door codes. They think they can get him to flip.

A few days after we get back to Alex's house, one of Mr. Benson's nephews knocks on the door with a piece of mail for us that was delivered to their house.

"We really can't take Mr. Talon or Thorn with us," he says, handing me a postcard. "Do you know anyone who'd be willing to take them?"

He looks from me to Alex. And, of course, Alex says we will. Lindsey's going to absolutely kill me.

Alex and I agree that we should wait to tell her parents what happened until they're back in the country. It's not something you really want to relay over the phone.

I am glad we do, because tears flow, and hugs abound. After everything they hear, the business of the motorcycle rides with

Alex doesn't even register and I'm given permission to give both kids rides, as long as they wear helmets.

At the conclusion of camp a few weeks later, Jimmy is upset that he's "missed all the fun." Alex dedicates some time to patching things up with her friend, Chloe, who's devastated that Camryn has ghosted her, until she hears what happened, of course.

I am leaning more and more toward moving closer to Tom, now that Mom will be heading this way. And when Becca finally gets back to our home (she made her peace with the things that will never change regarding her parents), she makes plans to fly out so that we can ride the FCC back together. Well, the three of us. Randy set me up with a dealer out here and I purchased a sweet little side car. I'm currently training Thorn to ride in it, so he can become the Thorn *by* my side.

Two days before Becca is set to arrive, Alex and I are walking along the gulch trail. She's telling me about how she and Chloe have patched things up.

"You should try to find your best friend to see how she's doing," she says out of nowhere.

"Auntie Becca's my best friend," I say, ruffling her hair.

She ducks away and runs a hand over her head to make sure everything is in its place.

"No, your best friend when you were a kid. Sarah, right? Didn't you say she wanted to come to Colorado?"

I stop and fiddle with the chain around my neck. "Yeah, but I don't know where she is now. It's been a long time."

"Seriously, Auntie C, I bet I can find her with a little bit of information. You can find pretty much everyone on the internet."

Chapter 45

New Beginnings

I walk up the path to the front door, still deciding whether or not I'm actually going to go through with this. We haven't seen each other in forever. Maybe I'll leave a note on the door or in the mailbox or something. I reach into my bag to see if I have a scrap of paper and a pen. Yeah, that's what I should do. Leave a note on the door and see if she reaches out. After years chained to my past, I have no right to pull on any loose threads that may be dangling from anyone else's.

I find an old sticky note and tear off the portion where I've scribbled down a phone number. I don't even remember whose number it is. Then, I fidget with the ballpoint pen I retrieved from the bottom of the bag, trying to think of what to write.

A dog appears at the window in the sidelite panel. It's an old black lab, his muzzle streaked with splashes of white fur. He looks up at me, unimpressed, then turns his head and barks three times. He looks back at me with soulful eyes, as if chastising me for forcing him to leave a well-deserved nap to do his guard dog duties. I shrug and take a step back. I can write the note in the coffee shop I saw just outside the neighborhood and drop it off in the mailbox later.

I'm turning to leave when a familiar face appears in the upper portion of the panel, above the weary lab. We stare at each other for a moment, our eyes wide with mutual surprise, and my heart thumps double-time, pulsating in my ears and muffling the sounds around me. A latch clicks, the doorknob turns, and I'm face to face with Sarah.

She looks almost identical to when I last saw her waving back at me before she hopped up the steps to her apartment complex. Almost. When I look closer, I notice thin lines branching from the outer corners of her eyes. Bill called them crow's feet. Mom prefers laughter lines. She's also a lot tanner than she was when we were younger, most likely a result of living the outdoorsy life of a Coloradan. My eyes drift to another novelty, one that catches me by surprise. Sarah is expecting a child.

"Charlie?" Her voice slides out in a whisper, like she's not quite sure if she believes what she's seeing. "Charlie? Is that you?"

Her eyes sweep from my head all the way to my feet, like a laser scanner in a sci-fi movie. I should say something, but a lump the size of Texas is lodged in my throat. Tears well in my eyes, a million different lenses warping my perspective.

"Close your mouth, Charlie. You're doing that daydreaming thing again," she says, opening her arms and launching herself toward me.

I receive her just in time and sob as we embrace. After what seems like an eternity wrapped in a millisecond, we each take a step back, letting our arms slide until we are holding hands.

"Sarah, it's really good to see you," I say. "I didn't think I'd see you again, after ..."

I pull one hand away, wiping the back of it across both eyes.

"I came to look for you when my mom passed away a few years ago," Sarah says, her own eyes glistening. "You weren't home. Your husband told me you didn't want to see me, that you were starting a new life and wanted nothing to do with the past."

"I'm sorry about your mom," I reply, not sure what else to say on the matter. I had never met the woman. "And I'm sorry about my asshole *ex*-husband."

We both laugh, our nervous energy converting into something more familiar, something comfortable.

"Watch the potty mouth," says Sarah, chuckling. "You need to protect your pristine, Goody Two-shoes reputation." She's lowered the tone of her voice to better mirror a certain someone from our past.

"Come on in, old friend." She steps aside and directs me to the door. "I'll make you some coffee."

The foyer is bright and cheery, flooded with natural light through a generous transom window. Photographs of wildlife line the walls on both sides of me.

"Lucas took all those," she says from behind me.

I whip around to face her. "Lucas? *The* Lucas?"

A rosy hue lights up her sun-kissed cheeks and she casts her gaze to the floor. She grins, reminding me of the first time she mentioned his name, this guy she had a mad crush on, the one that made her want to venture out into the world.

"Yes, *the* Lucas. After ... well, the thing with Bill, I skipped town. I wanted to ask you to come, Charlie, but then I heard you were all tangled up in his will. Plus, your parents would have freaked. I knew you couldn't come."

I nodded. Sarah loved my parents, especially my mom. She would've never done anything to hurt them.

"It's ok. I get it. I was kind of a mess. Everything was kind of a mess. You needed to get away."

Sarah directs me into a living room graced with more beautiful nature photos. There's one of a waterfall that has to be at least ten feet tall, hung over a stone fireplace with what looks like half of a polished tree trunk acting as a mantle. The whole room is fashioned to look like a remote mountain cabin. A coffee table riddled with papers sits in front of a set of brown leather sofas angled to enjoy the warm cozy fires that surely grace the fireplace on cold winter evenings.

"Sit, I'll bring coffee for us both. I just brewed some."

Sarah rushes from the room and I sit, sinking into the soft, supple lap of the nearest sofa. I lean forward and pick up a large sheet of paper that looks like it's about to slip off the pile of documents strewn every which way on the table, examining it before I return it to its friends. It's some kind of blueprint. The table is filled with them, all marked up with undecipherable notes in dark pencil.

Sarah appears holding a tray topped with two large coffee cups, a porcelain sugar bowl and tiny pitcher, all with matching designs, and a pile of cookies. She pushes the papers to the side, clearing a space, and sets it down before sitting next to me.

"Almost feels like old times." She sighs. "But it's not hot chocolate, and this time I made the cookies instead of your mom."

"You made these?" I say, crumbs tumbling from my lips. I cup a hand to limit the mess and brush what I've managed to catch onto the tray. "They're awesome." I pick up one of the papers off the table. "I thought Lucas was in law school," I say, holding it up.

Sarah blushes once again. "Those are mine. I'm an architect, Charlie. I went to college and studied my ass off, and I'm an architect." Her smile is so wide, the chandelier is reflecting off her pearly whites.

My jaw drops. A freaking architect. "Wow, you *are* a badass," I say. "Well, I guess I know who's going to design our house when we move to Colorado."

"We? Who's the other half of this we?" Now it's her turn to look inquisitive.

I pull out my phone and show her a selfie I took with Becca in our new jackets. "Her name's Becca, and she's a keeper."

Sarah nods and her easy, familiar smile appears. "She looks like a keeper."

"When are you due?" I ask, nodding at her belly while I add sugar and cream to my cup.

"A month from tomorrow. I'm ready to get this little man out now."

"Mamma?"

A high, faint voice floats in from behind us. I turn just as a tiny figure toddles into the room, her golden locks bouncing against her brow. She scuttles past me, not turning her deep, suspicious brown eyes from mine until she's safely in her mother's arms.

"Look who's up from her nap," Sarah says in a voice that sounds so foreign from her lips. It's the voice of a mother, the voice of unconditional love and protection. "Do you want to meet mommy's friend?"

I didn't know Sarah when she was a toddler, but now I know exactly what she looked like. The girl considers me for a moment, nose crinkled, examining me like I'm a bug under a magnifying glass. Then her expression lightens and she nods at her mom.

"Yesth," she says. "I want to meet your fwend." She holds out her small hand and I give it a light shake.

Sarah gives the girl a few bounces on her knee. "Charlie, this is Charlotte, but everyone calls her Charlie."

A warm feeling spreads through me from the very center of my soul. I instinctively reach for the chain on my neck, grinning at Sarah, then move my attention to the little girl gazing up at me.

"Awesome name," I say, with a slow steady nod.

Charlie giggles and reaches up for me. Sarah stands and surrenders her into my arms and I'm surprised at the ease I feel holding her. Sure, I picked up my niece and nephew when they were little ... that's what aunties do. But I've never felt compelled to hold someone else's child or even comfortable doing it. This feels different. It doesn't feel like I just met her and she's leaning into me, chatting like she's known me forever.

I feel a tug on my necklace as Sarah's daughter fiddles with the chain. She snakes it up and out into the open.

"Ooooh, pwetty," she says, holding it out toward her mom.

"Is that...?" Sarah reaches for the pendant, a hint of alarm in her eyes. She leans in for a closer look. "Never mind, I thought it was something else," she says, handing it to me. "Charlie's right. It is pretty."

I nod, gazing at the treasure dangling from my sleek silver chain: a smokey glass lens in the shape of a teardrop with, at its center, a small white flower resembling a baby's breath blossom.

I still hear Bill's voice occasionally, though it seems to get weaker as time goes by, with each step I take away from my past. I don't honestly think it will ever completely leave me. He's a part of who I am, and I've come to accept that. Just as I've come to accept the things I've done to survive.

But, I also know these are not the only things that define who I am. And I revel in the things that make the voice try to scream out in anger. My hand drifts down to pat my wallet, snuggly tucked into my back pocket. The sticky paper that had entrapped my soul for so many years is long gone now. Since replaced by a postcard, its glossy image lined with the folds required to make it part of me. Which is fine because it's not the picture I treasure, not the picture that I wish to preserve, but its significance.

It's addressed to *Charlie and Alex down the street*, but the address is that of Mr. Benson. The back isn't signed. It doesn't need to be. In the top left corner is the name of the town depicted on the front: Robbins, CA. Below it, in neat, precise handwriting similar to what one might find in a composition book of old, a recipe for *Empanadas de pino*.

How's my *life of crime* going, Bill? I'd say it's going just fine.

Acknowledgments

You may have noticed the it takes a village theme throughout A Twist of the Lens. Well, it also takes a village to get a book published. From my family and the people who inspire me to write to everyone involved in the publishing process, my village is important to me. And, the readers! They are a huge part of my village once the book wanders out into the world. I am in awe of the insight offered by authors I have met along the way. Inspired by my readers and their

support.

When I am writing, I often dive head first into the many rabbits holes I encounter while researching in the pursuit of authenticity. If I mention a camera, I want to know how it works. If I mention a place, I want to accurately describe it and relay the feel of it. In this novel, a gorgeous 1952 Indian Roadmaster is practically a character in the story: The Flying Candy Cane. I knew next to nothing about motorcycles, aside from having been a passenger a few times. I knew even less about a classic like the 1952 Indian Roadmaster. So, off I went to the nearest Indian motorcycle dealer for some help. There I found a wonderful gentleman by the name of Ryan Russell who let me pick his brain. I got to see a vintage Indian bike first hand (though not the exact year of Charlie's FCC, I was told the mechanics were the same) and ask questions about it.

Thank you, Russell! I would also like to thank Xavier Muniz, who I encountered at a Harley Davidson shop while I was editing and who graciously answered some additional questions I had about motorcycles and elevation. And, a big thank you to Damian and Chris at G-Force Powersports. When I wandered back into Indian Motorcycle of the Rockies in Denver hoping for some photos for promo, you guys were awesome!

Last but not least, I want to thank the ladies in my accountability group, Teresa, Shauna, Robi, Christine, and Melissa for helping me to stay organized. And of course, a shoutout to Becky and Lauren, my long-distance friends who are always there to read my drafts, talk me down, or give me a nudge.

About the Author

Elizabeth Devecchi spent her formative years in Rhode Island, setting out after high school to travel and gather degrees. She holds a BA in French from Wittenberg University, a Law Degree from the Univeristà di Torino in Turin, Italy, and an L.LM in International Law from The University of Iowa College of Law.

Though she writes in a variety of genres, Elizabeth has had a special affinity to horror and suspense since first wandering into her parents' basement, furnace room library and getting her hands on such classics as *Jaws*, *The Omen*, *Audrey Rose*, and *The Amityville Horror*. With her discovery of Stephen King sealing the deal. She currently resides in Colorado with her family and a menagerie of pets and "guest animals," where she plays tennis, frequents book clubs, and bakes focaccias in her free time.

Find out more about her past and future projects at
www.elizabethdevecchi.com

Wicked House Publishing

Come find us!

Amazon: Wicked House Publishing
Mailing List: Sign Up Here!
Facebook Group: The Wicked House Cult of Slightly Insane Readers

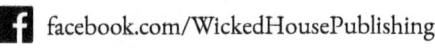

facebook.com/WickedHousePublishing
x.com/WickedHousePub
instagram.com/wicked_house_publishing